D1526027

ALIYA
A Love Story

BRENDA LESLEY SEGAL
in association with
MARIANNE KANTER

ST. MARTIN'S PRESS
NEW YORK

Library of Congress Cataloging in Publication Data

Segal, Brenda Lesley.
  Aliya : a love story.

    I. Kanter, Marianne, joint author.   II.   Title.
  PZ4.S4543Al   [PS3569.E37]   813'.5'4   77-9217

ISBN 0-312-01865-7

In memory of
Lieutenant Colonel Yonatan Natanyahu
killed at Entebbe,
July 4, 1976

ALIYA
A Love Story

1

At first she thought she was dreaming. There were these men huddled together, chanting softly as they swayed back and forth, the great shawls across their shoulders dripping fringe. They looked like blackbirds in their ghetto hats and coats, blackbirds with white wings, mumbling to themselves, bobbing back and forth with funny little boxes tied around their heads and laced to their arms.

The stewardess picked up a pillow that had fallen into the aisle and smiled at her. "Morning prayers," she said. "You've never seen the laying on of *tefelin* before, have you?"

"Uh, no, I can't say that I have."

That is for sure, she thought, unfolding her legs and stretching a bit. Meredith Anne Sloane had seen many things in her twenty-five years, but never, absolutely never the laying on of . . . whatchamacallits.

She stood up, blinking at the light that now filled the 747. Pulled up window shades were making little popping sounds all around her and the passengers on the big plane were starting to stretch and stand and ask about coffee.

Having finished their prayers, the group of men in the aisle removed the great white shawls (like birds taking off their wings, she thought) and folded them into neat little bundles. The boxes and thongs were also removed and put into their proper containers. As the group disbanded and "disrobed," Meri saw with a slight shock that it included several well-dressed businessmen and a long-haired young man in blue jeans as well as the black-hatted and bearded Jews she had noticed at the El Al terminal the night before. "*Hasidim*," she'd heard them called; and they had been dancing, a circle of young men, none older than she and most younger—pale-faced boys with scraggly beards and ridiculous curls hanging over their ears, dressed in these ridiculous black coats and hats which smelled none too fresh, but dancing and singing with a joy and an energy that seemed to infect everyone in the place with renewed excitement. We are going to the Holy Land, they sang. We are going to Eretz Israel. We are going home.

Only Roger and Meri had stood apart from the spectacle of the rejoicing Yeshiva students and clapping bystanders. Roger was not even charitable enough to affect the smile of amused tolerance he usually adopted when he felt out of place. "Spare me, please," he muttered.

"Why? It's interesting."

He raised his eyebrows. "I've seen *Fiddler*." He took her hands in his. "I wish you had taken another airline. It could easily have been arranged. Midnight flight to Tel Aviv! Lord, this is as bad as that 'Vomit Comet' we took to Miami."

"Yes, but think of the Spanish you picked up then, darling. Think how handy that will come in when you talk to your future constituents."

"There are such things as language records, you know. God!" A three-year-old in jeans hurled herself at his knees in frantic flight from a little boy chasing her with a cup of ice water. Roger returned the child to her mother. "I promise you," he said out of the corner of his mouth, "there will be chickens running loose in the aisles."

2

She laughed. "And I suppose all the stewardesses will look like Mrs. Goldblatt."

"No doubt. 'Coffee? Tea? Pastrami?' "

"You are terrible."

"Well, you don't expect me to be ecstatic, do you?"

"It won't be long, Roger. The museum isn't sending me on this trip for fun. Ben Levi is one of the finest archaeologists in the world. If he's on to something, we want to know."

"Okay, okay. I just don't like the idea of you being out there in the middle of—Well, let's be frank, Meri. Israel is not the safest place in the world."

"Neither is Central Park. If you're so worried, why don't you come along?"

"I wish I could," he said solemnly. "I really wish I could. But you know I have my work."

"Exactly. And I have mine. And my work," she said slowly, giving great care to each word so that there should be no mistaking her feelings, "is as important to me as yours is to you."

He laughed hurriedly. "Oh come on, love. I wasn't trying to put you down. You're a very talented and capable young lady. And a beautiful one. As well as being the love of my life." He lowered his voice. "I'm going to miss you, baby."

"Well," she murmured, "I'm sure Kay will console you. Or is she pregnant again?"

"Don't be bitchy, Meri. It doesn't become you. Besides, you know you only have to say the word—"

She yawned. It was almost midnight. It had been a long day and she was suddenly very tired. "No," she said with a slight smile, "I wouldn't dream of breaking up your happy home. And neither would you."

She yawned again as she made her way to one of the lines that were forming in front of the rest rooms. She hated sleeping in planes. Where were the days of long sea voyages and staterooms filled with flowers and Fred Astaire? Instead of

3

gowns of tulle and ostrich feathers billowing out of steamer trunks, the one suitcase with the initials M.S. tucked away in the belly of the jumbo jet held a wardrobe consisting of cotton and denim and soft little jersey tops. Who could know that the slender girl in the space-age knit was, in her heart, Ginger Rogers?

The young steward, mistaking Meri's smile as being meant for him, immediately jumped to his feet. "You had a good rest?" he inquired enthusiastically.

"Wha—oh, yes. Thank you." Breeding decided to give way to honesty. "Actually, I can think of better ways to sleep. Like in a bed."

He laughed. "What are you talking about? This is fantastic. Try sleeping in a trench in the Sinai or in the Golan when there's snow. This is fantastic," he repeated, stretching his arms as if to embrace the plane. "Warm. Dry. Plenty of pillows and blankets. The trouble with you Americans is you're all spoiled," he said good-naturedly. Waving congenially, he went off to serve breakfast.

Meri stared after him appreciatively. He certainly didn't look like Mrs. Goldblatt or her husband, proprietors of the dry cleaning establishment in her apartment building. She looked around now at the other members of the El Al crew. They were young, good-looking, some dark-haired and tanned, some fair and freckled, some with deep accents, some sounding rather British. What they all seemed to have in common was a kind of easy, almost arrogant energy. Roger had been wrong about the stewardesses. He would really have been upset if he had seen the stewards.

She looked back again at the young man she had spoken to. He was of average height, a bit stocky, with very wide shoulders and a mop of black, curly hair. His dark eyes had flashed their appreciation of the honey blonde with the long legs as soon as she made her way into the plane, and he had been most solicitous throughout the flight. Meri was amused by the attention. He was not at all subtle, but his flirting had

been so good-humored, so—well, friendly—that she was not the least put off by it. So now, her glance back at him rewarded him with the knowledge that he had not been unnoticed after all. He had just mentally awarded himself another ten points when Uri, the other steward in Economy, slapped him on the shoulder. Uri had noticed too.

"*Col hacavod,*" he said. "All honor to you. The *blondini* is some piece."

Moshi shrugged casually. "Tourists," he said in a markedly bored tone. "They all want to fuck."

Uri laughed a bit grudgingly. He was surprised that this one was not in First Class. "Especially the *shiksas.* They love you *sephardim.*" Uri was tall and thin; he looked very much like the philosophy student at a German university that his father had once been.

Moshi merely grinned. He threw a cup into the air, then spun it neatly on his finger. "Oopah!"

Meri washed her face, brushed her hair. She was too weary to bother with makeup, but applied some lip gloss in honor of Moshi—despite his lack of sympathy for her discomfort. She did not know that the steward—when he was not pouring drinks for El Al passengers, or conducting personal tours for the Swedes and Dutch girls with whom he shared a mutual admiration, served at least three months each year in Israel's battle-ready infantry. In the Golani Brigade Moshi had long ago mastered the fine art of sleeping while standing. There had been desert nights so cold his unit had taken turns sleeping on the hood of the half-track with the engine running.

The seat belt sign flashed on. "Damn," she said aloud, and quickly got out of the cubicle. She hated airplane lavatories. That sign always went on at the most inopportune moments. What a way to go. She could just see the headlines: Meredith Sloane, daughter of Philadelphia banker, Jonathan Harris Sloane, and Main Line hostess, the former Patricia Meredith, found dead, decapitated, mangled—whatever—in the wreck-

age of an El Al jumbo jet somewhere in the Swiss Alps. The post-deb's body was identified by her school ring (Bryn Mawr, Class of '73) and a pornographic letter from her married lover, Roger Logan, Rich Young Lawyer, potential Congressional Candidate, and Father of Three. Maybe Four.

Oh Daddy, she thought, wouldn't you just love that. Tish, too. Tish! How could anyone feel anything for a mother every-one called "Tishie," for God's sake? Tishie. It was obscene. But then everyone at home was either Bitsy, Betsy, Mimsy, or Boo. And Meri, of course. How wonderful they all looked together, that contingent of young colts in their cashmere sweaters and plaid kilts, their long silky manes flying as they cut a cool swathe through the crowds of Center City when they ventured forth downtown for lunch or a matinee. And of course they all had to go together, as if there were something to be feared by going alone into the midst of everyday mortals, those poor gray creatures who rode buses instead of the Paoli or the Chestnut Hill local; as if one of them might be con-taminated by contact with the blacks that crossed over from Market to Chestnut Street or even, God forbid, to Walnut.

God, she thought, it was a good thing she'd taken the apartment in New York. Sometimes it bothered her, though, that her friends in Manhattan didn't seem to be all that differ-ent from the ones she'd left behind.

It bothered her that she had never seemed to be able to commit herself to anything or anyone. Even the affair with Roger was little more than another experience. It had been time to have a married man, just as in school it had been time for the Princeton senior, and then the visiting professor, and the New York film-maker. Had any of them really touched her? Even in the intimacy of passion had she ever really opened herself to anything beyond the experience of the mo-ment?

A handsome gentleman in his fifties nodded politely as their paths crossed in the aisle. She watched him climb the

stairs back to First Class, the neatly folded prayer shawl tucked under his arm. He might have been one of her father's associates. Certainly she would not have guessed that he was Jewish.

Of course she had come into contact with Jews—at school, later on in New York. Somehow, though, those people had never really impressed her as being, well, Jewish. The young actors and artists and film-makers were a world unto themselves; and the brokers and lawyers and publishers had long been carefully assimilated into the private world of wealth and prestige, so that no vestige of their heritage remained for any to see but the yearly contributions to their particular charities and the political support of a sandy slice of land somewhere in the Middle East. Was it possible that such men had ever worn a prayer shawl and skullcap to welcome their God with the dawning sun? It was difficult to imagine. Why the Serfes, for example, gave the best parties. . . . Of course there were still social events where even Unitarians were barred, not to mention advocates of Ethical Culture—especially at Woodside, the family estate. Only last weekend, there had been the usual Saturday night gathering of that particular set which Meri always privately thought of as the Great White Clan, a group bound together by bridge and blue chip stocks, immune and seemingly oblivious to the ills that beset more ordinary mortals. Disaster to someone like Chessie Greene meant having an eligible bachelor cancel out an hour before her dinner party; while inflation to Yvonne Hadley (Vonnie, of course) meant serving California wine, instead of French, to her women's consciousness-raising group. Still, Meri mused, Vonnie wasn't all that bad. She had been the first to applaud Meri's working at the museum and had been genuinely enthusiastic about this trip.

"I think it's wonderful, the museum sending you, dear," the woman had said emphatically. "It's about time they started taking us gals seriously."

"Why not?" Alex Merrill boomed. "Couldn't have picked

7

a better legman." He winked; and Meri moved quickly to avoid the little pat he was about to bestow on her behind.

Tish, of course, was worried—not just about bombs going off in the plane or terrorist attacks on the Hilton: "The food is just awful, darling. Margaret Drew took one of those Holy Land tours last summer—the Church sponsored it. She said there was a little shop you must visit—oh God, what was the name of it? She wrote it down somewhere. Anyway, do be careful what you eat, darling. Margaret said her group came down with something that made 'Montezuma's Revenge' look like hiccoughs."

" 'Jew's Revenge'! Ha!"

"Don't be vulgar, Alex," Tish Sloane said sternly.

"Well, I wouldn't be at all surprised if they did try to poison us," Alison Morris said with a shrug. "I mean, they're just fanatics about their precious little Israel. Look how they've behaved toward the poor Arabs, kicking them out like that."

"They didn't kick them out, Alison."

"Now don't tell me you're a Zionist, Meri. Although, I suppose, living in New York . . ."

"I'm a Zionist," Chessie Greene broke in cheerfully. "I love Jewish men."

"You love anything that—oh, never mind. Really, Chessie," Alison drawled, "don't you think it's time you outgrew your bus boys and tour guides?"

"Not a chance." She turned to Meri with a wink. "You know what would really be perfect? A half-black, Jewish, Puerto Rican." She sighed. "I don't think I'll settle for anything less as husband number five."

"If I come across one, I'll let you know," Meri said with a laugh.

Chessie popped a macadamia nut into her mouth. "Anyway, Israelis are out."

"What?"

"Israelis are out. On the cocktail circuit, anyway. Palestinians are in." Her long red nails scraped the nut dish clean. "I

can see you now in the refugee camp," she said dreamily, munching away. "His eyes are very dark, very soulful. God, I could come just thinking about it."

"Thinking about what?" Drew Paine, unpublished novelist, joined them. His family had made a fortune in real estate.

"You, of course, darling. What else? Meri's going to Israel," she added.

He raised his eyebrows. "I thought everyone was going to Rio, this year. The museum doesn't mind?"

"The museum is sending her," Vonnie Hadley explained. "Some of us have jobs, Drew."

"Can't imagine why." He turned to Meri. "What are you going to do, luv, pick oranges on some whadayacallem—oh yes—a *kibbutz?*"

Meri sighed. Didn't anyone around here ever take anyone—or anything beside the Devon Horse Show—seriously? "I happen to be going to Israel as a representative of the Metropolitan Museum of New York," she said as calmly as she could, "to investigate the progress Dr. Eleazar Ben Levi is making in his excavation of one Tel Shalazar, said dig being sponsored in part by said museum. I am not going to pick oranges nor do I intend to administer to the emotional wounds of any grieving Palestinians. I have no political leanings one way or the other, if you must know—and the only extraneous thing I hope to pick up is a nice tan."

"Somebody picking on my little girl?" Jonathan Sloane joined them now.

Fortified by her father's arm around her, Meri turned to Alison Morris. "And I think it's wrong to be contemptuous of the deep feelings I imagine Jewish people must have for Israel. For us it's just another place, but for them, why, I should imagine it's a symbol of their very survival as a people."

"She's right," her father seconded.

"Come now, Jonathan," Drew Paine said. "The Jews don't need any symbol. They have an absolute instinct for survival."

"How can you say that, Drew?" Vonnie Hadley asked. "After Hitler—"

"Exactly. They're still around, aren't they? No, my darlings, if the world as we know it were to end tomorrow either by war or natural disaster, I can assure you that when the last great rumble of thunder subsided, out of the smoke and ashes three creatures would emerge: A rat, a cockroach, and a Jew."

They were singing. A group of students in the rear of the plane had gathered around the bearded young man in blue jeans and work shirt whom she had earlier seen in the midst of the praying men. He was a burly fellow who might have been a farm laborer or truck driver; he was, in fact, an ordained rabbi taking a year's sabbatical from his Massachusetts congregation to study in Jerusalem. His muscular arms cradled the guitar lovingly as the youngsters around him sang and clapped. He threw back his head, laughing, as they stumbled over the Hebrew words to the song.

"*Chai,*" he corrected them, rolling the "h" sound at the back of his throat. "Not 'hi,' like 'hello.' "

"Hello is *shalom*," one of the boys shouted, eager to show what he knew.

"Yea, Larry!" The others applauded and cheered, to which the boy responded by giving a victory salute.

"Okay, now, c'mon," the guitar player said. "*Chai. Am Yisroel Chai.*"

"What does it mean, do you know?" The blue-haired lady next to her whispered politely to Meri.

The girl was surprised. "I really don't know."

"We're Baptists, you see," the woman apologized, nodding toward the man next to her.

Before Meri could answer, a man across the aisle said to them, "What do you want to know? What they are singing?" He had a heavy accent.

"Why, yes," the woman said timidly. "It's the Hebrew language, isn't it?"

"Of course it's *Ivrit*," the Israeli said brusquely. "What do you think, it's Japanese? It's Hebrew. *Am Yisroel Chai*. Israel lives."

"Oh," the woman said brightly. "Thank you very much." Once he'd turned away, she raised her eyebrows, murmuring to her husband, "Edna said they were arrogant. Did you ever hear such rudeness in your life?"

"Wha—? What?" The man looked up hurriedly from the *Playboy* magazine he was engrossed in. He cleared his throat. "Interesting article here. Very interesting."

The blue-haired lady sighed.

"They are the most arrogant bastards you will ever wish to meet," Diane Whitney had warned Meri. "I am absolutely delighted Max is sending you this time. After last year, I have not the slightest desire to ever visit Israel again."

"That bad?"

"Don't get me started. You'll just end up thinking I'm anti-Semitic. And I'm not, really, I'm not. But even the shop-girls there do their best to make you feel absolutely insignificant."

Meri laughed. "I've always felt that about the ones at Gucci."

"Just wait, my girl. Tell an Israeli your father is Jonathan Harris Sloane, and he'll ask if he's a trio. Now here"—she handed her a folder—"here is the last report we had from Jerusalem. You will note the date. Three months ago. Ben Levi knows we are under pressure with the UNESCO investigation and still no word from him. Typical. The Israelis don't give a damn what anyone thinks. Has Max briefed you?"

"He called from the hospital. I didn't realize this dig meant so much to him."

"Max has always been enamored of the Holy Land. Maybe it's that Episcopalian minister father of his. He was active in Palestine long before it became a Jewish state, and was very instrumental in getting certain moneyed parties to back expe-

11

ditions there. That's why the Israelis are allowing us now"—
she snorted at the word "allowing"—"to fund this one. They're
very possessive about exploration. And of course we get the
first outside exhibit. All right, now, here's the story. What
we're dealing with is the possibility of a Christian community
outside Jerusalem dating roughly to the time of our Lord.
There seems to be evidence," she said carefully, "—and here is
where we are particularly interested—pointing to the existence of some silver artifacts."

"The chalice."

"I didn't say that. Did Max?"

"You know that's what he thinks."

Diane sighed. "Dreamers. All of you. Anyway, you know
what's going on in the UN now. UNESCO has received word
that Ben Levi's expedition is disrupting the Arab community in
the area—something like that. Accordingly, some very important people whom we are depending on for some very important acquisitions—I cannot disclose their names but I can tell
you they owe heart, soul, and bank account to the oil cartel—
are on our backs. Of course if an important Christian relic is
discovered at the site we would carry on regardless of UN
condemnation. The Israelis will in any event. However, we
haven't heard a word from Ben Levi. It's impossible to do
anything over the phone, and the upshot is you had better get
your size nine behind over there and come up with some
answers for us. Think you can handle it?"

"I don't see why not."

"Yes, well, you've never been to Israel. Come up with a
million dollar grant for those s.o.b.'s and they act as if they are
doing you a favor by accepting it. Spend weeks arranging an
important meeting and discover at the last moment that your
key person has been called up for reserve duty. Everywhere
you turn you're either frustrated, insulted, or robbed."

"Max certainly doesn't seem to share your opinions."

"You will like Israel," the department head had told her
just before he was stricken with the heart attack. His eyes had

taken on a very special gleam. "You know, Meri," he had said, "there is a passion for life among some people that you and I were never heir to. It is something we ought to acquire along with all the social graces. I have the feeling that Israel will be good for you, as it was for me."

"Max is blinded by the Mediterranean sun," Diane Whitney said. He's such a good-hearted fool he doesn't know when he's being insulted. Fortunately, the Arabs still have a sense of courtesy. Whatever you do, don't turn down the cup of coffee or tea they will offer when you enter their shops." She paused. "Stick with the tea. Arab coffee works like melted Ex-Lax."

"You wish to eat?" the stewardess asked.

"What? Oh. Yes. Thank you."

She accepted the tray mechanically. Why had Max spoken to her that way? What had he seen to prompt that statement about some people having a "passion for life"? Did he think she was just another cold, shallow "society girl"? Or was that what she herself feared? No, she thought suddenly, fiercely, seeing the faces of Alison Morris and Chessie Greene and her own good-natured but frivolous mother. She wanted more from life—and from herself—than that. She wanted something . . . more.

She really was hungry. She looked down at the food before her. Coffee. Juice. Cream cheese. Smoked salmon. The stewardess was coming down the aisle with a basket of bagels. Meri had to smile.

Mrs. Goldblatt, after all.

13

2

Eleazar Ben Levi brushed one thousand nine hundred and seven years worth of dirt from the clay fragment and held it up to the light. His hands were as tender as a lover's. Yes, there it was. An *aleph*, the first letter of the Hebrew alphabet. A scratch to the left of the shard—was that another letter? He threw every bit of his energy into concentrating on the object. Yes, yes it was. It had to be. . . .

"Hallo! Hallo!"

He sighed. "What is it, Raffi?"

The boy was very excited. His dark eyes were like two big black buttons in the small face. He gestured wildly with his dirty hands. "Come! The *jinji* has found something!"

The *jinji*. That would be the redhead from South Africa. Amazing how the Arab child had picked up so much Israeli slang.

The red-haired girl in question was surrounded by a group of student "diggers." She handed what looked to be a greenish jewel to the archaeologist. It had been smoothed by time, its gleam softened by age. "I think it's Roman glass." She tried not

to sound too excited. "That would support your theory, wouldn't it? It was over there, where we found the parchment." She was watching his face intently.

Ben Levi turned the fragment in his hand. "Good specimen," he said at last. "Coca-Cola bottle. Circa 1949-1950, C.E." He smiled at the crestfallen girl. "*Lo hashuv*. Don't worry. There are plenty of these in private collections." He tossed the glass back to the girl who, disgusted, let it drop to the ground.

Raffi snatched it up. "Give it to me!"

"Why, what will you do with it?" one of the boys teased him. "Keep it for good luck?"

"Stupid. I will sell it to the tourists." He was off, his long legs kicking up stones and sand as he flew toward the marketplace of Jerusalem.

Ben Levi was less amused than the others. "Keep him out of here," he told Uri, the young Israeli who was the unofficial leader of the students.

"He does no harm," the *sabra* said mildly. "He makes us laugh. He's a good kid."

"And probably stealing us blind."

"Not Raffi, He's okay. One hundred percent."

Ben Levi raised his eyebrows. "Since when did you become such a lover of Arabs? Maybe you should be in the Knesset instead of in the field."

Uri reddened but said nothing.

"Just keep him out of my way."

"As you wish," the boy said coldly and went back to his group.

Angry with himself, Ben Levi stalked to his car, cursing himself all the way back to the university. What idiotic things to say. He must have sounded like a complete fool. Leah would really have taken him to task for it. My wife the social worker, he thought. It never failed to amaze him that she could still go into the Arab community of the Old City the way she did,

getting the women to the clinics, getting the children to attend the schools. . . .

The children. How could she even look at them?

There was a message for him back at his office. Miss Sloane had arrived from New York. She was at the King David.

"Miss Sloane?"

Terza, his secretary, looked up from her lunch. He wished she wouldn't balance the Tempo soft drink bottle on the typewriter carriage.

"The one they sent from the Metropolitan."

"Ah, yes. Poor Radnor. So what does she want?"

Terza shrugged. "I don't know. We sent a report. I typed it myself before I went to *meloim* last month."

He pulled a cola-stained document from the pile on his desk and held it up. "This one?"

"Oy-va-voy! Didn't you send it?"

"I meant to."

She shook her head. "Oy-va-voy!"

He tossed the report onto the table between them. "Sorry, Miss Sloane. We are not usually so disorganized. My secretary was called away by the army last month, and then there was this business of the UN commission, so—" He spread his hands in apology.

"Yes, that's why the board was so anxious to hear from you. If there's going to be a UNESCO condemnation, it may get sticky for us. Of course, if you are really on to something—"

"There will be a condemnation, as you call it. Rest assured. Whether or not it is warranted is another matter. For nearly twenty years following our War of Independence, the Jordanians systematically destroyed all traces of Jewish life in the part of Jerusalem they controlled. Tombstones from Jewish cemeteries were ripped out to pave their lavatories—the closest, I can assure you, they have ever come to defecating

upon us. The ancient Jewish Quarter, which we are now in the process of restoring, and where, incidentally, I am fortunate enough to live, was for all purposes demolished. Yet, strangely, in all the time that was going on and people were being driven from their homes—Jews, not Arabs, you understand—their holy places desecrated or destroyed, no one said a word. Not one speech from all the righteous delegates to the world body about how the 'character of the city' was being altered and changed." He lit a cigarette and smiled at her. "Don't worry. You will see for yourself that we have done nothing to warrant the wrath of Rumania and Tanzania. In any case, there is indeed evidence of an early Christian settlement in Tel Shalazar, so that should make everything all right. It's a matter of priorities. What, after all, is the western wall of Solomon's Temple compared to the humble stall of an Arab shopkeeper?" he commented wryly, recalling world indignation when the area surrounding the Temple Mount was cleared so that the people should not be interrupted in their prayers by sniper fire. "But then, what is the stall of an Arab shopkeeper compared to a fragment of a bowl touched perhaps by the Nazarene himself? Would you like more coffee?"

"Thank you, no." She leaned closer. "Have you really found—"

"I speak in parables. Like your Christ."

They strolled out onto the balcony of the hotel. The view was breathtaking.

"*Yerushalayim Shel Zahav*. Jerusalem of Gold." He took a deep breath, seemed to drink in the melting sun that spread a veil of gold over the hills of the city. "I have been all over the world, but never have I found a city as seductive as this, the city where I was born. Jerusalem," he said softly to the walled city, "you are not ours so much as we are yours."

She stood transfixed by the panorama before her. The fatigue and tension of her journey now left her; she felt her body relax in the sweet, cool mountain air. For a moment she

18

had the strange sensation that she was being drawn up into the golden sky, that, had she wished, she could fly.

Ben Levi turned to her. "You must be tired."

"No, I'm fine. I want very much to see the Tel."

"Tomorrow. It will be dark soon. Night falls very quickly here. Read your report. I will bring you up to date tomorrow. Meanwhile, rest, have a good dinner. The fish is good, the chicken not so good. I will come for you myself. No," he remembered, "I can't. I have classes in the morning."

"The afternoon?"

"No good. Tomorrow is Friday. *Shabbat.* Everything stops at two. Never mind. You will walk around the city, do some shopping, as you women like. You will find what to do," he said matter-of-factly. "In the evening you will come to us for dinner. I will pick you up here at the hotel."

"Professor—"

He was already half across the lobby. Suddenly, he stopped, turned as though he had remembered something else. "You have everything? Did Linda fix you up all right? You have everything you Americans need?"

"Everything is fine." Linda Meyers, of the university's public relations department, had picked her up at the airport, driven her to Jerusalem, checked her in, was meeting her for dinner that evening.

"*Yoffi.* Great. See you tomorrow. *Shalom.*" A wave of his hand, and he was gone.

Meri took a deep breath. She felt as though she had been dropped into the midst of a whirlwind.

Linda Meyers was a large chunk of woman with a warm smile and the sort of sympathetic, friendly manner that soothed the frayed nerves of visiting "hotshots" and made her indispensable to the public relations office. The famous Meyers smile was a bit forced now. She always felt uncomfortable in the presence of small-boned females. Meredith Sloane

19

was nearly as tall as she; but the girl's long, slender legs and patrician good looks made her uneasy about her own Amazon-like stature and reminded her unhappily of the WASP lovelies back in Ohio who had seemed to exist in a perpetual state of blue-eyed grace. Surreptitiously, she studied the ivory silk blouse, the little "nothing knit" skirt and sweater. Nice. Understated, casual but chic, and very, very expensive.

"If there is anything in particular you'd like to see during your visit with us, just let me know," she said enthusiastically. "There are some wonderful tours. . . ."

"Thank you, I thought I'd just wander around, get the feel of things. I seem to have the day off tomorrow."

"Yes, the professor lectures in the morning." Was that supposed to be funny, or not? You never could tell with the *goyim* what they really meant.

"I thought I'd rent a car."

"I've arranged that. The Fiat we drove up in—you can use that. You have your license, of course?"

They went over a few more details. Linda Meyers made a point of describing the various sites that held particular attention for the Christian world.

"I'm not very religious," Meri confessed. "Frankly, I've seen all the churches I care to see in Italy and France."

Linda was taken aback by this. "Oh."

Meri smiled at her. "Look, just think of me as another American. Like you. After all, we come from the same world—"

Not in a million years, Linda Meyers thought. Aloud, she said politely, "I wasn't thinking of you as a Christian. The Via Dolorosa, Bethlehem, Nazareth—why, everybody wants to go there. Don't you think it's fascinating to see all the places mentioned in the Bible?"

"Yes, of course. I didn't mean to sound rude. Please forgive me if I did. I've always had a horror of guided tours and, well, organized sightseeing. And for once I'd just like to find my own way."

Holly Golightly with bread, huh? Lotsa luck. Linda Meyers cleared her throat, smiled her most dazzling smile. "Of course. This is a very exciting country. I'm sure you will find much to interest you."

She started off early the next morning. The road leading from the city was an empty highway cutting into the silent desert. Signs pointed the way to Jericho, the Dead Sea, Masada.

She turned on the car radio, and an Israeli pop tune filled the morning air. It was a typical Israeli song, the kind they seemed to like because it was good to clap hands and march to. She did not know that the words to the infectious tune were those of the twenty-first psalm. The *sabra* liked his Bible best accompanied by electric guitar.

On the outskirts of Jerusalem, an Arab woman crossed the road with a basket of oranges on her head. Meri stopped the car and managed to make the woman understand that she wanted to buy some. She went off at last with half a dozen oranges wrapped in her scarf, having cheerfully paid many times the amount the woman would receive in the marketplace. Meri did not care. She felt good, eager for adventure, for whatever the Jericho Highway might hold in store. She patted the Bazak guide to Israel in the seat beside her. She'd done her home-work. The little Fiat flew along the road in time, it seemed, to the music.

Another sign. Wadi Kelt. She had heard about that from Max. What was it? An oasis at the bottom of a deep ravine? A monastery? She ought to have let Linda Meyers arrange a tour. No. She wanted to be alone. The morning was too perfect, she felt too fine to trust this outing to a commercialized venture. She would trust her instinct, go wherever the feeling took her. And right now, that seemed to be to Wadi Kelt.

The sand alongside the road began to be littered here and there with a few silent, rusting tanks. The road dipped like a roller coaster; signs marking the drop in elevation began to

21

appear. Suddenly, as if sensing a presence, she turned off the road and onto the sand and dirt. It was here. She was sure of it.

Like an apparition emerging from a mist of dust, the jeep appeared.

"*Atzor!* Halt!"

She leaned her head out the car window. "Something wrong?"

One of the two young soldiers in the command car leaped out, the gun moving from his shoulder to his hands. He peered into the Fiat before answering. Satisfied she was alone, he said, "No good. You cannot be here."

"I was looking for Wadi Kelt—"

The other soldier began to speak into a walkie-talkie.

"Please. Out." He beckoned her out of the car.

"Look, I just wanted to—"

"Identification, please. You have papers?"

With a sigh, she handed him her wallet. "My passport is at the hotel."

He nodded, walked to the rear of the car, studied the license plate, studied her driver's license and Social Security card.

She was getting annoyed. "Do you mind telling me what all this is about? No, wait. I'll tell you. I've stumbled onto your nuclear reactor, right? This is where you make the bombs, right? Let's see, *Time* magazine said that was in Dimona. This wouldn't be Dimona, by any chance?"

The soldier looked up from her papers. "English?"

"American."

"I have an uncle in America. New Jersey. You know New Jersey?"

"Not intimately."

"She make belts." He pointed to her waist.

"Who, me? I—oh, you mean your uncle. Your uncle makes belts."

"*Ken.* My uncle."

"Terrific."

22

Another jeep pulled up. Two more soldiers. The Israeli in the first car said something to the newcomers. The driver grinned at her. She smiled back. "Hi."

The young soldier handed back her wallet. "Okay. Tourist. Okay. But not to be here. Could be mines." He pointed to the ground. "Okay?" He smiled.

"Mines?"

He shrugged apologetically.

She looked up at the two jeeps. The grinning driver was still grinning. The Israeli beside him sat impassively, his arms folded across his chest, his eyes hidden behind aviator sunglasses. The third soldier was still on his walkie-talkie.

"Well, thanks, I guess. I just wanted to see Wadi Kelt," she called out lamely, adding to herself, "whatever that is." Suddenly an idea occurred to her. She reached into the car for the camera. "How about a picture for your uncle in New Jersey?"

With what sounded very much like an oath, the Israeli in the sunglasses leaped from the jeep and grabbed the camera from her hands.

"Hey—" she started to say.

The voice was low and terse. The words were clear and spoken without the slightest trace of any accent. "Lady," the man said, "will you kindly get the hell out of here?"

She was so surprised that she just stood there with her mouth open.

"You are damn near a restricted area as well as in the vicinity of what we suspect may be a *Fatah* mine field. Now, for my sake and your mother's—go home."

"My mother is in Philadelphia. Which makes 'home' rather a long distance for now. Would you mind terribly if I just went on to, say, Jericho?"

He took the glasses off, wiped the sweat from the bridge of his nose. His eyes were a startling shade of blue green. Quite deliberately he looked her over, making a point of studying her legs, her denim shorts and halter top. He finally reached her

23

face and shook his head. "You're going to Jericho," he echoed, "like that?"

She felt herself redden. "Come now, Captain, you're not going to feed me some story about the natives going berserk at the sight of bare legs and dragging me off to some alley."

He shrugged. "I'm not going to tell you any stories at all. You obviously know all there is to know."

"I know you Israelis would like to have everyone think the worst of the people whose land you occupy." If she thought this would anger him she was mistaken.

"On the contrary," he replied calmly. "I have a great deal of respect for our Arab citizens—which is more than you exhibit by dressing like that."

"I am not an idiot, Sergeant. I have a skirt in the car."

"I see I've been demoted." He grinned and turned to the other soldiers, saying something to them in Hebrew. They laughed.

"May I have my camera please?" The tone of her voice could have frozen the streets of Philadelphia in July.

He flipped it open, removed the film, tossed the Nikon back to her. "Sure."

He was in the jeep again as quickly as he had left it, leaving her standing beside the little Fiat, camera in one hand, roll of exposed film in the other.

"Go home," he said once more; and though he pointed to Jerusalem, she would often wonder if he meant Philadelphia.

She waved at the soldiers who had escorted her back to the main road, then quite deliberately set the car toward Jericho. The morning stillness soon quieted her pique, and as she flipped on the radio again, she told herself that the men had only been doing what they considered to be their duty. It was just that one who had been so unpleasant. After all, it wasn't as though she had deliberately tried to be troublesome or to pry into their precious military secrets. She could have sworn he was an American—those blue green eyes. He was all of a shade of dusty brown—the uniform, the taut skin, the thick curly hair

24

he'd run his hand through. Tall, well built. The color of his eyes was startling in that tanned face.

Jericho was full of palm trees. There were signs all over the place pointing to the "Ruins." She parked the Fiat, then noticed what appeared to be a restaurant across the way and went over to it. The place was cool and shadowed inside. A huge ceiling fan turned slowly overhead. A dark young man in jeans and a University of Michigan T-shirt lounged sullenly behind a counter.

"Good morning."

He nodded.

"You speak English."

He nodded again.

"Can I get something to drink here?"

"Coke?"

"All right."

He watched her down the soda greedily. "You're American," he declared.

"Yes." She was eager to make friends. "Have you ever been to the States?"

"I go to school in America."

"How do you like it?"

He shrugged. "I learn more than I can here."

"Well, yes, I suppose the opportunities are greater."

"I'm Arab. There are no opportunities here for me at all."

"Oh." She looked around. "This is a very nice place."

"It belongs to my family. We have an arrangement since '67 with Eged Tours. All the buses stop here."

"That's very nice for you."

"Everyone knows us. We give good price. Believe me, anything you see"— he waved at the shelves of dolls dressed like Arab women, the letter openers of olive wood, the boxes inlaid with mother-of-pearl—"Anything here, I give you a good price. You tell me what you want, I give you the best

25

possible price. You won't do better in the street. Also we have very clean rest rooms. American-style toilets. Very nice."

An ornate box inlaid with dark wood and mother-of-pearl caught her eye. "That's lovely."

He brought the box down from the shelf, opened it for her.

"It's a backgammon board," she exclaimed with pleasure.

He smiled for the first time. "*Shesh-besh*. We call it *shesh-besh*. It's a very old game."

"Yes, I know."

"You want it? I make you a very good price. Twenty-five percent off for dollars."

"Well, I wasn't really thinking of buying anything now, although it is beautiful."

"Sixty dollars. All handmade. Real mother-of-pearl."

"It's lovely."

"Fifty dollars. For you. Because you're American."

"Thank you, that's very nice of you. Look, I really don't want to carry anything around. I'll stop back in a little while. How much for the Coke?"

"On the house. I told you, I like Americans."

"Thank you. You're very kind."

He leaned closer. "You stop back. I give it to you for forty-five dollars. I tell my father I know you from the States."

"Oh. Well, okay. Um. Okay." She moved to the door, turned back. "You mentioned bus tours. Am I going to run into any now?"

"No. There are none due for an hour or so."

"Good," she said, smiling at him. "I hate crowds," she added conspiratorially.

There were signs all over the place leading down to the excavated ruins of ancient Jericho. She descended the steps that led to the past. Like many tourists, Meri found her first view of an excavated site a bit disappointing, since here was not a Ben Hur Hollywood set, but only the foundations of what had once been cities, streets, temples, and palaces. On the whole,

she had to admit she preferred reconstructed models. She was about to turn back when she saw the young man in the college shirt standing a few feet away.

"You are disappointed."

"Somehow, I thought there'd be more."

"Because you don't know where to look." He came close to her. "Come, I'll show you." He took her arm, began to lead her deeper into the maze of ruins.

"That's all right," she said hastily, gently pulling free. "Actually, I have a number of places to see today."

"What's your hurry? You must never hurry in the Middle East." He smiled at her. "We do things nice and slow here."

Something in the tone of his voice made her uneasy.

"I have a girl friend in America," he said suddenly. "She's blonde too. Much blonder than you."

She cleared her throat. "How nice."

He grinned. "I teach her the way we do things in the Middle East. She likes it very much."

"Will she be coming here to live?" She was trying to think of something to say.

He shrugged. "What do I need her here for? Come. I show you the ruins." He smiled again. "You like the *sheshbesh*? Maybe I give it to you as a present. For a kiss. What do you say?"

"I—I—"

"Looks like rain."

Startled, she looked in the direction of the voice. A man in a khaki uniform stood some ten yards away from them. He was tall, broad-shouldered, with a mop of thick, golden brown curly hair. The eyes behind the aviator sunglasses were, she knew, a vivid shade of blue green.

He took a cigarette from the pack in his shirt pocket and casually lit it.

She looked up at the bright blue sky. The sun blazed down upon them. White cotton clouds floated languidly by.

27

"Definitely going to rain," the soldier said. "I can always tell."

The Arab had disappeared like a magician's rabbit. They were alone in a crossword puzzle outline of sand and heaped stone. She stared at him.

"Don't tell me I'm in a restricted area," she finally managed to say with what she thought was a fine degree of irony.

"You never know."

"Or have you come to deliver the weather report—sort of a special service for tourists?"

He exhaled a ring of smoke.

"You needn't have interfered. I was quite all right. The boy was only trying to show me around."

"Sure he was."

"You have an evil mind. Or is it because he's an Arab?"

He sighed. "Lady, do you have any idea how many dumb broads come skipping around here looking for fun and games? Sooner or later one of you gets raped by some fifteen-year-old warrior with a mustache who just wants to show you a short cut to the Wailing Wall, or beat up by some Moroccan pimp who expected a higher return on the coffee he bought you than you'd probably care to give. Now I don't give a damn what you do in Chicago—"

"Philadelphia. New York."

"But you are not going to bust up some cop's *Shabbat* by provoking an incident."

"Provoking!" He had led her back to the open square in front of the souvenir shop.

"I suggest you let the hotel arrange a group tour for you— damn!" He threw down the cigarette. "I knew it."

The Arab student had returned followed by a small crowd of angry men. They were all exclaiming wildly in Arabic. "Militarist pig!" the boy shouted, suddenly breaking into English. "Fascist oppressor! Take the whore before we kill you both!"

The crowd of men began to close in on them, shouting and

shaking their fists. Women began to appear in the windows of houses. A group of children ran toward them, excited by the noise.

The Israeli said something in Arabic. Meri marveled at the calm, easy tone of his voice. He had removed the sunglasses. Quietly, the Israeli continued to talk to the emerging mob; he sounded almost apologetic.

The Arab boy in the T-shirt spat on the ground. His voice became more and more shrill; he turned to the townspeople, his arms flailing the air, as though orchestrating their fury to even greater heights. Someone bent down, found a rock, raised it in the air. . . .

A warning shot fired from an M-16 froze the scene. A jeep had pulled into the open square. Meri recognized the driver. He was not grinning now. He held a walkie-talkie to his mouth. The rifle was propped in his lap, barrel straight up in the air, his finger held firm on the trigger. The soldier with Meri said something to him in Hebrew; the driver of the jeep nodded, his eyes never leaving the crowd.

"Where's your car?"

"Right there. To your left."

"Get the keys out of your bag. Are the doors locked?"

"I don't know. No, not on the driver's side."

"Good. Walk slowly. Get in first. Slide over. Okay?"

"Yes."

"Good. That's it. Slowly. Give me the keys."

The mob, undecided whether to go after the couple on foot or the soldier in the jeep, now began to quarrel among themselves. The appearance of two more cars filled with uniformed men seemed to settle the question. Stones began to fly through the air at the police as the force moved to disperse the rioters.

Meri slipped into the Fiat, scrambled over the gearshift into the adjoining seat as the Israeli moved in and started the car. As they pulled out of Jericho they could hear the sounds of a full-scale melee behind them.

29

Neither spoke for some time. The road stretched ahead silently, the stillness of the desert enveloping them. She wanted to say something, didn't know what. Finally she murmured, "It's all your fault. Nothing would have happened if you hadn't followed me."

Without answering, he took the pack of cigarettes from his shirt pocket and held it out to her. She shook her head. Still without a word he took one for himself and lit it, inhaling deeply.

"After all," she continued," we don't really know the boy intended to do anything, uh, funny."

Still, he said nothing.

"I admit I was beginning to feel a bit nervous, but I could have handled him."

He shot her a look. "The way you handle your boyfriends in Philadelphia?"

"I live in New York. Anyway, he may very well have thought I was leading him on. I was trying to be friendly. Oh God," she remembered, "I said I hated crowds. . . ."

Another look.

"Nothing would have happened," she repeated firmly. "I know it. You shouldn't have followed me."

He adjusted the rearview mirror. "I didn't follow you," he responded calmly. "We had reason to believe your friend was going to stir things up today one way or another. There's a television crew from London filming in the area. Give the folks at home a nice look at Israeli police clubbing sweet little Arab kids over the head. We managed to divert the tour buses." He paused. "I had an idea to check around myself."

"I didn't realize . . . I really am sorry. I didn't mean to cause any trouble."

"You're right, I'm the one that triggered it off. One look at this uniform was all they needed." He shook his head. "Stupid of me. I should have let Mohammed grab you. The worst that could happen was we'd be out one tourist." He turned to look at her briefly, then smiled. Only this time, it was not a sardonic

half-smile, nor an insolent grin. He had, she thought, a very nice smile indeed. "Where do you want to go?"

"I'm staying at the King David."

"I thought you wanted to see the country."

She stared at him in surprise.

"Trying to make amends. You held up well back there."

"I was in a state of shock. I think I still am."

"Well, you didn't faint. That's good."

"I've never fainted in my life."

"Good. You want the five dollar tour or the ten?"

"The ten. By all means."

"Right." He switched on the radio. Like all Israelis, he rarely rode in any kind of vehicle without the radio blaring out music and, more importantly, news. She leaned back in her seat, watching him. He drove fast but with a relaxed surety, as though the terrain were part of him and he a part of it. The road continued to dip downward to the Dead Sea. The palm trees of Jericho had long given way to the barren hills of the Judean desert, that wilderness of sand and rock, where jackals howled at night, where gazelles sometimes leaped into view, where, once, lions and prophets had roamed.

Here I am, she thought, in the middle of nowhere, with a stranger, truly a stranger, a man of whom I know nothing and who knows me not at all. I don't know where I'm going or whom I'm with or even what the words are to the song on the radio—and why do I feel so . . . so . . . content?

More than content. Excited, yes. Scared, maybe. Not scared of him, not really—no, not scared at all.

The hot, dry, desert wind whipped her hair about her face. She felt flushed all over.

She took an orange from the scarf on the floor and clumsily began to peel it. He took it from her, bit off a piece at one end and spat that out the window. Bracing his elbow against the steering wheel, he stuck his thumb into the place he'd bit, making a hole there, then handed the orange back to her. "Roll it on your thighs."

31

"I beg your pardon?"

"Sorry. Between your hands. Go on. Do it."

Wondering, she rolled the orange between her palms. "Now what?"

He shook his head at her ignorance, retrieved the fruit, and held it aloft, squeezing the juice into his mouth. "Like that."

She liked it.

Afterward he split the orange open for her. "Tell me something," she said mischievously, chewing on the pulp. "What is the difference between an Arab wanting to show me around—and an Israeli?"

He took another orange from the scarf, bit a piece off the end, and spat that out the window before answering. "Style, lady," he said cheerfully. "Simply a matter of style."

The tour buses were already parked at Qumran, their occupants milling around the refreshment stand before inspecting the remains of the Essene community, a sect of Christian-like ascetics who had lived in the area until the Roman conquest of Judea in 70 C.E.

The soldier pointed to the cliffs behind this National Parks Authority "oasis." "The Scroll caves are over there." Then he gestured toward an area off to the side. "The toilets are over there."

She stared at him, speechless.

"Don't look so shocked. Everyone pees. Even in Philadelphia. Go wash your face. I'll meet you back here."

When she returned from the restroom area, she found that he had bought lunch for them: the round, flat bread called *pita*, slit open and filled with thin slices of grilled meat, chopped cucumbers, onions and tomatoes, and a sauce of sesame seed paste he said was *tahina*. Meri followed him to one of the picnic tables, watched him set the food out on an improvised tablecloth of small paper napkins. She was amused

32

at how neatly he placed everything. She was also, she discovered, quite hungry.

Two young women joined them at the table, drinking cola, smoking cigarettes, and chatting away in French. They spoke rather loudly and laughed quite often, all the while casting little sidelong glances at the soldier who sat across from Meri and seemed oblivious to them.

"How is it you didn't come with a group?" he asked her.

It was the first time either of them had even come close to asking who or what the other one was. In the car he had revealed nothing of his identity and made no effort to learn hers. They did not even know each other's names. They had seemed to have an unspoken agreement not to ask questions. Now, he was breaking the silence; and it pleased her that he should seek her out first. She decided, however, to be as reticent as he.

"I'm a loner."

He gave her an appreciative look, but did not question her further.

She could not help herself. "There's something I'd like to ask you."

He raised his chin as though to say, "Go ahead."

"What's your name?"

He seemed surprised. "Arik."

"Arik. That's nice."

"*Todah rabah.* Thanks."

"Just . . . Arik?"

"We're very informal here."

"Oh." She was confused.

"Come on." He got up, led her from the table. She could not be sure whether or not he was laughing at her.

"You know," she mentioned, "those girls at the table thought you were pretty terrific."

"I know."

"You're awfully sure of yourself, aren't you?"

He laughed. "I speak French. Not as well as you, I'm sure,

but enough. They thought you were a model," he added casually. "Are you?"

She smiled sweetly. "No."

"Period. All right. Hey, hold on." He caught her by the arm. "What do they call you?"

"Any number of things, I should imagine. My name is . . . Meri."

"Just . . . Meri?" he said teasingly.

"Meredith Sloane."

"Of Philadelphia." He nodded. "Figures."

She was surprised. "You know my family?"

"No. Why? Should I?"

"The way you said—"

He shrugged. "It just goes together. Your face. Your name." He lit another cigarette. "Your attitude." He studied her with that maddening half-smile. "I had a feeling you didn't come from an old Zionist family."

She had to laugh. "Hardly."

"Then what are you doing in Israel? Who are you working for?"

"I'm with the Metropolitan Museum in New York. I'm here to coordinate some information regarding a particular expedition, the results of which we hope to exhibit in the States."

"Tel Shalazar?"

"How did you know?"

"It's a small country. Besides, everyone here is an amateur archaeologist. The national pastime is digging. Almost as popular as soccer. How long will you be around?"

"Depends. A few weeks, I suppose."

"Good." Having led her through the excavated sites and reconstructed dwellings of the Essenes as they spoke, he now pointed to the cliffs behind them that were dotted with caves like so many dark eyes. "There's where they found the Scrolls." He turned. "Damn glad I kept my mouth shut and let

you read the signs. I bet you know as much about all this as I do."

"Probably not. I've only been in my particular department a little over a year. Where to now?"

"A place I know well. Masada."

An isolated mountain, surrounded on all sides by a huge void, cut off from the Judean wilderness by deep canyons, the fortress of Masada rose majestically above the western shore of the Dead Sea. Eternal symbol of freedom, site of the last significant stand against Rome by Jewish Zealots after the fall of Jerusalem in 70 C.E., Masada had long been a challenge to Israeli youths who had climbed its rocky flanks even before the tremendous, historic expedition led by Professor Yigal Yadin in the early sixties.

In the days of Herod and later in that fateful time of Jewish rebellion, two paths had led to the summit: the tortuous "snake path," winding around the eastern escarpment facing the Dead Sea in a precipitous climb of over twelve hundred feet, and the ancient western path, a somewhat easier approach rising approximately seven hundred and forty feet. To these, the Israeli government had added a third and most popular means of ascent: a cable car.

"Come on." He took her hand, bought tickets for the ride, and managed to get them on the cable car before it took off. The conductor smiled at them.

"Lay-at, lay-at," he said. "Slowly, slowly." He spoke in Hebrew to the soldier who nodded and said, *"Todah."*

Meri looked inquisitively at him.

"He said we didn't have to run," Arik explained. "He would have waited for us."

"For him," the conductor said in English, his eyes shining, "I would wait. For soldier, always." He touched his chest. "My son is also soldier. He is with Air Force."

Arik nodded appreciatively.

35

"Doesn't matter," the old man said. "Air Force, Navy. Walk with guns. Doesn't matter. They are all the best. Our boys are the best," he told Meri. "They are our pride. They are our wealth. Nothing too good for them. You understand?" They had reached the end of the ride. "Go. Enjoy. But three o'clock is last ride back. Never mind. A couple minutes I wait for you. For soldier I wait. But only couple minutes," he apologized. "Is *Shabbat*."

They thanked him, Arik assuring him they would not make him wait. "Anyway," he told Meri, "we can always walk."

"You must be kidding."

"Nope. I let you take it easy now because we only have about an hour. Next time, no ride up. We climb."

She looked at the ground below the cable car station. It was a long way down.

The Israeli laughed. "It's easy without a backpack and rifle. You just have to pace yourself." He helped her up the flight of steps cut into the rock. "Come on." He put out his hand, leading her through the same gate where, a thousand years before, refugees from the devastated cities of Judea, escaped slaves, and rebel fighters also ended their ascent, waiting on stone benches built against the walls for permission from the fortress's Zealot guards to proceed inside. The area beyond was surrounded by the vast casemate walls and their towers. For some nineteen centuries, these had been little more than a shapeless chain of stone heaps; now they had been restored in the shape of an outer and inner wall with the intervening space cut up into the chambers that had housed the majority of Masada's defenders. Meri could see the niches in the walls that had been used as cupboards, recesses that had once held lamps, bowls, cooking utensils, and food. Ten centuries after their use, the plastered walls above the cooking stoves and clay furnaces were still smudged with soot. Nearby were large "rolling stones," primitive cannon balls, which the defenders had heaped on top of the walls and towers to hurl down upon the Romans. "They were never able to use them,"

36

Arik told her, explaining that Flavius Silva, after establishing eight camps around the base of the mountain and building a circumvallation three miles long to prevent the besieged Jews from fleeing or attacking, had chosen for his assault the western side where a white promontory rose. Here, the general of the Tenth Legion had ordered thousands of Jewish slaves to pile up an embarkment of beaten earth and stone which rose toward the walls, close to the west gate. The only way the defenders of Masada could have stopped the Romans from building this platform for the dreaded battering ram would have been to hurl their missiles upon their own people. Helpless, they could only watch and wait.

Meri followed the soldier as he led her to the southern casemate wall with its tower lookout; they could see the excavated Roman camps beneath. He showed her the *mikveh* or ritual bath, the huge underground cisterns cut in the rock whereby the ingenuity of Herod's engineers had succeeded in capturing the winter floodwaters, the palatial villas which the Zealots had converted into humble living quarters. There was even a massive swimming pool and Roman bath.

In the great Western Palace, she saw columns with painted Ionian capitals, the king's bedroom, its walls covered by frescoes, and the throne room, paved by a wonderful, colored mosaic floor. "Herod was afraid of Cleopatra," Arik explained, "and probably of his own people as well. That's why he had all this built. As a refuge for himself and his family. I doubt if he ever thought it would become a camp for Jewish freedom fighters. Here, look at this."

Close to a beautiful mosaic were the remains of a stone cupboard or stove which the Zealots had built; it was a startling contrast to the luxurious Herodian floor on which it rested.

"Tired?" he asked as they emerged from the maze of rooms.

"I should be, but I'm not. Imagine, a palace on a mountain top. It's really incredible."

"If you like palaces so much, come see the best one."

37

It was a building constructed in three tiers at the northern end of the mountain. From a terrace supported by an artificial platform devised by Herod's engineers upon the narrowest tip of Masada, surrounded by columns crowned with Corinthian capitals and rows of pillars, they stared outward at an awesome silent beauty. To the north lay the oasis of Ein Gedi; eastward, the eye stretched across the Dead Sea to the mountains of Moab, westward to the hills of Judea. The cool northern breezes ruffled her hair, soothed the sun-ache of her warm skin.

"You are very quiet," he remarked.

"I don't know what to say. I've never seen anything so beautiful. One could find courage . . . even God . . . looking out at that." She turned to him. "They killed themselves, didn't they?"

He nodded. "The battering ram finally breached the casemate wall. They tried to seal the breach by building an inner stockade of wood beams, filling the intervening space with earth. But the Romans catapulted flaming missiles at the wall, setting it on fire. The Zealots thought the Northern wind would blow the fire back, but suddenly the wind shifted and carried the flame against the wall. The Romans went back to camp, figuring the fire would take its toll through the night and they would attack in the morning. The commander of Masada was a man named Eleazar Ben Yair. Evidently he had no plan of escape, no hope of leniency. Don't forget, his men had resisted Rome for seven years. Masada was more than a mop-up operation for Silva, it was a real thorn in the Roman pride. The Tenth Legion was a crack unit, ten thousand tough legionaries all in a nice temper out in that hot desert sun for some ten months or so, and with strict orders to finish off this last outpost of rebellion. No, Ben Yair had no reason to expect mercy. The Romans had already massacred the men at Machareus, the other Zealot stronghold, and enslaved the women and children there. Surrender was out of the question. So they decided to kill themselves, to cheat the Romans of their victory and escape slavery . . . or worse." His voice was

thoughtful, matter-of-fact. "Any men that survived the battle would probably have been crucified. The women would have been used, then killed. The children—who knows?" He shook his head. "I've sometimes wondered what I would have done. I don't know. I really don't know. Anyway, the inhabitants of Masada drew lots. Each man would kill his wife, children, then himself. Whoever was left would be taken care of by one of Ben Yair's ten captains, chosen by lot. Then, one last man would take care of the rest before falling on his sword—as the saying goes."

"Do you think that's how it really was?"

"Do you see those steps? They lead to a small bathhouse. There, and on the ground nearby, we found the remains of three skeletons—a man, a woman, and a child. There were arrows nearby, a remnant of a prayer shawl, a shard with Hebrew inscription. The plaster was stained with blood."

As they drove back to Jerusalem she watched the receding hills with some regret. The afternoon sun had fallen like slices of gold upon the tawny cliffs. She felt tired yet possessed of a strange energy unlike any sensation she had ever before known. She could feel his presence like something on her skin. She wondered what it would be like to touch him.

Something in her was opening up; she could feel it unfolding in the middle of her being, a strange sensation but rather a lovely one, a kind of languid letting go.

In school they'd called her the golden girl until someone pointed out that platinum was a more suitable analogy. She didn't like to think of herself as cold and was hurt that she should be thought so. It was true that everything had come easy for her; she'd never had to go out on much of a limb for anyone or anything. But, she thought defensively, there was after all so little one could be honestly passionate about, knowing the feeling was not just a fashionable pose or a shabby pretense in order to be one of the gang. Anyway, she thought with a sigh, men always had to feed their own egos by believing

you were madly in love with them—and that was one thing she knew without a doubt she had never been.

Platinum. Diamonds and platinum. She'd always hated them both. She looked up at the rosy sky, thinking lazily that she would never wear anything but pearls and molten gold from now on, pearls for the sea, and gold for the sky above Israel. She would be naked except for ropes of pearls and chains of rosy gold. . . .

She cast a quick glance at the man beside her as if to see whether he had fathomed her thoughts. What strange thoughts they were, so different from the way she usually thought of herself.

His presence was really disconcerting, though not unpleasantly so. He had taken her hand several times during the day, his grip firm as steel, but warm, so warm.

They had stood together alone on a mountaintop, just as long ago, others must have stood, with no world before them but this and a past burned to memory.

"I wonder how it was for them," she had mused. "I know it must have been difficult, yet, in a way, I envy them."

"Do you?"

"To see these hills every day, the sky, the sea. To breathe this air. . . ."

"Yes, it's beautiful. It's also hard. Harder than anything you can imagine. In winter, the rains turn everything to mud, the dampness goes right through you—you think you'll never feel warm or dry again. The wind cuts you to pieces. Summer is so brutal you start wishing for the wind and rain again. Then there is *hamsin*, the dry, hot wind of the desert that drives some people crazy. Others just get headaches. Bad ones."

"I wasn't thinking of that."

"I know. Well, I can tell you what the people on Masada probably thought—all of them must have wished a hundred times each day they'd never seen this place. Or each other." He laughed at her expression. "Why so shocked? They were only people."

40

He was amazing. This was his legend, after all. "Well, a little more than that. They were heroes."

"Heroes are people. At least, our heroes are."

"What does that mean?"

"It means we have no need for saints. Look, there were nine hundred and sixty men, women, and children here, holding out against the entire Roman Empire for a full two years after the rest of the country—and in fact the world—had been conquered. Outnumbered ten to one, every hope of victory smashed, every avenue of escape gone, they chose to die by their own hand. A heroic decision?" He shrugged. "What choice did they have? You have to remember these were refugees, survivors of massacres, escaped slaves, veterans of who knows how many battles. All of them had seen people they knew and loved abused or tortured or murdered. It would have been like asking someone with a tattoo on his forearm to take the chance of going back to Auschwitz." He lit another cigarette. "Anyway, that's beside the point. What interests me is that between the birth of these people as a *chevra*—a group of comrades—and their death as heroes, they were like everybody else in the world. Probably lived here as best they could, made love, had babies, fought among themselves, stole from each other, lied to each other, cheated each other—people, not saints."

"Well, maybe that's what makes them great."

He had rewarded her with an appreciative look. "Now you're thinking like an Israeli. Of course it's what makes them great. It's what makes *us* great."

"You are incredibly arrogant," she said suddenly.

"Excuse me, were we talking?"

"I was thinking of some of the things you've said to me today."

"Today's not done." They had reached the outskirts of Jerusalem. He pulled over to the side of the road and parked

there. "Just follow the yellow brick road. Should take you straight to the King David."

"What about you?"

He raised his thumb. "I can always get a ride." He extended his arm along the back of the seat, touched a tendril of hair that fell loose on her shoulder. "I'll see you tonight. Pick you up at seven. Arab food. You'll like it."

"I can't. I have an engagement."

"Break it."

"I really can't. I'm invited to someone's home for—what do you call it?—*Shabbat* dinner."

"Fine. I'll come along."

"Oh no you won't."

"Sure." He pulled her hair. "Haven't you heard? Nothing too good for us soldiers." He winked. "Seven. Wait for me."

"You can't—it just isn't done—"

"Where? In Philadelphia? This is Israel."

"But—"

"Forget it. Do you want to see me or not? If you don't, just say so and that's it."

"I—"

"Say it, lady. I don't like hesitation and I don't like games. If you don't know what you want it's as good as not wanting at all—and so long, as far as I'm concerned."

"I—" She sighed. "You know . . . you speak English awfully well."

He grinned. "Thanks. So do you." He opened the car door. "Seven. Wait."

She found the hotel easily enough, went straight to her room and took a long bath. She fell asleep on top of the bedcover, dreaming strange wonderful dreams about the sea and all kinds of naked people.

Brigadier General Benjamin Hatar was waiting for him. "So?"

42

"She's all right. Works with a museum in New York. Something to do with Elie Levi's dig."

Hatar nodded. "We did a check while you were playing tour guide. Intelligence agrees. No previous dealings with our little friend in Jericho. Anyway, MOSAD tells us now the *blondini* they're interested in is a Hollander. This one's clean." He looked over a typed document. "Rich papa, social background, the works. No Arab boyfriends." He held out the sheet. "Interested?"

"Why not?" He scanned the paper. "Meredith Sloane. Age twenty-five. Caucasian. Blonde hair. Blue eyes." He looked up. "Blue gray."

"I see you did a thorough reconnaissance."

"I'm seeing her tonight."

"Mazal tov."

"No objections, then?"

The officer shrugged. "I should stand in the way of international relations? Besides, if it turns out she's not okay you can be the first to let us know." He paused. "Did she ask any questions?"

"No, she just thinks I'm some wise guy looking to bed her."

Hatar raised his eyebrows. "The ideas some women have."

"Imagine."

"What if she wants to know more?"

He spread his hands. "What do you want me to do? Tell her I lead a special unit of skilled executioners, escape artists, and combat agents? Come on, Beni. You've known me for over twenty years, when I was just a kid. I've been working directly under you since '67. You have to ask?"

"To the PLO and the Popular Front, a commando officer like you is worth his weight in gold. Dead or alive." He shrugged. "To me you're no godsend. Just another one of my guys. But for some people you'd make a nice fat prize—especially dead, with your schmuck cut off and stuck in your

mouth in that nice little way they have of telling us how much they like us."

"Thanks. Nice to know I'm appreciated."

"You're a first-class officer, Arik. There isn't one of your men who wouldn't follow you anywhere. Good! But you take risks. A successful mission is one in which everyone comes back."

"What the hell does that mean? My gang has never taken a loss."

"You've been lucky. All I'm saying is, don't be glib." He looked again at the dossier. "The Sloane girl seems okay. Someone else might not be. You never know. It's what you don't know. . . ." He sighed. "The hell with it. *Shabbat shalom*. Have fun."

It was dark when she awoke. She dressed quickly, wondering if he would really show up. She didn't doubt he had the nerve. But what if he simply decided not to come—or couldn't come. She had spent a full day with the man and really knew as little about him as she did when he first took the camera from her hands. She knew he was some kind of officer. He seemed terribly American, but he had said he was a seventh-generation, native-born Israeli. Funny, she'd always thought of *sabras* as being dark or red-haired. Yes, wasn't David (or was it Moses) supposed to have "hair touched by flame"? Oh, what did it matter? He probably wouldn't come. (She knew in her heart he would.) It was just as well. She really had to start getting down to business with Ben Levi. The museum wasn't sponsoring a singles trip.

He wasn't in the lobby. At seven-fifteen, Eleazar Ben Levi came striding through the door, waving to her as he made his way across the room. "*Shalom, shalom.* How are you? Good, you are ready. I have the car outside. The management is not happy about it, but it's all right—you are ready so we can go."

44

"Would you mind waiting a bit? I know it's crazy but I met someone today who said he'd be here—"

Ben Levi didn't understand.

"Well, look, never mind. I told him I had a dinner engagement so he probably realized he shouldn't come. Yes. All right. We'd better go. Of course. The car. Yes. I'm ready."

Ben Levi looked puzzled. "You're waiting for someone?"

"No, it's all right. Forget it. Please."

"Someone from the museum?"

"No, no. Please. Forget it. It was just—oh. . . ."

There he was. Coming toward them now. The beret tucked into the epaulet, shirt pocket bulging with a cigarette pack. Blue green eyes in a tanned face. A tall, erect figure oblivious to the admiring stares of the tourists in the lobby.

He extended his hand, speaking to Ben Levi in a crisp Hebrew. The archaeologist stared at the officer a moment, then smiled in recognition, shook hands with him, spoke with him before turning again to Meri. "Lieutenant Colonel Ariel Vashinsky," he said, introducing the soldier to her. "This is the son of Dr. Chaim Vashinsky, one of our leading mathematicians—now lecturing, I believe, in your Princeton." He clapped the six-footer on the shoulder. "Believe it or not, this giant was once upon a time a student of mine."

"Miss Sloane and I have met."

"Oh?" Ben Levi looked at him in surprise, then at the American girl. A slow smiled spread over his face. "Come on, then. The car is parked at the entrance." He shook his head at Arik. *"Mumser,"* he said, grinning.

"Why didn't you tell me you knew the professor?"

"You didn't say you were seeing him tonight."

"You mean you would have come anyway?"

"Sure. Why? Didn't you want me to come?"

She decided not to answer that. "Why didn't you tell me you were a lieutenant colonel?"

"Do you know what a lieutenant colonel is?"

"No."

"Do you care?"

"Not really."

"Okay, then. Anyway, the only thing you really want to know is whether or not I'm married."

"I should think you would want to know that about me."

"I know. You're not."

"Why? Because I'm not wearing a ring?"

"You don't have the look."

"I didn't know married women had a particular 'look.'"

"Ones traveling by themselves do. You're not divorced either."

"Suppose you stop right there."

"I wasn't going to continue."

"Well, you can if you like. I don't answer to anyone."

"Except Mommy and Daddy."

"I beg your pardon."

"No, make that just Daddy, right?"

She was prevented from answering him by Leah's return with the after-dinner tea. The professor's wife was a warm and charming woman who had been unperturbed by the arrival of an uninvited guest. "You see," she had said, "we even set a place for you." The extra place setting was in fact meant for her soldier daughter. Leah never gave up hope that each *Shabbat* would see the arrival of Tal, home for a weekend off. "We are having some friends drop by," she told Meri. "I told them they must all speak English tonight. It's terrible to be in a room where everyone is chatting away and you don't know what is being said. But this one"—she indicated Arik—"could easily translate. You went to school in America, didn't you, Arik?"

"High school, yes. My father was teaching at Harvard," he explained to Meri.

"What do you hear from your parents?" Leah sat down beside them. "How is your mother? Is she well?"

"*Beseder. Hacol beseder.* Everything's fine."

46

Leah studied him. His expression was pleasant enough, but she sensed that he did not wish to prolong this particular conversation. She knew that Rina Vashinsky had suffered a nervous collapse after the death of Arik's younger brother in the Yom Kippur War, and that it was concern for his wife's well-being that kept Chaim Vashinsky abroad. It was rumored that the woman had vowed never to set foot again on Israeli soil even though she had a son and a married daughter there. As the sole surviving son, Arik was legally exempt from military service, but he refused to give up his commission; and it was rumored too that this had added to his mother's melancholy.

Leah turned her attention to Meri. "Tell me, how did you like the *shuk*?"

"The *shuk*?"

"Forgive me. The marketplace in the Old City."

"I didn't stay in town. Arik took me to Masada."

"Masada! An auspicious beginning." Ben Levi set a dish of sunflower seeds on the teak coffee table before them.

Leah was curious. "Had you two known each other in America?"

"No," Arik said politely. "We met, ah, on the road."

Leah laughed. "Ah, you were tramping!"

"Hitchhiking," Arik explained quickly to Meri.

"Hitchhiking—is that what they call it in the States? What a funny name. But everyone does it here."

"I'm glad you weren't alone," Ben Levi said. "There was some trouble in Jericho today. I heard of it this afternoon on the radio."

His wife looked dismayed. "Now what?"

"Who knows? Some stone-throwing. Nothing serious. An Arab policeman got cut a little. He's all right."

"An Arab policeman?" Meri asked.

"Yes. The government tries as much as possible to keep to a self-rule policy. Arab mayors, Arab police in Arab towns."

"But not the army."

"Oh yes, we have many *Druze* in *Zahal*. They are excel-

lent soldiers and officers." Leah turned to Arik. "Our Tal is with the Tank Corps. I hoped she would be in tonight. We haven't seen her for three weeks. Well, what can one do? It's just a pity she had to miss a nice dinner. My daughter," she turned to Meri, "as I told you, is serving her military duty."

"Then little Gabi has a big sister." She had wondered about the two-year-old. Leah had to be in her late forties.

"Yes, and a big brother as well. Yigael is with the consulate in London. He is married to a lovely girl, and I expect I shall be a grandmother soon." She paused. "We had another child. Assaf. He was killed by a terrorist bomb on Jaffa Road. Four years ago this spring. He was eleven years old."

"I'm sorry."

The woman tried a small smile. "We all have our losses. It is part of life here. It is hard, but we go on." For a moment her eyes locked into Arik's.

As though to confirm the continuation of life, little Gabi ran barefoot into the room. Leah pretended to be shocked by this after-bedtime appearance, scolding the toddler in a voice that tried hard to sound angry.

"Abba, Abba," the little girl called, stretching out her arms to Eleazar Ben Levi.

"All right, all right. Another kiss and then to bed." He carried her off, Leah trailing with a steady stream of instructions to him.

"Israeli women think nothing of having children at an age when most women stop," Arik noted. He paused. "After the Yom Kippur War, we had almost as many pregnant grandmothers as we had widows. Like the woman said, life goes on." He poured a cup of tea for her. "Lemon?"

"No thanks. One sugar."

"You know you could be doing this."

"Not on your life. I haven't the slightest desire to impress you with any so-called feminine ways."

"So I noticed. Don't worry. I'm not very interested in any

48

so-called feminine ways. I can think of better things to do with my free time than spend it on home cooking."

The reappearance of their host and hostess precluded any elaboration of how he did care to spend his free time.

Leah was curious. In her daughter's bedroom she had interrogated her husband with the determination of a MOSAD agent. "How did those two get together? She's not Jewish, is she? Well, at least she's nicer than the other one. But with Arik! What do you think?"

"I know as much as you, my dear wife—and before the evening is over, probably less. If Max sent her, it's good enough."

"Max sent the last one."

"No, he had nothing to do with that. He was in South America. Leah, we can't always expect to have dealings with people who like us. You should know that by now. Anyway, it isn't important. Only the truth is important."

"I know, I know," she said impatiently. "I just can't picture them together."

"Who?"

She jerked her head in the direction of the room they had just left. "She's the kind that marries senators, not Israeli soldiers."

"Arik is more than a soldier," Ben Levi said thoughtfully.

"What do you mean?"

"Nothing. Something I remembered hearing. . . ."

"Of course he's not just a soldier. He's Israeli. It's just—"

"It's just that you want him for one of our own," her husband teased.

She reddened. "Why not? So many beautiful war widows, twenty, twenty-one years old. It breaks your heart. Arik must be over thirty; why do you suppose he's never married? He's certainly old enough—"

"And getting older waiting for us to return." He bestowed a final kiss upon his little daughter, who had been watching

49

wide-eyed. "Gabi, Gabi," he said, stroking the child's curls. "Whatever you do, don't grow up to be a *yenta*."

While chatting away in her charming British accent, Leah studied the girl. Any fool could see she was a beauty; Leah was looking for other qualities. Leah was a Palestinian, a Jew born in the British mandate that would become the state of Israel. As a teenager she had smuggled weapons in her kibbutz's produce-ladened trucks, brought food and clothing to the beaches when boatloads of illegal immigrants sailed in on moonless nights, fought in the war of '48 alongside the man who would become her husband. Next to her family, she loved Israel. It was therefore second nature to ascertain right away whether the Anglo-Saxons she met were friend or foe. She had satisfied herself that Meri, while not a passionate friend to Israel, was not its enemy either. She had the feeling the girl had simply never concerned herself with the problems of the tiny Jewish state. Well, Leah had to admit, why should she? Leah had been to America, spent some time in New York, met museum board members and personnel. Ms. Sloane's biggest worry in life, she was sure, was getting a cab on a rainy day. Yet she liked the American. The aristocratic features imparted a certain coolness, but the girl was actually quite warm and open. She gave the impression of being very willing to listen. It was almost as if she were seeking something, Leah thought, and wondered if she had found it with Arik. The magnetic field set up by those two was unmistakable; the air was hot around them, though in fact they seemed to pay little mind to each other. Leah recognized the signs well. It starts in primary school, she thought, when the fellow who likes you is always the one pushing you down so you go home with scraped knees. Arik was still giving little pushes, gentle, teasing shoves to a proud young lady whose chin rose high above her slender neck. Leah remembered how Elie used to find fault with her transmission of the coded messages, always scolding her for driving the jeeps recklessly. . . . It was good with such begin-

nings. You fought and then you made love. What was the fighting after all but a scratching at the bite from Cupid's arrow? Elie thought she was a *yenta*, a busybody. So Miss Sloane has a good time, he said. Good for her. Good for Arik. Let him keep her busy and off his neck with her reports. No, Leah thought, those two were swimming out to deep water. He doesn't know it and she doesn't know it, but *I* know it, she told herself. And one of them is bound to get hurt.

Meri laughed at something her host said, answering the remark with pretty wit. If only our girls had that kind of grace, Leah thought enviously. Israeli girls were beautiful, but rarely did they possess the soft charm that seemed so natural to their counterparts abroad. At that moment, the door was flung open and a sparkling, smiling creature burst in upon them.

"Tal! Tali!" She ran to embrace her daughter.

"*Shalom*, Corporal," Eleazar opened his arms.

Words in Hebrew flew among the three. Meri turned again to Arik. "She's telling them how she managed to get home," he explained.

"Oh, sorry." Leah said breathlessly. "It's just that I'm so excited! We haven't seen her for three weeks. Tal, this is Miss Sloane from America. She's with the museum."

The girl stuck her hand out. "Hullo," she said in English. "How do you like Israel?" Without waiting for a reply, she turned back to her father. "*Abba*, you wouldn't believe what a time I had getting here. I came part of the way with a French millionaire and his wife in a Mercedes. Can you imagine? A Mercedes! It was fantastic!" Suddenly she turned to Arik. "Must I salute? It's my own house." Her long eyelashes fluttered as she closed her eyes dramatically. "Please God, don't let it be they've come to take me back. At least not until I've washed my hair."

Having been assured by the officer that his presence was purely social, Tal went off with her mother to the kitchen. Meri leaned forward. "Professor—"

"Elie. Please."

"Thank you. I thought perhaps we might talk a bit now about Tel Shalazar. You've been avoiding it all evening. I'm very excited about what's happening, but also a bit confused. You hint at the possibility of what could be terribly significant discoveries—not in the sense of uncovering something new to our knowledge but in the realization of an ageless quest." She spoke carefully, anxious to find the truth yet aware that he might not wish to reveal his thoughts in these surroundings. Ben Levi appreciated her tact, but he chose to be reticent nonetheless. A word here, a word there, and the people from New York became too excited—which was all right, except that they started jumping on his back to produce results. Americans wanted everything quickly. Still, the UNESCO people could be troublesome—even though their reports were such rubbish. "We have already found various artifacts pointing to the Christian community of which I wrote. This particular sect seems to have set up house about the time of the war with Rome. No doubt they fled Jerusalem before the siege of the city, hurriedly taking their belongings with them. Among those belongings were, it seems, certain articles of great importance to them. Religious articles. Vessels of metal, not clay."

"Oh, why won't any of you say it? Even Max won't come out with it. Is it the chalice then?"

"We have found certain writings in which an article such as the one which you have in mind is mentioned," Ben Levi said carefully. "That is why this dig was initiated. But tell me," he said, suddenly breaking out in a smile, "what do you think? How do you think the world would take an old Jew finding the Grail itself?"

"Who's an old Jew?" Tal had returned, munching on a sandwich.

"Your father."

"Silly. All your girl students are in love with you."

"How do you know that?"

She shrugged. "Everyone knows."

Smiling, he shook his head, raising a finger to his lips as Leah returned with a plate heaped high with food for her ravenous daughter.

If one could tell how a girl would mature by looking at the mother, one could also see from the daughter what the woman was like as a girl. Tal was a nineteen-year-old version of Leah, slim, yet full-breasted, her large eyes sparkling with health and fun. The dark hair was pulled back in a ponytail, unlike her mother's, which was cut fashionably short and curled, and the eyes were hazel like her father's; but in all other ways she was Leah as she had been when Eleazar met her thirty years ago, the two of them fighting together in the *Haganah*. Only the uniforms weren't so good then, he thought, looking at his daughter with a kind of salty-sweet nostalgia. Yes, it was Leah all over again. He could remember even now the taste of her in his arms as they lay together in the Judean hills. He looked more closely at his daughter. So now who was this one with when they both were supposed to be on duty? Never mind, he told himself with a sigh. Life was short, let it be sweet. Who knew what tomorrow would bring? How many had already been taken from them? And always, it seemed, the brightest, the bravest, the best. Three years of military service for the boys, then ninety days reserve duty every year until the age of fifty-three. And in between, hijacked planes, bombs in super-markets, grenades tossed into open cars. . . . It must be nice, he thought, watching his daughter, to live in a country where all you had to worry about was whether your children smoked marijuana, dated gangsters, or might run away to join some *meshuga* religious cult.

Tal was chattering away to Arik when her mother inter-rupted: "English tonight, my girl. You're being rude."

"Oh. Sorry. I forgot." She turned to Meri. "Don't you know any *Ivrit* at all?"

"Afraid not."

"Pity. We could talk much more. *Abba*," she went over to Ben Levi, plopped herself in his lap. "Doron is thinking of

studying abroad. He says Italy is the best place for design. What do you think?" Before he could reply, she turned, beaming, to Meri. "Doron is my boyfriend."

"This week," her father explained.

"This week and next week and all the weeks after that."

"Is that what you say?"

"Well, I'm saying it this week anyway."

They all laughed.

Friends arrived. Dov was an Eged driver; his wife Miriam, secretary to a city official, was delighted to see Professor Cahane of the university's literature department, as they had both grown up on the same kibbutz. Yeshua Mezin was a lawyer with a very sweet and very pregnant little wife who spoke no English. Yeshua had been active in the Soldiers' Movement, a reform political group that had emerged after the Yom Kippur War, and he got into a spirited discussion with Arik now. Leah was telling his wife how to make apple cake; and suddenly everyone in the room was chatting madly away in Hebrew. At this point, Meri sort of wandered into the kitchen where Tal was rinsing coffee cups. She had changed from her army uniform to blue jeans and a man's sweater.

"Here, let me help."

"Never mind. It's nothing to do." She sighed. "I thought Doron was getting off this weekend but at the last minute they wouldn't let him go. They want him to be a tank commander," she added proudly.

"And stay in the military?"

"Not forever. But it is a great honor. *Zahal* is a civilian army. That is why our officers are so important. They must always be first into battle. No, Doron will study to be an architect. He will make beautiful flats that young people can afford."

"Is Arik a reservist then?"

The girl was astounded. "Don't you know?"

"We only met this afternoon."

"He is an officer."

54

"Like your Doron will be."

"No, no. You really don't know anything, do you? I shall try to explain." She sighed. "It would be much easier in *Ivrit*. Never mind." She dried her hands. "The *Gan-Aluf* is with Special Forces. They have the hardest missions. They are the very best." She paused. "I really can't say any more. You must ask him yourself."

"Oh, it really doesn't matter. I was just curious."

"Don't you care?"

Meri shrugged like an Israeli. She was quick to adapt. "I'm just passing through, as they say."

Tal looked at her admiringly. "Fantastic! All the girls are dying for Arik Blue-Eyes and you don't even care."

"Is that what they call him?"

"He is quite famous. The girl who went to the Miss Universe contest two years ago was mad for him."

"How do you know that?"

"Oh, it's a very small country. Everyone knows everything here. It's really a disgrace. Do you know Yordana Yadin?"

"No."

"You don't know Yordana Yadin? She's a very big movie star. Absolutely fantastic. Everyone thought they were going to get married. But he dropped her for a girl soldier. Can you believe it? Fantastic."

"What's going on?" Arik stuck his head in the door. Tal responded pertly in Hebrew. He merely grinned at her and said to Meri, "Come on. They're all watching the news on television. It's all Hebrew. You won't understand any of it. Let's go."

The night was cool. In the summers of biblical times, wealthy merchants from Tyre and Joffa had traveled to the mountain city of David that they might partake of the pure air and cool winds that rustled through the pines and cypress. Now, in late October, the days were still warm; but at night,

55

Jerusalemites got out their electric heaters while the people of Tel Aviv had yet no need of theirs.

But she was not cold. She had never felt the presence of any male so strongly as she did now. She felt warm beside him.

They walked together through the deserted streets of the Old City, the shops of the marketplace locked and boarded for the night, their footsteps echoing down the narrow passageways, along the stone-paved alleys and streets of steps. Jesus had walked here. Crusaders had ridden their horses beneath these same stone arches. In the days of the Temple, perfumers and artisans and merchants of all wares had each had his own section even as now there were stalls of Bedouin rugs and sheepskin pelts, donkey harnesses woven with bells, baskets, bolts of goods, and grocer stalls of nuts and spices, flours, fruits, and vegetables, pens of live chickens and pigeons, bakeries, and butcher stalls with great hanging slabs of beef. In the day, the narrow streets were packed with men in black caftans and white headdresses, their women in embroidered robes with coin-edged veils covering their hair, and baskets on their heads that they balanced without touching. Donkeys still clip-clopped up and down the steps as in ancient times, but now they nudged past tourists in Chanel suits and drip-dry shirts, mini-skirted Army girls, and Israeli teenagers in blue jeans and sweaters. But that was in the day. Now, the streets were still, dark with the velvety night of the Middle East, that soft, heavy curtain that hung so sweetly until dawn.

Again she had the feeling that it was all a dream, that time and space had lost their references for her, that she was walking to some place in time that she had lived before or never even imagined. He had taken her hand; and though they walked by each other's side, she felt that he was leading her to something. Again, she felt something in her fly out, this time into the night, up into that black sky dotted with a hundred stars.

No words passed between them; it was not necessary. There was only the sound of their footsteps on the narrow,

cobbled streets. It seemed as if as many years had passed as there were miles between this place and home. Home. Had this once been home to her? Had some early Meri—Mari, then, perhaps—walked along these passageways, hurrying beneath the stone arches to a Christian meeting place, listening to plans to leave the doomed city, then running home to gather up the belongings that could be taken to the "New Jerusalem"? Strange, it was the first time she had ever felt a real sense of Christianity, of something more than Santa Claus and chocolate Easter bunnies.

. . . The Christian Mari, she thought suddenly, must once have been the Jewess, Miriam. . . .

Miri. Mari. Meri. . . .

She shivered.

"Cold?"

"I'm all right." She was grateful, though, that he put his arm around her, drawing her closer to his side. Her hip, her leg seemed bonded to his as they walked on. She could feel an unmistakable heat traveling up the length of her body. She shook her head as if to clear it.

"Tired?"

"I'm all right," she said again. "It's just that today has been so incredible. So much has happened, I've hardly had time to breathe."

"That's the way it is here. The days are always full."

"Of what?"

"Whatever you like. Laughter, sorrow, adventure—love." He had stopped. Now he pulled her around to him. Tenderly, almost casually, he brushed her lips with his.

She pulled back a bit to look at him. Suddenly she thought of Miss Universe, and the movie star, and the girl soldier; and a wicked little smile crossed her face. Slowly, carefully, she put her arms around his neck and slowly, carefully, she put her mouth to his. It was some time before he drew back to look at her. Then, without a word, he took her hand and led her back to the hotel and up to her room.

* * *

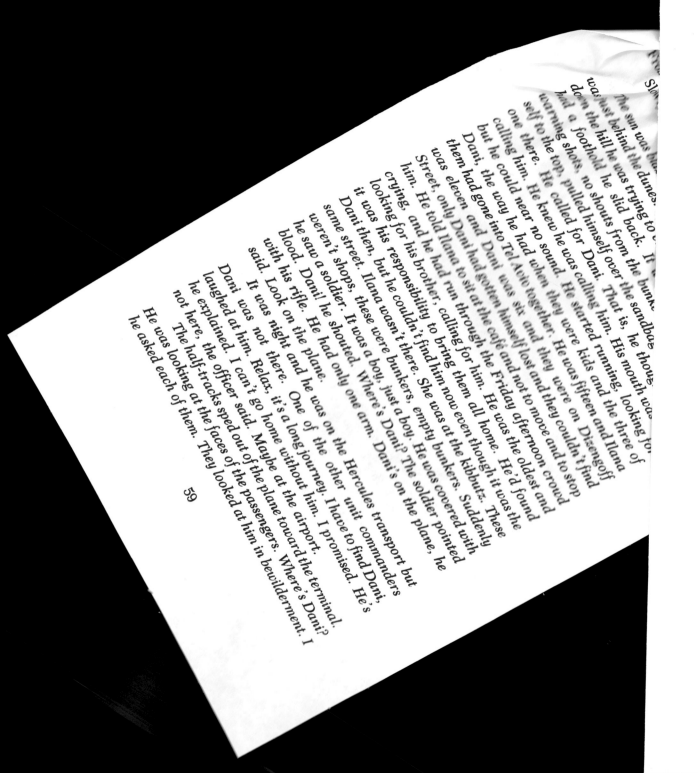

The key slid into the lock, the door opened; she heard
close it behind them. She reached for the light switch, [ ]
hand covered hers before she could flick it on, drew [ ]
away from the wall, and turned her around to him. E[ ]
darkness she could feel his eyes on her. Every tim[ ]
at her it was as if he were in her.

He took her in his arms now, brushing his f[ ]
hair. Like a cat she stretched against him, he[ ]
around his neck, her teeth reaching for his e[ ]
she felt his hand twist in her hair, drawing[ ]
then his mouth was on hers and the f[ ]
beneath them and she was falling, fallin[ ]
been wading playfully at water's edg[ ]
the tops of the waves, and now she w[ ]
the force of it pulling her away f[ ]
pulling her deep, deep into the [ ]

Frightened, she pulled a[ ]
bumping against the wall.

He did not move. Agai[ ]
and for a moment she hat[ ]
mand, for having this power ov[ ]
for what seemed a long time and [ ]
games. Not with me. Not ever."

She heard the breath escape her body in [ ]
the fluttering of wings in a still place. And sud[ ]
understood. She knew. With him it would be something [ ]
never been. With him there would be no mirrors in the mind,
no air-brushed poses, no glib little tricks to disguise the sense
she'd always had that it was all slightly ridiculous and rather a
lot of bother for such a short moment of pleasure. It would not
be like that with him. She would never be able to pretend with
him, to lie to him, or to manipulate him.

But there was no turning back. Even now, with this
distance between them, she could feel herself being drawn
into him. They were not even touching and she hardly knew
where she stopped and he began.

don't know," a woman said. Was he supposed to come? "There
he is," one of the men said, pointing to the doorway. Dani! he
cried. Dani! His brother smiled at him. Then a shot rang out
from the control tower and Dani fell forward. It's Yoni, one
of the soldiers shouted. Yoni's been hit! He ran forward,
turned the body over. . . .

Move! Move! To the plane! they were shouting. They
started pushing the passengers out the terminal but he was on
the ground, aiming the Kalechnikov at the control tower. One
of the passengers was in the way. He sat up, trying to push her
away.

"Lishkav artza! Lishkav artza!"

The girl was bewildered. She tried to take his face in her
hands.

"Are you crazy?" he shouted in Hebrew. "Get down!"
She didn't understand. He couldn't make her understand.
He pushed her down, rolling on top of her, covering her body
with his. He suddenly realized she was naked; they were both
naked. He pulled back, confused, trying to bring her face into
focus.

"Arik, Arik," she called softly. "You're dreaming. It's a
dream. Only a dream." He rolled over on his back, closed his eyes. When he
opened them, she was looking down at him, her face half-
shrouded in a curtain of hair. He reached up for her, brushing
the hair from her face, bringing her mouth down on his,
pulling her on top of him as if to blot out the images that filled
the night, blanketing his body with the warmth of hers. His
hands went over her hungrily. He rolled over and on her again,
brutally possessing her. She gasped, a small sound, but he
stopped as suddenly as if he'd heard a shot. "I'm sorry," he
whispered. "I didn't mean to hurt you." She put her hand to his face. There was
"It's all right." She put her hand to his face. There was
nothing he could not do to her. Nothing. She seemed so fragile.
He stared at the girl beneath him.

He shifted his weight from her but she pulled him back. "No," she murmured. "Don't go away."

It was almost dawn. He could see her face now, calm and strangely pure. Her eyes were large and clear, more gray than blue, he thought. He had known they would be good together, but he had been surprised by the extent of his desire for her throughout the night as well as the heat of her response. They had come together as perfectly as two people could.

He slid his hand under her body, his fingers encompassing the slender waist. "You're very beautiful," he said solemnly.

She wanted him to smile. "Thanks. So are you."

She watched him as he slept, wanting to touch him yet fearing to wake him. His features were relaxed; if he was deep in a dream again, then this time it was pleasant. He looked so young, like the boy he must have been. What had his childhood been like? she wondered. Was it full of baseball and Saturday afternoon movies and, later on, Friday night dating? Or was it made up of other things, things she had no knowledge of, no feeling for?

The room was filled with light. In the distance came the call from the Mosque of Omar, upon the Dome of the Rock that was the Temple Mount, the call of the faithful to Allah. . . .

She bent her head and lightly kissed his shoulder. Then she lay down beside him and closed her eyes.

3

Ben Levi was waiting in his office. "*Shalom*. How was your weekend?"

"Half a weekend, you mean. It feels funny going to work on Sunday."

"Well, we are not a rich country like America. We can't afford two days of leisure here."

"The campus is quite beautiful. The view is extraordinary."

"Yes, the hills of Jerusalem are rather nice, aren't they? I am particularly fond of the view of Bethlehem as one approaches it from here."

"We drove there yesterday," she said eagerly, then reddened.

Ben Levi smiled. "Very wise. The Arab cities are the only ones with any activity on *Shabbat*."

She cleared her throat. "Well, shall we be on our way? I'm quite anxious to see the Tel."

"Yes, of course."

*   *   *

"I imagine you may be disappointed," he said later, in the car. "To the untrained eye there isn't much to see but piles of dirt and sand and perhaps a few pieces of broken pottery."

"I'm beginning to realize that. Of course, it wasn't hard to visualize Masada as it was once."

"Well, Masada is something special. An extraordinary effort, coupled with an extraordinary desire, on the part of a great many people. Hundreds of volunteers from all over the world came to dig on that mountaintop."

"You could have that same kind of response if people knew what it is you are seeking."

"Exactly. Which is why I have no desire to advertise. Masada could accommodate thousands—well, at least nine hundred and sixty or so at one time. It is an isolated area fairly easy to maintain control of. What we are concerned with is a small patch of land on the outskirts of the city of Jerusalem. If it were to be made public that we are involved in a search for one of Christianity's holiest relics, we would be flooded with well-meaning pilgrims and volunteer workers, which would raise all kinds of security problems. Members of various terrorist ogranizations could see fit to enter the country in this manner. The site itself could be sabotaged in order to blacken the government's eye, to make Israel look bad to the Christian world. All kinds of nonsense could begin. The Pope might start calling for internationalization of the area again—who knows? They might start another Crusade, God forbid. No, this must appear to be a rather routine excavation, a more or less scholarly exercise—part of the general archaeological activity around Jerusalem."

"What about UNESCO?"

"Another routine exercise, part of the general anti-Israel activity centering around the United Nations. They're worried we may disrupt the outdoor toilet facilities of a few residents of the village of Rannon, thereby altering the true character of 'Israeli-occupied Arab lands.' As my American students say—'Far out!'"

She tried not to smile. "But if you revealed the true nature of this exploration—"

"My dear girl, the communist nations would rail against the exploitation of the peoples' land for purposes totally meaningless in terms of socialist values. The Third World, as those other nations call themselves, would denounce the project as a quest for a white man's toy. Don't worry about the UNESCO report. Nobody listens to it except the people who want to hear that sort of thing. It's all nonsense. Rubbish."

"I'm afraid some people do pay heed to it," she said ruefully. "That's one of the reasons I'm here."

"No doubt there are a few contributors to the museum who find it necessary to remain in the good graces of the international oil cartel," the archaeologist said bluntly. "If they are putting pressure on you now, it's merely an exercise in power. They are finding all kinds of ways to test their leverage these days. Give in to them now and there will be no end to it."

"Today Tel Shalazar, tomorrow the world?"

"Don't be surprised. The next time you look at a map, take note of Israel's size and the vastness of the Arab lands surrounding us. You must admit, there's a great deal of money and power going to so much bother over such a tiny spot."

"What about the Palestinians?"

"I'm a Palestinian, Miss Sloane. So is my wife. Both of us were born in Israel before it became a Jewish state. Ah, here we are. Watch out for those stones. It's very easy to turn an ankle."

It was soon apparent to Meri that no one connected with Tel Shalazar had any real desire to have her around the site. They were all pleasant enough, but she had the feeling that she was only tolerated as a visiting dignitary. She was beginning to share Diane Whitney's frustration. After all, the museum was paying for a good part of this; certainly she deserved something more in the way of cooperation.

"I'm beginning to wonder what it is I'm supposed to be doing here," she said to Linda Meyers.

"Going to cocktail parties, touring, meeting the V.I.P.'s, falling for an Israeli. . . ."

Meri looked up sharply.

"Just have a good time, that's all."

"I didn't come here for a good time."

"Didn't you? Sorry. I didn't know."

"Oh look, I didn't mean to give you that. Of course I was looking forward to the trip. And everyone's been terribly nice, really. It's just that I get the feeling that no one here takes me seriously." She paused. "Well, maybe that's my problem. I always seem to be saying that."

Linda Meyers looked more closely at the American girl; despite herself, she was beginning to like her. They had spent the day together, visiting some artist friends of Linda's, going to smart boutiques, lunching with some people at the *Jerusalem Post*. They were in a café now, on Jaffa Road, polishing off a plate of pastries and mugs of Viennese coffee. "Keep her busy," Elie had said. "See that she has a pleasant time and goes home happy. I'll have Terza type up a nice summary for her to take back to Max."

It was an old story for the p.r. woman. The congressmen and civic leaders on "fact-finding missions," the "in memoriam" contributors to the university scholarship fund, the presidents of Hadassah and Devorah and ORT and Christians for Israel and Baptist Women for Peace, the industrial magnates and the black journalists and the Japanese filmmakers. . . . "Keep 'em happy and keep 'em busy," said the generals and the university presidents and the hospital administrators and the scientists and the *kibbutz* secretaries. "Keep 'em off our backs so we can get on with the business of running our own country and living our own lives."

"My schedule calls for me to stay here ten days to two weeks—as long as I need, actually. I could make out a report in a day or two. It doesn't make sense. Unless. . . ." Meri had a

sudden thought. "Unless Max thinks Elie is about to strike gold."

"You mean silver, don't you?"

"You know?"

Linda Meyers licked a blob of whipped cream off her mouth. "Uh huh."

"Well, why didn't you just write everything up and send it to us?"

"Not my job. I just keep visitors happy."

"It doesn't make sense," Meri repeated, reaching for an apple tart.

"Aren't you enjoying yourself?"

"Fantastic—as you say. I just feel guilty. I'm hardly doing any work at all."

"You're not supposed to. Relax. Fringe benefits of a good job."

"I just keep thinking of Diane Whitney and all her meetings. According to her she was always arranging conferences of one sort or another."

"Who asked her? Let me give you a small tip. Nobody here likes being told how to run things. It's bad enough with every other Israeli setting up his own political party. I mean, we have the only symphony orchestra in the world with fourteen first violinists. Everyone's a prime minister. Everyone's an organizer. We tolerate it among ourselves as an idiosyncracy in the national character. But from outsiders—forget it."

"And I'm an outsider."

"Yes, you are." She immediately regretted her words, though they had given her a certain satisfaction. She was warm-hearted, not at all unkind. Still, in the small Ohio town where she'd grown up, it was she who had been "different," a big, dark girl who had exasperated her own friends with her talk of *kibbutzim* and Zionist pioneers and her knowledge of Herzl and Weitzman. While the other Jewish girls in town were doing their best to look like Debbie Reynolds, humming "Tammy" as they decorated their "Hanukkah bushes," she

bought a guitar and learned Israeli folk songs. She had a good voice, and after the mandatory college (her mother had started saving the day she was born) she did what many bright, discontented kids were doing: she took her B.A. and her guitar to Greenwich Village and sang for her supper in small cafés for rotten agents and a succession of lovers, each one of whom left her a little more lonely, a little more ready for the next. The second Kennedy was killed; she watched her friends on television getting beaten up in Chicago; the Vietnam war was getting her down. She was into astrology, Tarot, the I Ching, and organic food. She wanted to have a baby. On a lonely autumn night, the sounds of the Puerto Rican faggots across the street finally got to her. Her apartment had been ripped off again and the t.v. set was gone along with a new jacket she hadn't even paid for. She reached for a book; it was *The Last of the Just*, by André Schwartz-Bart. She had read it in college. She stayed up all night rereading it. The next day she went over to the Jewish Agency on Park Avenue and arranged to emigrate to Israel. She left two months later for a *kibbutz ulpan* near Ashkelon where she worked half a day and learned Hebrew the other half. Three months later she was in Tel Aviv working for a travel agency. Five months later, she was married to an Israeli. They went back to Ohio for the wedding and stayed there two years while her parents put him through junior college. He wanted to go on for his engineering degree so she taught school until he graduated. He wanted his Master's degree. She wanted a divorce. Back in New York again, she worked awhile for the Jewish Agency. When the Yom Kippur War broke out, she went back to Israel. He stayed in America. The last she heard he was living in Delaware, married to a sweet little Jewish girl whose father contributed heavily to the UJA. A little girl. Size five junior petite no doubt. The son of a bitch.

"You're pretty direct, aren't you?" Meri was saying. "What am I? The Great American WASP?"

"You're pretty direct yourself."

68

"Yankee heritage."

Linda nodded. "Ham on Sundays—the kind with cloves stuck in it. Thanksgiving turkey with chestnut stuffing. I bet your mother made turkey with chestnut stuffing."

"My mother has never made anything but a cup of instant coffee for herself—and that under duress."

Linda Meyers laughed. "We had Thanksgiving," she said. "My mother always stuffed the turkey with matzoh meal. She always made creamed corn in honor of the Indians. We all hated it."

"Creamed corn. I loathe it. Did you ever have chipped beef on toast?"

"Never."

"It's disgusting. That was our Saturday night supper, while you were having corned beef with cole slaw and Russian dressing on rye bread. And sour tomatoes. And ginger ale."

Linda Meyers's eyes widened. "How did you know—" She laughed. "I guess it's true. If you live in New York, you're Jewish."

"And if you live in Israel—"

"You're Israeli. It's not the same. Believe me."

"I'm beginning to see that." Meri paused. "Israeli men. . . ."

So that was it. "Whom have you met?" Linda asked kindly.

"Oh . . . just a soldier. An officer, actually."

"Well, I can tell you this—he's lying about his age or he's married."

"Oh no, I don't think so. He's about thirty-three, I think. A lieutenant colonel."

Linda nodded. "He's married. They're all married."

"No. I don't think so."

"What unit? What color beret?"

"Red."

"Paratrooper. Wow."

"I think he's with something called Special Forces."

69

"Hmmm. Could be divorced. Gorgeous?"

"Yes, he's quite good-looking."

Linda Meyers smiled. "You know, for a while there you were becoming a real person, and now you're back with that finishing school voice again."

"Defense mechanism." She sighed. "I've never had any real friends, someone I could really talk to. Everyone I've known has always been afraid of me, even the girls I went to school with. I've never known why. Maybe it has something to do with my father." She pursed her lips. "I have no brothers or sisters, and my cousins are all idiots. My mother thinks she's Myrna Loy. Still sound like finishing school?"

"I don't know." She laughed. "You're really different from what I thought you were. Or maybe it's just that for the first time I'm giving myself the chance to know someone like you." She smiled warmly, as though to reassure Meri that her next words held no rancor. "You see, I've always hated girls like you. You were the ones in the movies with the Christmas trees and the ice skates and 'little cottages by the lake.' Your parents called each other 'dear' and you always had a date New Year's Eve. Before, when I called you an outsider, I didn't intend to hurt you. I didn't think people like you could be hurt."

Meri smiled ruefully. "Well, as Clarence Darrow once said, 'Even the rich are entitled to a defense.'"

"I hope I didn't sound like the proverbial poor little rich girl," she said later, outside the café. "I'm not. I have my share of fun. It's just that I've never been all that close to anyone— except maybe Max Radnor. He's been super to me. That's why I want so much to do a good job."

"From what I understand, Radnor is on Elie's side. All you have to do is document his faith in the project."

"Not if it would mean deceiving him. He's too fine to be made a fool of before the board—and fools are what we'll all look like if this turns out to be a wild goose chase."

"Excuse me," Linda Meyers said carefully, "but it seems

to me that you are the one who's turning this thing into a chase. The Tel Shalazar project was begun simply as an exploration of a site thought to be an early Christian settlement. As far as the UNESCO committee report goes—it's a lot of garbage, it's not going to stop us from continuing our work. You've picked up on the chalice bit to justify your own involvement. Do you need that kind of justification? Suppose Elie found instead the missing Temple candelabra, the one Titus is supposed to have carried off to Rome? Would that hold no weight against your UN blackmailers?"

"That's not what I meant," she said hurriedly. "Of course we're in this, no matter what. But I do have to make it clear to the powers that be just exactly what it is we are involved in." She was quiet a moment. "What do you think? Will he find it?"

"I don't really care," the woman said mildly. "To me, it's just an historic artifact. I think it's trouble, if you really want to know. The Arabs have one holy war going against us now. All we need is a new bunch of fanatics claiming their piece of sanctified ground." She buttoned her sweater. It would be dark soon; it was growing cool. "The missing menorah . . . the Messiah . . . your Holy Grail . . . they're all dreams." She gestured toward the busy street of shoppers hurrying home, buses blocking traffic, cars honking. "This is real. Eretz Israel is real."

"The reality of life in Israel is usually a shock to the Western immigrant who comes here out of a sense of some kind of lofty Zionism," Tom Jordan was saying. He was an editor with the *Jerusalem Post*, a transplanted Englishman who had settled in Jerusalem after the Six-Day War. "The people here are tough. They have to be. And they can be quite petty and mean. Of course they can also be magnificent on occasion." He smiled at Linda, who had returned from powdering her nose. "I suppose that's what makes them fascinating," he continued. "People all over the world have their petty

71

moments, but rarely do they have many magnificent ones as well."

They were in The Black Cat, a disco-nightclub run by an Israeli Arab called Salim. Salim was one of the city's minor celebrities; his place was a top hangout. Linda and he were old friends; sometimes she sang to entertain the customers. The place was always full. There were a few uniforms scattered among the crowd; Meri jumped whenever she saw one.

It was three days since they'd been together. He'd said he would see her Friday evening, they'd be together on *Shabbat*. Still, she thought, he might have called. There had to be a phone on the base. Unless he was "in the field"—whatever that was. Where the hell was he anyway? Was there an army base in Jerusalem? The city was full of soldiers; they were so polite about taking their rifles out of your face when they queued up at the bus stops with everyone else.

The music was good; she would have liked to dance. She wondered what it would be like to dance with him, if they would move together as easily, as freely as they made love.

She had to stop thinking of him; it was making her ache. She leaned forward, trying very hard to concentrate on what Tom Jordan was saying, fighting the distraction of the music and her own fugitive thoughts, so that she did not hear the scraping of the chair beside her. It was, rather, the startled expressions on the faces of the others at the table that caused her to turn around.

"*Shalom.*"

A light went on under her skin. "Hi."

"How are you?"

"Fine. You?"

"*Mea huse.* A hundred percent."

"Tom Jordan. *Jerusalem Post.*" He extended his hand.

"*Shalom.*" He shook the reporter's hand, nodded at a wide-eyed Linda Meyers, then turned back to Meri. "Let's dance. I like this song."

She was in his arms again and the world was lovely—what a good song it was. And he smelled of the night air—he must have walked, he always wanted to walk. . . .

"Where are you coming from?"

"My base."

"Where's that?"

"Not too far."

"How did you know I was here?"

"What makes you think I was looking for you?"

She tilted her head back to look at him. "Weren't you?"

He smiled and kissed her.

"How did you know where to find me?" They were walking back to the hotel, their arms around each other.

"I have friends in high places." He smiled. "The desk captain told me you went out."

"But how did you know where I'd gone?"

"Other friends . . . in higher places."

"Arik. . . ." He had swung her around to him and was kissing her again. "How long can you stay?"

"I have to be back by six."

"Then we have all day. . . ."

"Six in the morning, lady. I'm just a foot soldier, not a diplomat."

"You're in Paratroops. You have a red beret. And wings." She put her finger to his chest.

"Been asking questions, I see."

"Um."

"A little knowledge is a dangerous thing."

"Then tell me more."

He took her hand, led her again down the quiet street. "What do you want to know?" he asked warily.

Everything, she thought. "Who's Donny?"

"Who?"

"Donny." She hesitated. "In your sleep. . . ."

"Dani." He drew out the "a," Americanizing the name. "My brother. He was killed in '73."

"Oh. I'm sorry."

"I have a sister," he went on cheerfully. "Ilana. She's on a *kibbutz* up north. My parents are in the States now. That's it. No dogs, cats, goldfish, or wives—present or ex."

She started to laugh.

"Your turn."

"Well . . . I had a dog once, when I was little. A golden retriever. She used to sleep by my bed." She sighed. "I loved that dog. She died finally of old age while I was in college. I was so upset I flunked my English midterms."

"Americans." He shook his head. "You spend more time and money on your pets than you do on people."

She pulled away from him, slightly shocked. "What an awful thing to say. And it's untrue."

"Name one person you've loved as much as that dog."

She was silent a moment. "I . . . I'm . . . a special case. I've never known . . . I was raised . . . I mean, my family. . . ."

"Yeah, I know," he said, not unkindly. "The air on Mount Olympus is kind of cold." He brushed his face against her hair. "But you're not," he whispered.

She felt her knees go weak, but again she pulled away from him. "No," she said in a low, firm voice. "I . . . I told you something that was important to me. My dog . . . Lady. . . . Maybe it sounded stupid to you but it meant something to me—and you shouldn't have ridiculed it."

He stared at her. "I'm sorry," he said finally, simply. "You're right. It was wrong of me."

She let out her breath. "Okay, then."

He pulled her around to him and looked deeply into the blue gray eyes that unhesitatingly met his gaze. "You're pretty straight, aren't you?"

"You laid down the rules, remembers? 'No games.' "

He nodded, a slow smile beginning to cross his face. "So I

74

did." He cupped her face in his hands and bent his head toward hers. "So I did," he murmured again just as his lips touched her mouth.

She was at the university by eight the next morning. Her early appearance in Ben Levi's office startled the archaeologist and his secretary. She handed the man a telegram. "UNESCO is going to make a formal condemnation. What do you want to do?"

He read the piece of paper, handed it back to her, shrugged. "The government will issue a formal denial, and so forth." He turned to the secretary. "Terza, *bavakasha*, call Leah and tell her the Gorens want us over Friday night. I'm going out." He turned to Meri. "You wish to come? I'm going to the Tel."

"Of course I wish to come. Elie . . . is that it? Is that all?"

He was geniunely confused. "Is what all?"

"A formal denial by the government, that's it?"

He sighed. "I've tried to tell you. There was never any doubt in anyone's mind—from the first day, the first minute those pale faces and big behinds showed up—what the outcome would be. The script had been written, the actors knew their parts. It's a show, that's all."

"A very sad and dangerous show, I'm afraid."

"I'm pleased you see it that way."

"If you would only explain to the world what it is you are seeking—"

"Miss Sloane." The hazel eyes, usually fixed on some far horizon, pinned her now like a shaft of steel. "Meri. Do you believe the allegations made against us are true? That in our work we have disrupted the lives and 'natural character' of the inhabitants and village of Rannon? That we have desecrated land holy to Islam?"

"Of course not—'

"Then why do you insist on an apology? That's what your

so-called 'explanation' is. Are we only to be allowed to live so long as what we do is beneficial to the Western, Christian world?"

"You're twisting it all around—"

"Am I?" He nodded. "All right. But the answer is still no. We deny the UN's charges, but we will issue no explanation of the project other than that which has already been given to the public. To hell with them. Let them do as they wish."

She was silent in the car.

"You are angry, Miss Meredith Sloane?" he said good-naturedly.

"Yes. I am. I'm angry with you just as much as I am with this stupid UNESCO business. Why don't you fight back?"

"That's quite funny, telling an Israeli to fight back."

"Well, why don't you? I know the report is nonsense— rubbish, as you say. Why don't you prepare a counterreport?"

"And who will read it?" he asked wearily. "Do you think anyone cares?"

"They'll cut off your funds."

"They already have. We have always given far more than we have received from the United Nations. Do you buy UN-ICEF cards for your Christmas?"

"As a matter of fact I do."

"Charming, aren't they? Ask the UNICEF people what portion—if any—of their services are extended to Israeli children."

She was silent again. "You really don't care what the world thinks, do you?" she said at last.

"The world thinks very little about us until their petrol tanks are empty."

"Well, I'm not going to let it go. Look, it's part of my job in any case. Just let me come up with something that's a little more than a departmental memo. Maybe I could get the museum to take a stand. Everyone expects a denial from Israeli

authorities. But if an outsider, a nonpolitical third party, were to issue a statement, come up with evidence—"

"It will be said that not only do the Jews own the newspapers and the banks but the museums as well. I appreciate the gesture, Meri, but you see, it really doesn't matter. It doesn't matter to *them*, because they will continue to say what they are told to say and to think what is expedient for them to think. And it doesn't matter to *us* because we will continue to do our work and live our lives as we see fit."

"Surely the truth matters."

"The truth. Yes, the truth matters." He smiled. "Set it forth then, that it may shine in the night like Demosthenes' lamp. 'For we shall be a light unto all the nations.' *Beseder*. All right. Do what you have to do."

Later, she would remember his words. At the time, she thought it was a strange way of putting things.

"Where is Raffi?" Ben Levi wanted to know.

"He hasn't shown up yet," Uri told him. "Has he done something?"

"Probably. When you see him, tell him to come to me."

"Tell him yourself. There he is."

A grinning ragamuffin came striding over the hill, his skinny arms swinging at his sides. He hesitated when he saw Meri. He had decided he was in love with the beautiful Anglo-Saxon, and he came forward now with some degree of shyness.

"Raffi!" Ben Levi waved him over.

Wondering, the boy ran toward them. Usually the professor wanted to get rid of him. He wondered if anything was missing from the camp and if they would blame him for it.

"Raffi." The professor spoke to him in English. "This is Miss Sloane. You've seen her before."

"Yes, yes." He nodded vigorously, his big eyes getting even bigger.

"I want you to help her. She may wish to ask questions of the townspeople. You will translate—say the words so that the

people understand what she says and she in turn understands them. Also you will see that she does not get lost in the back streets." He raised his eyebrows significantly. "You will be her protector."

"Yes, yes." He nodded again, excitedly. "Okay." He raised a hand, then lowered it. "No sweat," he added grandly.

Meri stifled a laugh. Ben Levi sighed. "*Shikrun*. Thank you, Raffi."

"But what will you give me? What do I get?"

"*Mumser,*" Ben Levi muttered. Aloud, he said, "You get a chance to help."

"What else?"

"I'll be glad to pay you for your time," Meri said, smiling at the child.

He shrugged. "Okay. I don't mind."

"What do you want? I mean, what do you think would be fair?"

He didn't hesitate a moment. "One hundred American dollars. Okay?"

Ben Levi answered this in a torrent of Hebrew and Arabic. Raffi looked up at Meri. "Too much?" he asked innocently.

"He wants you to sponsor him at the university," she told Ben Levi at dinner that evening. "Can you imagine? He's only ten or eleven and already planning his future. I mean, in detail. He wants to be an archaeologist. He's really an extraordinary little boy." She did not reveal the rest of her conversation with Raffi. "You are very beautiful," the child had said as they walked back to the Tel from the town of Rannon. Then, with great seriousness and deep respect, "I would like very much to fuck you." She had stumbled over a stone as much from surprise as lack of knowledge of the terrain. She hardly knew what to say, but Raffi was in total command of the situation. "I don't mind if there is something wrong with you," he assured her.

"What makes you think there is something wrong with me?" she managed to gasp.

The answer was obvious. "You are not married."

Meri smiled. "He really adores you," she told Ben Levi.

"Who is this?" Leah had entered the room with a tureen of soup.

"A little Arab boy who hangs around the Tel. He's crazy about Elie."

"He's not crazy about me," the man replied, edgily. "He is crazy about what he thinks I can do for him."

"Well, he is rather an opportunist," Meri admitted with a laugh. "But aside from that, I believe he's genuinely fond of you."

"My dear girl, when you have been here a little longer you will come to realize that none of those people are without motive."

"What do you mean?" Leah said. " 'Those people.' Because he's an Arab he's not entitled to any genuine feelings?"

"I didn't say that."

"Yes, you did."

"All right then."

"Elie—"

"Leah, *maspeak*. Enough. I don't wish to discuss it."

"*Beseder.*" She filled Meri's plate. "So who is he?"

"Leah!"

"Elie, you cannot let Assaf's death fill you with this poison." She stopped. His face had paled, and his lips had drawn into a thin, tight line. "Excuse me," he said quietly, and got up from the table and left the room.

Leah bit her lip. She finished ladling the soup into her plate, then sat down and stared at it. She sighed. "Elie was born in Jerusalem," she said slowly, passing a basket of bread to Meri. "His father was a great scholar, with a wonderful library of books from all over the world. In the War for Independence, the Jordanians destroyed the house, all the books. And in the fighting over the years—what is it, four wars in less than thirty years?—my husband has seen much blood spilled,

many friends gone. But he was never bitter, only sad that it should be so. He has always been a fair man. A . . . concerned man. When Assaf was killed, something in him died as well. Something that was good. Forgive me, I don't know if I make myself clear in English. For me, when Assaf . . . was taken from us . . . I screamed, do you understand?" She raised her hands in the air, her fists clenched. "I screamed, and I wept and I cursed. But when I had done with crying—only it is never really done, for a mother it can never be done—but when I had calmed myself, I felt this great emptiness and I had to be filled inside again. Do you understand? Gabi is not Assaf. No one is Assaf. Just as no one can be Gabi. But she is there to be loved and cared for, and she is so full of life that she sweeps away the sorrow. And I will not allow the legacy of my son's brief life to be one of bitterness. It is *haval*—a great shame—for this to be so. But," she sighed, "there is much bitterness and hatred on all sides. Friends—Arab people I have known since my child-hood—now speak in a way I cannot conceive as coming truly from their own hearts and brains. They do not talk to me anymore. They recite slogans. They make speeches." Absently she cleared the table. "People I have known all my life," she repeated, shaking her head. "And I don't know them any-more."

"But surely," Meri said softly, "they have their griev-ances."

"Of course. I work with the social welfare program. I know, believe me. But you see, one can only legislate civil justice. One cannot legislate goodwill. There is a great dispari-ty between the cultures. The Arab attitude toward women is still a horror to me. It is such a joke, really, at these internation-al meetings of women when the various representatives rail against Israel. We are the only country in the Middle East where a woman has half a chance to do something more than just have babies and be old and used up by the time she is in her twenties." She was angry now. "The men sit in the cafés all day with their hookahs, playing *shesh-besh*, bragging about the

mansions they lived in before the Israelis came—mansions, ha!—while the women are home with the children and the laundry and the cooking and everything else." She shook her head disgustedly. "They beat their wives whenever they wish, barter their daughters like chattel—and there is nothing one can do about it. Nothing."

"But it is the same with the Oriental Jews." Ben Levi had come back into the room. "What you are talking about, Leah, is a matter of culture and education, of accepted behavior patterns, not politics."

"What I am talking about," she responded with spirit, "is the fact that it is not Jews, Arabs, blacks, Indians, or Mongolians who are the true second-class citizens of the world—but, for the most part, women!"

"Oopah!" he grinned. "Miss Sloane, meet my wife, secretary-treasurer of the Jerusalem chapter of the Women's Liberation Society of Israel."

"Are you serious?" Meri laughed. "Women's lib in Israel?"

"Of course," Leah said proudly. "We are a democracy, aren't we?"

4

She missed him, counting time from weekend to week-end, filling up those long days they were not together with work and activity. She called Max in New York, informing him that she would be staying on longer than they had expected, and moved from the hotel into an apartment that Linda Meyers found for her. The "flat" consisted of the upper level of an old two-story house, a five-minute walk from the old walled city and surrounded by the towering, modern structures of the "New City." The place belonged to an artist friend who, Linda said, would be abroad a few months and was glad to rent it for American dollars.

Rickety wooden stairs led up from the outside of the vine-covered building. It was cool inside, the marble-tiled floors covered with small Bedouin rugs and a few, larger Oriental ones. The furniture was massive, antique, a memory of the Turkish past and the British presence that had once colored the land. The walls were covered with paintings, vivid canvases of yellow and orange and pink, all variations on the same theme: Jerusalem of Gold. Juxtaposed with these were

enormous pictures, mostly black and white or with very little color, of erotically postured men and women surrounded by missiles, guns, helmets, and other accouterments of war. There were also sketches of biblical figures with many studies of Jacob wrestling with the Angel, and in the bedroom, one large, lyrical painting of a man and woman embracing in an idyllic field of green misted with rain or dew. There was something written in Hebrew at the bottom of the canvas. Meri stood before it a long time.

"It's beautiful, isn't it?" Linda acknowledged. "Hard to believe Yossi did it. His other things are so much stronger. It's his only piece of work—at least the only one I've ever seen— that has no violence in it. He's a very strange man."

"Who did the other paintings, the ones of Jerusalem?"

"Oh, that's Sara's work. She sells very well. A number of exhibits have been set up for her in New York, Chicago, California. That's what keeps her and Yossi going, really. She should do very well this time. People always buy before Christmas."

"Yossi is her husband?"

"I don't know," Linda confessed. "I think they might just be living together. Yossi is a real character. He's like something out of the Bolshevik Revolution. You really like that painting, don't you?"

"Hmm."

Linda came to stand beside her. "It is beautiful. It's something to do with the 'Song of Songs,' I think." She peered more closely at the canvas. " 'Anni vedodi vedodi li. I am my beloved's and my beloved is mine,'" she translated. "Yes, that's from the 'Song of Songs,'"

"He's awfully good. Some of these paintings are museum quality. Does he sell?"

"He can't get arrested." She shrugged. "People don't want real art from Israel—or maybe they don't expect it. The tourists want scenes of Jerusalem, old rabbis praying at the Wall—cliché souvenirs." She smiled wryly. "They want to see

us dancing the *hora*, going off to war with a song on our tongues. They expect us to be kosher. They send us their messed-up kids as though picking oranges on some kibbutz will straighten them out. They don't want to think that maybe we have messed-up kids too, that Israelis get divorced, have breakdowns, eat bacon, and want to paint and write and sing of things that go beyond Israel and Judaism." She stopped. "I'm sorry, Meri. I don't know why I went off like that." She laughed apologetically. "The truth is I've got kind of a crush on Yossi. It just kills me to think how wasted he is here."

"Yes, I can understand that. You know, I don't mean to brag, but I think I can do something for him," Meri said thoughtfully. "In fact I'm sure I can. I know a great many gallery people. And he's really good. Very powerful. Where is he now?"

"Where else? *Meloim*. Reserves."

The place was green with plants hanging in baskets, perched on the window sills, set on tables. There were two sweet potato tops and three avocado pits rooting in water in the kitchen. Vines crept through the open windows, their leaves shadowing the glass, filtering the sun. The flat was always cold; she was rarely without a sweater. She had to go outside to get warm and there it was heavenly, bright with sunshine, the air tinged with a sweet, spicy scent. She bought an electric heater, kept it at the foot of the big brass bed. The comforter was thick, filled with down; in the mornings she hated to get out from under it. She ate Israeli yogurt and cheese and olives and crusty rolls that she bought each morning at the market. She wandered through the Old City, learning to bargain with the Arab merchants for candlesticks of olivewood, and a half-kilo of pistachio nuts, and a long, embroidered dress. She went with Raffi into the village of Rannon and spoke to the people there, had tea with university personnel, went to cocktail parties attended by Israeli political figures and American embassy personnel, moved rocks and stones with the students who

toiled at Tel Shalazar. At night, she lulled herself to sleep thinking of him, putting him in her fantasies, counting the days until Friday. Thursday night was the worst, a hundred hours long. Friday morning stretched into afternoon, the sky deepened into lavender, the thousand birds of the city set up their twilight racket, the religious hurried to the Wall, their black gabardine set aside for caftans of brown silk and mink-haloed hats, their beards and forelocks curled and perfumed for the coming of the Sabbath Queen—and still he was not there. She paced up and down the apartment, plumping the pillows, checking the refrigerator to make sure there was plenty of milk and cola, making herself a third cup of what would be untouched coffee. And at last there was the sound of his footsteps on the wooden stairs, bounding up the steps two at a time, and that moment before they were in each other's arms—a moment of him standing in the doorway with that grin of his as if to say, "Well, I made it again," looking into her eyes the color of violets in the fading light. And then they were together with his face in her freshly washed hair and her head against his chest smelling the desert and the gasoline and the khaki and metal and sweat.

She had never seen him with a gun, not even that first day. She wondered why. It was sort of sexy to think of him with an Uzi or Kalechnikov or—what was it?—the new Galil. He shed his uniform as soon as he could, changing to Levis and European-cut shirts, the cuffs always left unbuttoned.

Once, she asked him, "Have you ever killed anyone?"

His face was expressionless, without emotion of any kind. "I've seen men die." was all he'd say.

She knew she ought to feel ashamed, and wondered at herself, at the heat that surged through her at the thought of him in some murderous action. She had always hated the so-called sport of hunting, been against wars, killing, "loathed" military men. Had it been a pose, an easy, fashionable "right" sort of stance and nothing more? Was there some dark, bloody part of her soul that only now, in the glare of that white eye

blazing in the Mideast sky, had come to light? Why was it such a turn-on to think of him with a gun?

Down the street from the flat was a shop owned by a Yemenite family. The men were artisans; they fashioned jewelry, candlesticks, intricate goblets of silver, the working of which had been handed down from father to son, generation after generation. She would sometimes see the old man bent over his worktable, his beard spilling down to his busy hands, his head crowned with a velvet skullcap embroidered in silver thread.

One evening they passed the place and saw that it was full of light and people. They stopped, peering in the window, and were immediately pressed to enter by one of the five sons. There had been a birth—a new child had come into the family—and now there was wine and cakes and almonds mixed with raisins and honey to be offered to all who passed by. No one seemed to speak any English; Arik was taken aside by the men, and Meri was reduced to a great deal of nodding and smiling as she sipped sweet wine from a tiny silver goblet encrusted with blue-green stones. She was aware of Arik conferring with the man who had bid them enter and then talking with the old grandfather. The old man kept shaking his head at something Arik was urging him to do. Suddenly the old man appeared to agree, and an exchange of some sort took place between him and the tall officer. It was only later, when they were alone in the flat, that she discovered what it had all been about. In a curious, offhand manner Arik took from his pocket a pendant suspended from a silver chain. He had seen it on the old man's worktable and persuaded him to sell it. At first, it looked like a piece of exquisite silver filigree set with a blue green stone like the ones that had adorned the wine goblet. The stone was the same color as his eyes. As she examined the pendant with great wonder and delight, too overcome even to thank him, she saw that the design was actually made up

87

of Hebrew letters so artfully arranged they did not look like script at all.

"He didn't want to sell it because it was still *Shabbat*," Arik was saying. "Wanted me to come back tomorrow. I told him I wouldn't be here tomorrow. Anyway, *Shabbat* was over—they had the lights on." He wished she would say something. "That's an Eilat stone. It comes from the mines of King Solomon. It's fairly common around here." He cleared his throat. "The, uh, words are from the 'Song of Songs.' *'Anni vedodi vedodi li.'* " He stopped, suddenly hesitant to say it in English.

" 'I am my beloved's and my beloved is mine,' " she whispered, tracing the letters with her finger.

He was surprised. "You know it?"

"The Book of Solomon has reached our shores," she said, laughingly. She looked up at him and smiled. "The painting in the bedroom. It says the same thing." She threw her arms around his neck. "It's lovely, Arik. The most beautiful thing anyone's ever given me. I love it. And I—I—" She seemed to stumble over her words, and caught her breath. What was she about to say? "I want to wear it right now."

He let out a deep breath. She liked it. "Okay," he said, drawing her to him. "Wear it now. And nothing else."

Days passed, and although she always left word of her whereabouts on the chance she might see him, he rarely came into the city except on weekends. She had the feeling he was preparing for some kind of action; he'd seemed preoccupied the last time they'd spoken. Then suddenly, one day, he called her at Ben Levi's office. "Pack your gear. I've got three days' holiday. Take a bathing suit. We're going into Tel Aviv."

Time turned into a montage of scenes that would remain as memories: Coffee at Cafe Rowal on Dizengoff Street— sitting outside, of course, watching the whole world pass by, or, at the very least, the entire population of Tel Aviv. . . .

Tennis at a country club in the posh suburb of Kfar Shmaryahu (he beat her) surrounded by gardens and diplomats' villas. . . . Watching the sun fall like a red balloon into the sea as they walked the beach of Caesarea. . . . The flea market and the artists' quarters in Jaffa, an entire city within a city excavated and restored to the way it had been in the days of Peter—only now the ancient streets housed sculptors' studios and art galleries and all kinds of boutiques. They had iced coffee at an outdoor restaurant on a huge balcony over the sea, the lights of the hotels along the shoreline of Tel Aviv sparkling in the distance across the water. The place was packed with beautiful girls and good-looking men. They might easily have been in Cannes or St. Tropez, Meri thought.

They had shish kebab on the streets of Jaffa, not far from the clock tower that was the city landmark. The night was steamy with the smoke of the sidewalk vendors grilling their foodstuffs over open coals—Hot pita with hummus and tahina, shish kebab and shashlik, "white steak" (pork), baba gahnoujh or salat hatsalim, and assorted pickles, peppers, and honeyed cakes. Like most *sabras*, Arik had a decided preference for "Oriental" food—as Israelis called that mixture of Arabic, Yemenite, Moroccan, and Iraqi dishes that made up a good part of the national diet.

The Arab vendor pressed her to taste a particular red relish which made her nose run, her eyes tear, and nearly singed the tongue out of her mouth. "You rat," she gasped, coughing as she grabbed Arik's Coke. "Why didn't you say anything?"

"Just mean, I guess." He grinned. "Besides, that's terrific stuff. It's very good for you."

She never could tell if he was serious or not.

"That's tame compared to what the Yemenites eat," he was saying. "I had a little Yemenite girl friend when I was nineteen. Shoshana Hamezini," he recalled dreamily. "Fantastic. Molten lava. What are you doing?"

She had her finger over the opening of the Coke bottle

and was shaking it up. "Making an American fire extinguisher." She let him have it. "For you!"

Later, in their room in the small seaside hotel, she wanted to know if he missed his little Yemenite.

"Umm." He had his face between her breasts. "You smell like strawberries."

"Maybe I ought to try a Yemenite too," she said thoughtfully. "I'd hate to think I was missing something."

He raised his head, grinned. "I've got just the one for you. One of my guys. . . . He's maybe five feet tall. His rifle is about as big as he is. And his equipment is about the same size as his rifle." He laughed at her expression. "Now if I'm not insecure, you shouldn't be either."

"Well," she said grudgingly, eyeing his body, "I shouldn't think you had anything to be insecure about."

"Neither do you, lady. Neither do you."

They stayed at a small hotel on Hyarkon Street, by the sea, not far from the very busy Allenby, with its steady mob of shoppers, the stores of Ben Yehuda, the cafés of Dizengoff. A short walk down were the luxury hotels—the Dan, the Plaza, the Hilton, the Sheraton. Everyone kept saying it was a small country, Meri thought. Well, if there were only three million Jews in Israel then surely the were all in Tel Aviv today, out in the sunshine-filled streets, in the stores, sitting at the outdoor cafés with their *café hafuf.* It was a cosmopolitan city, a different world entirely from Jerusalem, with its mystical aura, and the *kibbutzim* and *moshavim*—collective farms—that surrounded the metropolis. Only the presence of soldier boys and girls drinking Coke and Tempo, eating pizza and falafel on street corners, reminded one that this was not New York or Paris. Back home, Meri thought, the leaves were brown, while here the hibiscus bloomed and bathers still swam in the sea a few blocks away from the hubbub of the city.

Their room was clean, pleasant in a rather spartan way. They pushed the two narrow cots together, the sound of the sea

carrying them off to sleep when at last they slept, entwined in each other's arms. She, who could never bear to be touched while she slept, now lay like a baby in the circle of his embrace.

Arik knew the proprietors of the hotel, an elderly couple with the tattoos of German concentration camps on their forearms. He spoke to them in Yiddish, which they seemed to prefer. Each had lost a spouse, children, in the camps. They had met after the war, in Israel, married, and had had a son, Dov, whom Arik had gone to school with. The boy had been killed in the Six-Day War, in the fighting on the Golan Heights.

"Do you come here often?" she asked Arik.

"Sometimes, when I'm in the city for a few days." He put his finger on her mouth. "No. I don't bring women here. I go to their place. Ouch! You have sharp teeth."

"What about tourists?"

"I don't know any tourists."

"You know me."

"You mean, in the biblical sense?"

She didn't understand.

He smiled. "In *Ivrit*—Hebrew—there is no word that means 'to make love.' There is only the verb 'to know.' " He paused. "The others that had you . . . they never knew you at all, did they? When it mattered . . . you always slipped away, didn't you?"

She closed her eyes. "Is that what you feel? Do I slip away . . . from you?"

"No. But I can see you doing it."

She opened her eyes. "And I can see you cutting notches in the bedpost."

"When I was a kid. Sure, everyone goes through that."

"And now?" She wanted him to say he loved her.

"Now I'm not a kid. I'm not saying there aren't a lot of people in this world who happen to be beautiful women. If they're interesting, I want to know them."

"In the biblical sense?"

"That's a part of it. Sure." He caught her by the arm. "You want me to say you're the best, don't you?" He pulled her down on the bed, under him. "The most beautiful, the most passionate, the most intelligent and sensitive—" His mouth came down hard on her. "Okay," he murmured at last. "Why not? You're perfect."

"Why am I perfect?" she prompted, running her finger down his back.

"Because . . . you don't talk too much. And when you do . . . you say the stupidest things."

"You really don't give a damn whether or not I say you are the best, do you?" She was watching him shave.

"Nope. I am the best."

She had to laugh. "Well, I walked into that one. You really are incredibly arrogant, you know."

"So you keep telling me. Get dressed. I told Micah we'd be there by six."

"I don't want to get dressed."

He rinsed the razor, set it carefully down. "I leave here in exactly twenty minutes."

"With or without me, right?"

"With, of course." He wiped his face with a towel. "How you look at that time depends on you." They were both naked.

"Suppose I don't want to go?"

Without a word he turned around to her. In a move so fast she could not see it coming, he caught her leg, grabbing her under the knee. His other arm caught her as she fell back, pinning her against the wall. She let out a gasp as her flesh hit the cold tile and then another as he rammed himself into her. It was over quickly, both of them spent by the shuddering climax that ripped through them. He let her leg drop. There would be a large black and blue mark where his thumb had been. He stood braced against the wall, bent over her. He was still breathing hard.

She swallowed. "I need a drink," she said huskily, finally

92

managing to peel herself off the wall. She staggered to the sink, bent her head to the tap, drinking greedily. Finally she straightened up. "And a bath," she added, going to the tub. He reached past her, turned on the water. She put her arms around his waist, pressed her lips to his ear. "I hate you," she whispered, and kissed him.

He was a desert animal. Some light went on behind his eyes when they left the cities and there was nothing but sand and sky and a windy silence around them.

She drove him to his pickup point in Beersheba, dropping him at a café already crowded with soldiers. It was dark when they left Tel Aviv, dawn by the time they arrived at the Negev settlement. Bedouin traders were already lining up for the twice-weekly market at which they gathered, grooming their camels for inspection and trade; silently, their women spread out embroidered pieces of fabric, brightly colored harnesses with tassels and bells, baskets and trays of woven raffia—misty silhouettes moving against the morning horizon, dreamlike figures from an ancient world. . . . Or were the jeeps, the trucks, the tall white apartment buildings with their laundry-adorned balconies in fact the anomaly here?

He grew restless as they approached the town. He fairly jumped from the car, anxious to resume whatever it was he did, kissing her hurriedly as he left to join his *chevra*.

She visited the Bedouin market, then drove back to Jerusalem, wondering at the beauty of the sun-streaked sky, the intricacy of light and shadow playing upon the rocks and sandy cliffs, thinking it was not difficult to see how an ancient desert tribe, called the Habiru, had come to thoughts of God.

The following Friday, he did not come. The gold of Jerusalem turned black with night and still he had not come. At ten o'clock she put the steaks back in the refrigerator (it had been such luck to find a butcher who had lived in New York) and went to bed, exhausted with waiting, totally drained from

the moment-to-moment anticipation of his arrival. She curled up beneath the comforter in an angry ball, furious with herself for the state she was in. By morning, she had transformed her rage to hurt and transferred her anger onto him. He might have had the decency to call. Okay, okay—so he was in the army. But don't tell her he couldn't call or get someone to notify her. She knew the men went out of their way to relay messages for one another. How many times had she waited while Arik called this one's wife or that one's mother, even going to their flats to say this one was well or that one would not be coming home just yet.

Maybe he had been hurt.

Oh God.

No, he was not going to get off that easy. There was nothing wrong with the bastard, he had just japped her, that's all, aced her for some hot little corporal. Yordana Yadin with a rifle. I wonder how I'd look with an M-16, she speculated. Stupid, she decided. A lifelong diet of Wonder Bread did not make for Wonder Woman.

There was a note from the hotel. Roger had called. Roger. He seemed so far away—in so many ways. She supposed she owed him a letter—he had written twice—but there really wasn't anything she felt like saying to him.

She moped around the flat, finally went out to the *shuk*, returning with a new treasure that she had bargained down to her liking. It was only a few dollars, but she was pleased with herself for finally getting the hang of Levantine haggling. It was time everyone stopped thinking they could take advantage of her.

She had been in the apartment only a short time when she heard footsteps on the wooden stairs. She ran to the door. A big black bear of a man in army fatigues, combat boots, and stocking cap burst into the place. A thick black beard covered most of his face. Two coal black eyes glared at her. *"Shalom,"* he grunted. "You are the American. I know, I know . . . Sara rented the flat to you. All I want is a bath and a night's sleep. I'll

be off in the morning, I promise." Mistaking her astonished silence for refusal, he suddenly swept the knitted cap from his head and threw it against the wall, cursing in Hebrew or Arabic, she was not sure which. "To hell with your money!" he thundered. "To hell with Sara! This is my home! A man spends six weeks on the Golan freezing his *tahat*, comes home to find his woman gone and his bed sold! To hell with all of you! I am not moving, I tell you, until I have a bath and some sleep!"

"Now wait a minute—"

"Not a minute, not a second!" Ripping off his shirt, he advanced toward her. Alarmed, she backed off against the wall, but he merely brushed past her, heading for the bathroom. She heard the water being turned on; soon there was a splashing sound and a loud contented grunt. For the first time in two days she hoped Arik would not show up.

He was much more pleasant after the bath, a grizzly turned into a teddy bear. "You must forgive me," he apologized. "I am an animal when I come back from *meloim*. It takes a bath, food, sleep, and Sara before I am a civilized creature again. But you must let me stay here tonight. Tomorrow I shall leave for Eilat. Don't worry, I shall sleep in the studio." He motioned to the adjoining room, a chamber filled with easels, paints, canvases, and a narrow cot pushed against one wall. "You may have my bed," he added grandly.

"You can stay," Meri said calmly. "I would have told you so if you'd given me half a chance. Actually, I'm kind of glad for the company. Would you like some dinner?"

White teeth split the beard in a huge grin. "You are a good girl. I knew it the moment I saw you."

The well-stocked refrigerator made him even happier. "God bless you Americans," he said admiringly. "You know how to do a thing. *Shmai Yisroel!* Is that meat?" He held up the package, smelled it, then unwrapped it tenderly. "Steak." His eyes rolled heavenward. "Blessed be the name of the Lord." He turned to her. "You know how to cook? Never mind, I do.

Better even than I paint. Sit down. Relax. I shall make a feast for us. Pity there is no wine."

"But there is." She held up the bottle of Carmel rosé. " 'The President's Finest.' "

"Fantastic. Sara, wherever you are, I bless you for renting to an American."

They sat lazily over coffee, candles burning on the table, the electric heater on the floor. She was wearing her Bedouin dress. Arik hated it. The silver pendant lay between her breasts.

"That was a wonderful dinner," she said, contentedly. "The pilaf was superb."

"It is Arabic. You make it with lemon, some garlic, yogurt. . . ."

"I must learn how to do it."

"I just told you."

"Israelis," she said, laughing. "You make everything so simple."

"Why not? Why complicate things?" He looked carefully at her. "This is all beautiful, but the dinner, the wine—they were not meant for Yossi Steiner, grateful though he may be. You were expecting someone."

"Yes."

"So?"

"He didn't show."

"He's crazy. A beauty like you . . . who can cook. . . ."

"I didn't make dinner," she reminded him. "You did."

"Never mind. We shall not tell him."

She smiled. "Yossi. I'm glad you are here."

"I as well. You can believe it."

"I was really feeling lonely."

"Well, we shall fix that."

She was silent.

He cleared his throat. "With conversation of course. Unless. . . ."

"I don't think so."

"Never mind then. As you like. Besides, we must consider Sara. It would not do for her to return to find you in love with me."

"You're very considerate, Yossi."

"Why not? I tell you this, I would not leave you lonely. Well . . . maybe I would. For a man there is always more than love. For a woman there is only that."

"And I was just beginning to like you."

"Ah, you think I am a male chauvinist pig. A *kosher* pig, ha? I am not. Believe me. No one is more in awe of women than I. You are sacred creatures, all of you. Even the ugly ones. Especially the ugly ones. The mystery of God lies between your thighs. You could rule the world had you not one small fatal weakness."

"Which is?"

"Men. It is a fact. We can live without you, but you cannot live without us. That is your weakness." He spread his hands. "When I paint, nothing else matters. Nothing. Only afterward. Sara paints—what is she doing? Sending messages out to one who will love her, take her in his arms, tell her she is beautiful. Do I need someone to tell me I am beautiful?"

"Everybody needs that," she said slowly. "All of us want to be loved."

"To be loved, okay. But to love—only women want that. For men it is a nuisance. Believe me."

She was silent. Was that it? Had she become a nuisance? No games, he'd said. Had it become too serious? Nervously, she fingered the silver pendant.

"He is also American?"

"No, although you wouldn't know it to hear him speak. He's Israeli."

"An Israeli that talks like an American. Dangerous. Very dangerous. He is a *yured*? One who makes his life away from *Eretz*?"

"Hardly. He's an officer in *Zahal*. Lieutenant Colonel

97

Ariel Vashinsky." She raised the glass of wine, toasted him in absentia. "A name, I might add, that has yet to make the Four Hundred."

"Arik Vashinsky?"

"Don't tell me you know him."

"You can be sure of it."

"But how? No, don't tell me." She held up her hand. "I know. It's a small country."

"That's for sure. I have a cousin lives on the same kibbutz as his sister. So. It is Arik Vashinsky for whom you wait. *Mazal tov.*"

"Why do you say that?"

"Saul had his thousands, David his tens of thousands, but Arik Blue-Eyes has his hundreds of thousands." The expression on her face made him stop. "Don't pay any attention to me," he said quickly, covering her hand with his. "I shall say anything to get you to bed with me."

She managed a faint smile, but she did not feel quite well.

"There, you see? Already we are touching." He raised her hand to his lips.

"Tell me about him," she whispered.

"It matters so much?"

"Yes, I guess it does."

"Well, I warned you. I shall have only bad things to say. Never mind. I am only joking." He poured more wine into her glass. "I don't really know so much. I do know that he ought to be more than a *Gan-Aluf.* By all that is right, he should be of higher rank. But he was put back. What is the word they use on television? Busted. Yes? Busted?"

"Why? Do you know?"

"Of course I know. As you say, it is a small country. It was during the Yom Kippur War. He disobeyed orders. I cannot recall the exact details but the general commission after the war found that he was quite right to have behaved as he did. Certainly his men, whose lives he saved, thought so. The

commission recommended that he be returned to his unit with all honor. Our glorious military establishment agreed that no charges be brought against him, but they—what was the word?—busted him on principle. The newspapers had a lovely time with it. Numerous fair maidens rushed with open arms to console him, but it seemed he had left the country, gone abroad—to America, I believe." He sighed. "That was a bad time for all of us. Very bad. Accusations. Recriminations. Investigations. Protests. It was a very bad war. Very bad. As if any of them are good. They are all stupid. Incredibly stupid. But at least one can derive some measure of satisfaction from an effort that produces some tranquility, some small amount of stability. After '73—technically, we had not been defeated— *Eretz* still remained on the map, autonomous, a free Jewish State. But there had been too many blunders, too many deaths—we turned on ourselves like a wounded scorpion. It was a very bad time. Very bad." He drained his glass of wine, poured the last of it from the bottle. "Then a few years back I heard that your Arik had returned. I saw his picture in the newspapers. Yes. . . . It was after some border raid. Some heroic, militarist action taken against the enemies of Israel and free men everywhere."

"You don't much like him, do you?"

He raised his eyebrows. "I have before me an exquisite creature—one who comes equipped with *steakim* no less— whom I seem to have no chance of getting my hands on. And you want me to like the *mumser*? It is enough I am forced to admire him."

"It seems to me," Elie was saying, "that your typing has lost a bit of its verve. I was getting accustomed to a much more sprightly sound from you." He raised his hands in imitation of a concert pianist. "Or is the machine broken again?"

"No . . . it's all right."

"What happened? Lovers' quarrel?"

"Not even that. He didn't get in this weekend."

99

"Ah. Well, now you know how Israeli women suffer. It happens all the time."

"He could have called."

"It is not always possible."

"Why not?"

"Various reasons. Something could be going on. . . . They could have sealed the base for one reason or another. It is not uncommon."

"You really think that's what happened?"

He was surprised by the urgency in her voice. "Of course. What else could it be?"

"I don't know. I thought . . . I thought . . . maybe. . . ." Her face flushed.

He shook his head. "Americans. You make everything so complicated. The man is in *Zahal*. He is an officer. His life does not belong to him."

"What do you mean?"

"Listen, my girl, in Isreal, you must be prepared for two inevitabilities. If you are a man, healthy, fit for military duty, then you must be prepared to be called up at any time. Never mind that the wife has bought a new gown for the party of the year, or that the firm is expecting a report on the new machinery, or that you've managed by means of blackmail, threats of physical violence, and an entire year's salary to obtain a ticket to the soccer play-off—never mind all of that. Someone on the radio says Red Lion or Cypress Tree, and it is good-bye to the wife, the boss, the soccer game, and off to *meloim*."

"And what is the second thing?"

"The second thing is if you are a woman. Then, you must be prepared to see your Red Lion or Cypress Tree take off with but a moment's notice, leaving you with the children, one of whom is teething and the other two with the virus, the broken 'fridge, and his aunt and uncle from Pittsburgh whom you must now entertain for the next two weeks."

Terza had come into the office during this. She frowned. "He makes it a joke," she said to Meri, "but it is not so funny.

100

All you can do is wait. It is a terrible business." Ben Levi said something in Hebrew; she shrugged her shoulders. "All right, we have to laugh a little. But really, it is not such a joke for the woman. I know each time how bad it was for my mother. And my brother's wife. He was not even there when the child was born. He was for months in Africa after the Yom Kippur War."

"Africa?" Meri's eyes widened.

"The other side of the Suez," Ben Levi explained.

"Africa. . . ."

"But we are speaking only of the average citizen, Miss Sloane. Your friend is permanently attached to *Zahal*. For him it is not a question of being called up, but of when he can get away for, shall we say, nonmilitary pursuits." He paused, as though weighing whether or not to continue. "He is an important officer, Meri," he said at last. "You may take my word for it. A very important officer." He sighed wistfully. "I can tell you one thing—he does not spend much of his time within the walls of offices such as this one."

Terza lifted her chin in that typical Israeli way, as though to say, "Listen to him. He'd rather be out in the desert or in the Golan wilderness than here in this nice, clean, comfortable place with its lovely telephones and typewriters." Which, in fact, he would.

"Enough with your typing," he said impatiently to Meri. "The United Nations can wait. Come with me out to the Tel. We shall see what is happening there. We both need some fresh air."

"You have a class," Terza reminded him.

"To hell with it," he replied in Hebrew. "I'm leaving."

"But what shall I say?" she asked, dismayed.

"Nothing. Why must you say anything at all? You are my keeper? Oh, all right. Tell them—tell them I've been called to *meloim*." The idea pleased him. "Yes, say I must report to *meloim*."

"You haven't been for two years. You're too old."

101

"As a consultant," he growled. "Now be still. You are a very fresh girl."

She lifted her chin again.

"I don't know if I could live with it," Meri said suddenly, as they approached Rannon. She had been silent for the duration of the ride, for once unconcerned with the speed with which the Israeli maneuvered the car around the narrow mountain curves. That speed usually left her white-knuckled and pale upon their arrival at the Tel; today, however, she was thinking of other things.

Startled, Ben Levi turned to her. He too had been lost in thought; and when he retreated into his mind, he went far, far away.

"I just don't know if I could take it," she said slowly, more to herself than to him. Living with a man, never knowing when you'd be together or when he'd be called away. What sort of life could it be? "What would I do while he was away?" She shook her head. "I don't even speak the language. . . ."

"You are thinking of staying in Israel?"

She was even more surprised than he, hearing it voiced at last. "I . . . I don't know," she stammered.

Ben Levi said nothing. So Leah had been right.

She fell silent again. To live in Israel . . . could she really consider it? Meredith Anne Vashinsky. . . . Oh no, it would never work.

Arik. . . .

Arik. . . .

God, what was happening to her?

"Do you find living here difficult?" she asked Linda Meyers. They were in the p.r. woman's flat, a small apartment furnished with Scandinavian pieces intermixed with Arab baskets and embroidered pillows and modern Israeli paintings.

"Well," Linda admitted, "it can be trying at times."

"Then why do you stay?"

"Well, there's this terrific view of Mount Scopus from my bedroom window. . . ." She smiled. "Why do I stay? Because for me, there is no other place. For me, this is where it all is."

"Because you're a Zionist?"

"No, there's more to it than politics and religion, although of course they are tied up in my feelings. It's hard to explain. I only know that I'm alive here. Oh sure, sometimes I miss the comforts of the States. But no, I don't really get homesick, in case you are wondering. Funny . . . when I went back to Ohio with my ex, for the first time in my life I knew what it meant to live in *Gola*—the Diaspora, you'd call it. All the time I was showing off for Shimon—five hundred channels on the color t.v., the big car, the big steaks—I was really homesick for Israel. I think I kept hoping he would turn around and say, 'Lindala, it's all very nice, the t.v. and the car and the rest. But there's more to life than this. There's Israel.'" She paused. "Only he didn't feel that way," she said simply. "I did."

"Was he religious?"

"No, he was just Israeli. Oh, he got a little crazy in the States. It always bothered him that McDonald's stayed open on the Day of Atonement. Then one year he decided we had to be kosher, but that didn't last very long, thank God."

"Do you still love him?"

"I never loved him, Meri. I loved Israel. Don't you see? I never really bothered to know Shimon, I was too busy being in love with Judah the Maccabee. Oh, it's a common enough syndrome among American Jewish girls." She laughed suddenly. "I don't expect that's the case with you and your Arik."

"Not my syndrome?" Meri smiled.

"Definitely not. Yours would . . . let's see. . . ."

"Lawrence of Arabia?"

"Right! Or the Sheik of Araby with billions in oil money."

"Well, if you run into any sheiks, give them my number, will you? Judah Maccabee stood me up last weekend and I still haven't heard from him."

"Arik? Oh, he probably just couldn't get off base."

103

"Then he might have called. And don't bother reminding me that there is no telephone in the apartment. He could have left a message at the university."

"It isn't always possible, Meri. I mean, to leave word. Sometimes things happen too quickly for that. That's the way it is here. Tell the truth, are you really angry—or maybe just a little scared?"

"Both," she admitted, with a sigh.

"Arik's all right," Linda said firmly, patting her hand. "I have nothing but positive vibrations. If he's in something . . . he'll get out okay. I know it." The doorbell rang at that moment, and turning to answer it she missed the look of confusion that came over Meri's face.

In something? Meri wondered. Get out? What was Linda talking about?

Linda's visitor was Tom Jordan, the *Post* editor. He was very excited. "Wait until you hear this, kiddies. There's been a rumor afloat the last few days that Hassan Hadad was knocked off in Lebanon. It's still not confirmed officially, but it is going out over the wires now. How do you like that? They finally got the bloody bugger. No, no coffee. Yes, I'll have a drink, thank you."

"Tom, that's fantastic!"

"Isn't it ever?" He was as pleased as could be. He raised the tumbler of Scotch. "To Colonel Mu'ammar al-Qaddafi. Soon may he choke on the hair up his arse."

"I'll drink to that," Linda whooped, pouring rounds for herself and Meri.

"Would someone please tell me why we are toasting—if we dare call it that—the president of Libya? And who on earth is Hassan Whoever?"

"Hadad. Oh, just one of the high muk-a-muks of the Diamond Sword of Islam, one of your basic terrorist organizations. Hadad flitted from Black September to Habash's Popular Front, to the PLO—you name it—before forming DSI. And believe me, next to him, Arafat is Mary Poppins."

104

"The Diamond Sword of Islam. Sounds like something out of Batman."

"Yes, well, Batman never massacred a bunch of school kids. Remember? That London suburb last year? Before that there was the Dutch minister of transportation, and the Israeli rock group at the San Remo festival, and, oh yes, the American major in Germany."

"Good Lord, they've been busy."

"Tell me about it. Hadad's buddies want a return to the Golden Age of Mohammed. I mean, the whole world, luv, under Arab domain, not just Israel."

"What's Qaddafi got to do with it?"

"He's been pouring millions into radical groups in Europe, Africa, and America, as well as supporting the various known terrorist organizations," Linda said.

"Oh, come on," Meri protested. "You can't honestly believe Colonel Qaddafi wants to rule the world?"

Tom and Linda exchanged looks. "Let's just say he'd like to unite the Arab world under his domination," Tom said gently. "Then, that under his belt, you know, maybe spread his wings a bit. Look, let's not get into any political discussions. Let's just be glad one murderer won't be taking tea tomorrow."

Meri sat cross-legged at the foot of the bed, staring up at Yossi's painting. The artist had left for a cousin's flat in Eilat, where, he said, the sun always shone and the beaches were full of Danish tourist girls.

What about Sara? she had teased him.

He seemed surprised. Sara wasn't here.

But didn't he love her?

Of course he loved her.

But?

But she wasn't here. He had looked at her as though she were a small child.

Meri studied the painting of the biblical lovers that hung

105

over the bed. She had the feeling it was Sara that had placed it there.

There was a candle in a clay holder. She lit it, and like the governesses in Gothic tales, held it before her as she walked silently through the dark apartment. The tile was cold under her bare feet; she hurried to stand on the wine-colored carpet, its intricate pattern a maze of Eastern thought. She was standing in the center of the room now. Slowly she began to turn, the candle making a circle of light around her, illuminating the pictures on the walls. There was Jacob, body bent backward, arms fending off the great-winged angel; a gaunt Moses with burning eyes casting down the tablets of stone; a young David, his lyre like a shield against the menacing, wild-eyed Saul; and the studies of lovers, figures of men and women, nude, locked in embrace, holding tight to each other in the midst of rockets, mortars, cannons, swords, bayonets . . . erotic figures of life set in an arid landscape of sand and blood and the rotting dead. And there were Sara's oils, like small jewels, colorful mosaics scattered among his stark paintings like flowers in the desert.

A sound outside the window made her jump. Recognizing the voices of the Israeli family that lived downstairs, she relaxed. They were Sephardic; she was not sure where they came from originally, but she was able to discern an Arabic sound to their Hebrew. They were fighting again, probably over the daughter coming home so late. There seemed to be a great many children in that family; Meri was not quite sure how many and which were the couple's children and which their children's children and which their children's friends. But one of the daughters was seeing a young soldier, and the father, a small, slight man who seemed to exert enormous power over the tribe, was evidently alarmed by his pretty young offspring's modern attitude. He and the blue-jeaned girl were always at it; and if the sounds that came up to Meri's window now were any indication, little Malka was getting a hiding to the accompaniment of her mother's screams and her sisters'

106

wailing. Meri knew that Malka would not cry. After a time the noise stopped and Meri went back to bed, burrowing under the down-filled comforter like a small lost animal. She envied Malka despite the beating. She, who had always prided herself on her independence, who had sent lovers on their way because she preferred to greet the mornings alone, now was jealous of a teenager's midnight groping. Ah, Arik . . . what had he done to her? If only he were here now . . . always . . . the two of them together. . . . Where was he? Why wasn't he here with her now? Where was he, dammit?

107

5

Twelve kilometers within the Lebanese border, a six-man commando unit escorted a top MOSAD agent to a prearranged spot where they would meet an Israeli patrol. The sun had barely dawned in the sky and the farmers of the village were already out in the fields. They waved to the soldiers, calling out greetings in their newly-learned Hebrew. The leader of the six-man team exchanged words with one of the farmers, then motioned his group to a clump of trees, where they immediately took up relaxed but alert positions. This was the area that had been called Fatahland, the border villages of southern Lebanon used by Palestinian guerrillas before the Lebanese civil war to stage such bloody raids on Israel as the Ma'alot massacre. Since then, tenuous links had been forged between the Lebanese Christians and the Israelis, both sides determined to establish the area as a terrorist-free zone.

The Israeli officer leaned back against a tree, his eyes scanning the horizon. He took off the green fatigue cap with its Christian Phalangist markings, and ran his fingers through thick, tawny hair. He held up his hand, checking his watch, its

face turned to the inside of his wrist. "Five minutes," he said. He reached into his shirt pocket and brought out a pack of cigarettes, offering one to the man beside him before taking one himself. The other man held the cigarette up, admired its markings. "Marlboro," he said. "You still have your taste for things American."

The officer shrugged.

"How do you afford these? They are a fortune."

"I save on rent."

"And clothing, too. Well, they say certain women like the uniform."

He did not answer.

"It is a pity, Arik, that you do not choose to join us. You could be very useful to us. To Israel."

"Cut the crap, Zadok. We've been through this before."

"Yes, well, it is not often one finds someone with your extraordinary qualifications, *Gan-Aluf* Vashinsky." He seemed to take a particular, personal enjoyment in reciting the other's title. Suddenly he grew serious. "I could set you up anywhere in Europe," he said in a low tone. "No one would doubt for a moment that you were an American. One hundred percent."

"I have a good memory, Zadok, and we've already had this conversation—right after the Yom Kippur War, wasn't it?"

"It was a good time for you to cut your ties with *Zahal*," the man said smoothly.

"A perfect time. Which you manipulated. I think you would have preferred to see me court-martialed. What happened? Couldn't you persuade the Commission of Investigation? For the good of Israel, of course."

"I don't like your attitude, *adoni*. You act as if we are too dirty for you. All right, you don't like me. I can understand that. Maybe you are right—we are the dirty fingers of the hand. But it is because of these dirty fingers that lives are saved. Good, clean, Israeli lives. In every one of your missions

our agents have been there first, feeding you the information you need for your glorious successes."

The soldier sighed. *"Col hacavod,"* he said softly. "All honor to you. But it is not my way."

The intelligence agent smiled wryly. "And what is your way? Fighting at the head of your unit, the sun shining on your weapons, the eye of God blazing down upon you?"

He flicked the ash from his cigarette. "Oh sure," he replied dryly. "Nothing like a nice war, your friends lying around with their guts spilling out and blood dripping where their eyes should be. *'Ta meshuga,* Zadok," he said, turning away. "You're crazy."

"Arik." He put his hand on the other's shoulder. "We need someone like you."

"You've got plenty of *olim* from the States, if you want an American. I can think of three guys right now who would jump through hoops for you." He smiled. "Just give them a 'double-0' number. They'll be happy as larks."

"That is not what I had in mind."

"Zadok, I'm beat. Look, we got you out of Beirut; now do me a favor and get off my back."

"Arik—"

"It's not for me," he said bluntly. "I don't like intrigue. And I don't like shooting people in their beds."

"People? You think an animal like Hadad is worthy of your feelings? Ask the parents of the schoolchildren he murdered in London last year if he is worthy of your noble sentiments. Ask them if they would wish to see him brought to trial in England or Holland or Italy only to be released at the demands of his skyjacking friends."

"I'm not the man's lawyer. In any case, he's dead. Unless you shot another waiter again."

The agent paled. "The Norwegian incident was a long time ago," he said stiffly.

"Yeah, well, I told you, I have a good memory. Now, if

111

you don't mind, I believe I hear some tanks and I think I'll just take a look and make sure they're ours."

"Tel Aviv is very pleased," General Hatar said. "They just called to offer congratulations. Any trouble?"

"No, but don't send Enosh out for awhile. His wife is due any minute and he's clutching up. It's their first, you know."

"Right."

"Samir is getting anxious about Marjayun again. He claims they could take it themselves but there aren't enough of them to keep it for any length of time."

"Samir always says that."

"Well, one hand scratches the other. He's a good man. I wouldn't want to lose his friendship—and Marjayun controls the road through Fatahland."

"I know, I know. Look, there's just so much we can do. Medical clinics, equipment, that's one thing. . . . Anything else?"

"Zadok tell you about the woman?"

"Leila Salemah. Black September."

"For sure?"

"Zadok fingerprinted the bodies. Arik. . . . He's pressing me again. I told him it's up to you."

"Thanks."

"I know you don't like him but—" he raised his hands. "Someone's got to do it."

"Sure."

"He wants to talk to you."

"Forget it. He already tried to sell me."

"I told him I'd keep you here—"

"No way. I'm taking off now. Right now."

"What do you want me to tell him?"

"Anything you like." He stopped at the door. "What about that leave you promised?"

"Five days."

"Ten." He spread his hands. "Beni . . ." he pleaded, "I haven't seen my sister in months."

The general grinned. "Your sister?"

"Of course," he said solemnly. "Beni . . . I'm the only family she's got."

Hatar shook his head and held out a slip of paper. "So give Ilana my love. Now take off."

He grinned. "Thanks. I knew you'd understand."

There was a jeep about to pull out of the military complex when he came out of Hatar's office. "Where to?" he called.

"Jerusalem," the driver answered.

"Great!" He jumped on just as Zadok entered the building.

She was changing to go out to a cocktail party given by the Ministry of Commerce when she heard the familiar bounding up the wooden stairs. A moment later she was swept up in the arms of a dirty character in the green fatigues common to the United States Army, the Israeli Defense Forces, and most recently, the right-wing Christian Lebanese militia.

"I thought I'd seen the last of you," she finally managed to gasp, trying hard to be indignant. "Where have you been?"

"Never mind that." He was exuberant. "I got a ride in with an AP reporter." He started taking off his clothes. "I love you. But I want a bath."

She had never seen anyone move so fast. The fatigues covered the floor, water was running in the bathroom. When she looked in on him he was lying back in a steamy tub, a look of bliss on his unshaven face. Gingerly, she held up his shirt and pants. "What do you want me to do with these?"

"Burn 'em."

"I'll see if I can get them cleaned up."

"You're beautiful."

113

"Do you want anything?"

"Yeah. A pack of Marlboros. And something to eat. Steak. Chips. Salad. The works."

"Anything else?"

"Yeah." He grinned. "Take off your clothes."

He slept like the dead. He hadn't moved for the last hour. Damn it, she thought. What did he think she was? Some broad waiting at the dock? She nudged him. He didn't move. She pinched his shoulder hard. He sat up so quickly she fell back, startled.

"*Mah zay?* What is it?"

"I . . . I just wondered how long you were going to sleep."

He fell back, yawning. "What time is it?"

"Eleven o'clock. You've been out for at least two hours."

"Sorry. I've been up the last thirty-six."

"You haven't slept for thirty-six hours?"

"I think so. What's today?"

"Wednesday."

"Wednesday." He thought that over. "Good." He rolled over and started to kiss her.

"I'm sorry, Arik. I didn't realize how tired you must be. It's just that I—"

"You were feeling neglected." He buried his face in her neck. "Spoiled brat."

"I'm not."

"Sure you are." His lips moved down her body.

"Look, if you're really tired—"

"The hell with that."

"That tickles. Arik. . . . Before . . . you said you loved me."

"Did I?"

"No games," she said solemnly. "Not now."

He stopped. "All right. No games."

"I hate this. I know I sound stupid."

"You are stupid. Don't you know?"

"I—"

"We belong with each other. That's all. That's the way it is."

She sighed. "I'm in love with you."

"Don't be in love with me, Meri. Just love me."

"And you?"

He shook his head. "American girls. You're so funny. You come on so cheeky and independent but you're so vulnerable. . . ."

"I'm an American girl then?"

"And I'm Israeli. Sure. That's part of it, isn't it?"

"No, it isn't. Not for me."

He stared at her.

"I don't think of you as being Israeli. I don't think of you as being anything but . . . Arik. Is that wrong?"

"No," he said quietly. "It's right. Very right."

"But I'm your 'American girl,' aren't I? I'm your . . . your shiska."

His eyes opened wide. "My what?"

"Your shiska. Isn't that what you call us?"

"Shiska? *Shiksa!* You mean *shiksa!*" He exploded with laughter. "Shiska! Oh my God. Oh no, no, don't cry. Oh Meri, no, don't cry for God's sake, no." He covered her eyes, her lips, her face with kisses. "Don't cry . . . Meri . . . no, no. . . . *Anni ohev otah.* . . . I love you. . . . Meri, Meri. . . . *Anni ohev otah.* . . ."

.

"Have you known many American girls?"

"A few."

"What's a few?"

"I've lived in the States, remember?"

"That's right, I forgot."

"That makes it all right then?"

"Don't tease me, Arik. I feel all funny and nervous inside. Dammit, what's happening to me? I don't like it." She swung

115

her feet off the bed and started pacing up and down the room. "Is this what happens when you fall in love?"

"Don't you know?"

She stopped. "What does that mean?"

"I'm not the first man you've had."

"Of course not," she snapped.

"Didn't you care for any of them?"

She stared at him. "I don't know. I can't remember. I can't remember any of them. God!"

He lit a cigarette. "Not even Roger?"

"Roger?" She moved closer to him. "How do you know about Roger?"

"You mentioned him once or twice."

"No, I didn't. I never did." One didn't discuss one's ex-lover with one's present lover, especially if the ex were married and fairly prominent. Besides, that sort of thing was not her style.

"Sure you did. Roger Logan. He's running for Congress. And he's married."

"I never told you that."

"How else would I know?"

Her eyes narrowed. "You tell me."

He put out the cigarette. "You were checked out by Intelligence."

"Bastard."

"I had nothing to do with it. It was before I really knew you. That's the truth, Meri. We were using Wadi Kelt for secret maneuvers that day you drove up. MOSAD had a report on a blonde tourist who was a courier for the Popular Front. They had to check you out."

"You read the report?"

"Sure."

She sat down on the edge of the bed.

"What are you thinking?"

She sighed. "I'm glad I didn't lie about my age."

He smiled, relieved. "Meri—"

"Meredith to you."

"Meredith Sloane. It sounds like a trust fund."

"I feel all shaky."

"I know."

"Take your arm away, please."

"Just let me hold you."

"No."

"Come on. Don't be stupid."

"I am stupid. You said it yourself."

"I didn't mean it. Come on, lie down."

"I don't want to lie down."

"Cousemmak!" He swore in Arabic and pushed her down on the bed, gripping her arms hard. For a moment they glared at each other, then he loosened his hold. "Meri . . . I'm not just an officer in Paratroops. I'm part of a commando unit. We strike primarily against terrorist operations. I can't take chances. It's not just me. The lives of my men are on the line. I read that report in the normal course of duty. I wasn't spying on you. And there was nothing in it, in case you are wondering, that turned me off and nothing that made me want you any more than I already did. I like you near me . . . I think about you when I'm away from you. At night, out in the desert, I want you with me. I go crazy sometimes thinking about it."

She put her arms around his neck. "Arik . . . I love you."

"I just don't know how far we can go with it. Doing what I do. . . . It's not just that. Let's face it, you'd have it easy anywhere in the world but here."

"It would work out. I know it would. Besides, we don't have to stay here forever. You could come to the States. My father would find something for you."

He removed her arms from his neck. "Wrong move," he said simply.

"You want to stay here all your life?"

"I'm Israeli."

"Oh, look, it's lovely and all that, but all your life? Always worrying about war? What about children? Do you want them

117

to live under that? There's so much more. We could have everything. We could go anywhere in the world."

"This is my home. This is my country. I don't need you or your father to go all over the world. I can go anywhere I like. But this is my home. This is where my children will be born, where they will grow up, where they will be free. I know the kind of life I could lead in America. It's beautiful. But this is my home and I stay here."

"Well," she said in a faint voice, "then I guess I stay too."

He stared at her. "You mean that?"

"Yes," she said, although she was not sure herself what she meant. She only knew she could not bear to lose him.

He took her in his arms. "Meri," he whispered. "Think about it. It won't be easy."

"Do you want me?"

"I want you with me. Yes, I want you. I just don't see what I can offer. It's not easy living here. It's hard for all of us. But it would be even more difficult for you. Think about it."

But all she could think of were his lips, his arms, his body warm on hers. "I'm not afraid," she murmured. "We'll work it out."

6

Although winter was near, the hills and fields of the Galilee were green; they made her think of spring. But that was the way it was in Israel, green in winter, when the rains came, and brown in summer. This land was lush, this northern territory, prized since biblical days for its fertile soil and its fresh-water lake, called the Kinneret because it was shaped like a harp but also known as the Sea of Galilee. For the most part the *kibbutzim* of Israel had been carved out of swamps and desert, worthless land bought for outrageous sums from Turkish and Arab landlords who never set foot on this property but resided in places like Cyprus and Beirut. The Zionist pioneers often died of the malaria they caught on their treasured plots, but still they bought the disease-plagued marshes as fast as the wealthy absentee landlords agreed to sell to "the crazy Jews." The crazy Jews had a saying then: "A piece of land here, a piece of land there, and we will build a homeland." The swamps had been cleared and filled, the desert irrigated to the verdant plenty of the days before the destruction of the Second Temple, when the Roman, Titus, needing wood for his great war

machines, had leveled Judea, stripping it of its beloved trees, starting the process of erosion that over the centuries would turn the land of milk and honey into a hard, inhospitable place.

But the Galilee had always been green, it seemed, abloom with poppies and anemones, the furrowed fields as they were when a man from Nazareth had walked the land. The wild almond flowering in spring, furrowed fields must have been like this for time past thought. Near Megiddo, Arik stopped the car and got out to bring bunches of great feathery stalks to her, weeds that grew by the roadside, dancing pale and beautiful in the wind. She watched him, standing for a moment on the hill above the Valley of Jezreel, looking out over the green land like the biblical kings who had stood in this same place. He was like a young king, she thought, and she couldn't wait for them to see him back home and in New York, ignoring the tiny voice somewhere in her mind that said, "He is what he is because he is here and part of this." She had known that he loved the desert wilderness; now she saw that this sweetly rolling land was also in his heart, as was the sea that touched the coast and the old cities and the new, modern ones.

"Which do you like best?" she asked him.

"What I like," he replied, "is that there is something for every way I feel. When I need to go alone into the Negev, I can. When I want the sea, it's there. I can go up to the mountains or nightclubbing in Tel Aviv. It's all here for me." He put his hand to her face. "And for you, I hope."

Later, he said, "If I'm ever unfaithful to you—and I don't mean sleeping around—it won't be for another woman." He paused. "I've been just about everywhere. Europe, the States, South America, Canada . . . you name it. But I always come back here. For Israelis, Israel is more than just home. *Eretz* is always there for us, no matter how far away we go. It's as though the land is our . . . self. Away from it, we become . . . something else."

She thought of Eleazar Ben Levi, standing on the balcony of the King David, looking out upon a city bathed in golden

light. "Jerusalem," he'd said. "You are not ours so much as we are yours."

"I can promise you only one thing about living here," Arik said. "And I give you my word on it. It will never be dull."

Kibbutz Galil-Bet was in the Upper Galilee, not many miles from the Lebanese border. It was a fairly young commune, having broken away from an older kibbutz, now called Galil-Aleph, when that settlement decided to concentrate on manufacturing radio parts. The members of Galil-Bet preferred agriculture to industry, some of them being Western immigrants from America, England, and South Africa who had left their industrialized professions to return to the soil on an Israeli kibbutz.

Arik's sister, Ilana, was in the laundry room; it was her week to do the ironing. She was a tall young woman with the same determined chin as her brother's but with straight dark hair and almond-shaped eyes. The smile was like Arik's, Meri thought, though it cooled considerably when its owner was introduced to her.

"*Shalom,*" Ilana said politely, extending her hand for a short, perfunctory shake.

"*Shalom.*" Meri smiled, trying to say many things with one word.

Ilana turned away. "How does it go with you?" she asked her brother in Hebrew. "Have you come for a visit or to stay awhile? The boys will be so happy to see you."

"In English. English, Ilana."

"Oh?" Her eyebrows lifted. "Sorry."

"I don't think she likes me," Meri remarked later, in the small room that had been found for them.

"Ilana? She's just shy." He was making up the narrow beds, arranging sheets and blankets with military precision.

"Did they teach you to cook in the army, too?"

"No, in school. I make first-class French toast." He

121

straightened up. "I know the Shipley School for Young Ladies never lectured on anything so mundane as housework, but how about moving your ass and giving me a hand?"

"How did you know about Shipley?" she asked, grabbing a pillow. "Oh, I forgot. The report."

"Just a guess. MOSAD didn't go back that far. There's just so much they can do in a couple of hours."

"That's a relief. I'd hate to think of all of you standing around reading how I wet my christening dress."

There was an awkward silence.

"I took out a Shipley girl once," he said, clearing his throat.

"Ah-hah!" She laughed nervously. "What happened? Did she rape you?"

"No. She was very nice. Very dull and very nice."

She nodded. "Arik . . ." she swallowed. "Is it because I'm not Jewish? Is Ilana—does she know I'm not Jewish?"

"She knows you're not Israeli."

"Does she know I'm not Jewish?" It would not be because of her looks; there were men and women throughout the small country whose physical appearance would fit the Nazi image of an Aryan super-race. Ilana knew Meri was American; only Arik could have told his sister that she was a Gentile.

"I think you're getting worked up over something that's not important," he said, taking the pillow from her and tossing it on the bed.

"If it's not important then why did you discuss it with your sister?"

"I didn't discuss it with Ilana. She asked me and I told her." He sat down on the bed and pulled out a cigarette. "There is no civil marriage in Israel, Meri. Not yet, anyway. There's no telling how long it will be before there is."

"Darling." She put her arms around his neck. "We don't have to get married in Israel."

"There's more. Children born of a marriage not recog-

nized by Jewish law are . . . not recognized by Jewish law. They are *mumserit*. Bastards."

"That's sort of archaic, isn't it?"

"Yeah. Part of our charm."

"Do you want me to convert?"

"Do you want me to?"

"No. Of course not."

"Then why ask such a stupid question?"

She sighed. "Well, I don't know what you want. What do you want?"

"Nothing," he said uneasily. "Let's not go into it now. This is a holiday, remember? Let's just have a good time."

"Well, for a holiday, I might have preferred the Hilton." She bounced ruefully on the foam slab set on a wooden frame that served as mattress and bed. "Which this certainly is not."

"Sure it is. The Galil Hilton. Didn't I tell you?"

"How's room service?"

"Fantastic. As long as you get it yourself."

"International cuisine, I suppose."

"All the oranges, tomatoes, and cucumbers you can eat."

"Recreational facilities?"

"You can work in the fields, gather eggs, wash dishes, iron shirts—whatever turns you on."

"Arik, are we supposed to work while we're here?"

"You're a guest, Meri. You're not expected to do anything."

"Why did you say 'you' and not 'we'?"

"I wouldn't feel right bumming around. They're always short of help, and we are eating their food."

"Oh, terrific."

"I told you, you don't have to do anything."

She was about to answer but decided not to say anything. She was beginning to have misgivings about this "holiday."

*   *   *

He was up early the next morning, hurriedly pulling on jeans and a heavy sweater to go out into the cold, gray dawn. He bent down and kissed her shoulder. "See you in the dining room at eight," he whispered. "Take your time. It's only six."

She managed to open one eye, but he was already gone. At quarter to eight he was back, pulling the covers off the bed. "Don't," she protested. "I'm freezing."

"You'll warm up. Here." He threw her his sweater. "Get dressed."

She sat up, shivering. "Couldn't we skip breakfast? We can always grab something later."

"We can, huh? Where? There's no Howard Johnson's down the road."

She held out her arms. "So who needs food?"

"I do. Get dressed and meet me in the dining hall. Do you remember where it is?"

She nodded glumly.

"Okay. Don't wear your good shoes. It was raining earlier and the ground is pretty muddy."

The dining room looked like a Broadway cafeteria, with its formica-topped tables and hard-seat chairs. Dishes clattered as they were passed along, and the rolling wheels of the serving carts being steered from table to table echoed above the muted conversations of the diners. A table full of teenagers was about the only lively spot in the place. Breakfast was plentiful: Bread, vegetables and fruit, hard-boiled eggs, cheese, yogurt. Lunch, served at one, would be the only hot meal of the day, with soup, and poultry or meat for the main course. Supper at seven was the same as breakfast.

"What a super, organic meal," Meri said brightly. "I have some friends in New York who are really into organic food. You know, everything natural, no preservatives."

The others at the table looked at her.

"I bet this is a fertile egg," she said, wondering why her voice sounded so loud.

rtile?" Ilana was puzzled. "No, there is no chicken
It's all right. You can eat it."
nd raw sugar!" Meri went on, spooning some into the
. "God, do you know how expensive that is in New
?"

Ilana's husband, Amos, looked up at Arik. "Tell me," he
said mildly in Hebrew, "does she always talk so much in the
morning?"

He was stocky and sandy-haired, a third-generation *kibbutznik* whose mild demeanor hid a first-rate, analytical mind.
Amos was the kind of man one could depend on, a reserve
officer highly thought of by his men as well as the high command. Ilana and Arik often teased him for his slowness to take
action, his unwillingness to come to any sort of decision without the most deliberate thought, his determination to follow
through with careful step-by-step planning. It was, however,
this very steadiness that had served his combat unit well. Amos
was not a man to lose his head; his calmness gave his men the
sense of security that enabled them to behave with the relaxed
precision that, they would later discover, had saved their
lives.

But as he sat in the kibbutz dining room, methodically
dicing tomatoes, cucumbers and onions into a confetti which
would then be thoroughly mixed with yogurt and sprinkled
with salt and pepper, speaking little and then in Hebrew, he
seemed to Meri little more than a country bore. Arik had told
her that Ilana was an accomplished musician and a writer
whose poems had been published; Meri found it difficult to
understand what the woman saw in this vegetable chopper or
why she had chosen to live with him on this remote settlement
instead of somewhere more sophisticated. Still, there must
have been some attraction; there were three children: eight-
year-old Assaf, six-year-old Gil, and two-year-old Daniella,
named for the brother killed in the Yom Kippur War.

"What do you think of our help?" Amos gestured toward

the workers in the orchard as they toured the ground
are Arabs," he said, before Meri could comment.

"I didn't know kibbutzes—I mean, *kibbutzim*—
laborers."

"They don't usually," Arik said. "These are Lebanes[e]
from across the border. Since the civil war, they are having [a]
hard time with unemployment there. We've instituted an open
fence policy as we did with Jordan after the Six-Day War.
You see, the more interaction we have between the Arabs
and ourselves, the better chance there is for us to lose
our hostility—and fear—of each other. It's just common
sense."

Meri nodded. "Leah was telling me how they integrated
the schools in Jerusalem. She said they're deliberately setting
up the well-baby clinics in East Jerusalem, so the Israeli
mothers have to get together with the Arab mothers."

He gave her a little hug, pleased that she had taken an
interest in the problems of his country.

"Amos," she asked, "don't Israelis resent the fact that jobs
are going to Arabs?"

He smiled. "We are not suffering here as you do in
America from the unemployment problems. With us, it is a
matter of too many jobs to do and not enough people. What has
been the problem is that some of us are against hiring anyone to
work on kibbutz. We do not like to be the employer. It is
against the *ethica*, the principle, of kibbutz." He turned to
Arik and spoke in Hebrew.

"There was a meeting," Arik translated for her, "like your
New England town meeting. The older members were against
the hiring of outsiders. They felt it turned them into capitalists.
But the young people felt it was important for building bridges
to peace. The government resolved the issue by agreeing to
pay the salaries of the Lebanese. That way, the State of Israel,
and not Kibbutz Galil-Bet, is in fact the employer."

"So then was another meeting," Amos continued. "Again
the *ethica*. To receive the profit of labor without to pay for it?

126

So was agreed the fruit and vegetables the Lebans pick is to send to *Zahal. Hacol beseder.* Everything is happy."

Somehow she found herself, like the proverbial partridge in a pear tree, picking fruit along with *kibbutzniks* and Lebanese workers. It was fun the first few minutes, but as her back and arms began to ache, the idea of "working the soil"—or the tree—began to lose its poetic appeal. Ilana was not in sight, but Meri was sure Arik's sister was aware of her early departure from the orchard. She tossed her head. So what? Arik had said she didn't have to work. It was just that there really wasn't anything else to do around the place. She went looking for him. The sun was out, everything was bright and green, although the ground was, as he had warned, quite muddy. For the next few days it would seem to her that she was constantly walking in mud or manure, chilled by the dampness of the unheated buildings and the less than overwhelming friendliness of the *kibbutzniks.* They were a closed group; it was the Lebanese workers who smiled at her or the teenagers who offered a warm "hi" or *"shalom."* The older members of Galil-Bet were as reserved as the Main Liners of the Hunt Club might be if one of their peers brought out a secretary from South Philadelphia. Meri did not know that these *kibbutzniks* were in fact the elite of Israel, sons and daughters of men and women who had shaped the neglected land into the soil that fed the nation, had defied the Turks to help the British, fought the British to gain their State, defended themselves against Bedouin raiders and the Arab Legion, not with the Uzis and Phantoms of *Zahal* but with the pitchforks and Molotov cocktails of *Palmach* and finally the guns of *Haganah.* They were unimpressed with foreigners who came shiny-eyed after the hard-won victories to "work for Israel"—as many a young, idealistic volunteer discovered. There was little glory in the day-to-day routine of kibbutz life. There were shirts to be ironed, dishes to be washed, animals to be fed, floors to be mopped, machinery to be repaired, crops to be planted, tended, harvested—all very

127

unglamorous stuff to the kids who came clutching *Exodus* or dreaming of the exploits of Kirk Douglas and Paul Newman. Great was the dismay of many volunteers who had flooded Israel in her hours of crisis to discover they were not to be given a gun and a Bible but rather sent to the fields and the factories; only citizens of the land were permitted by law to serve in the nation's army.

So Meri was not wrong to think she detected a coolness, a wariness on the part of her hosts. Had she come to them as a volunteer, she would have been put to work first in the kitchen before graduating to the more pleasant work in the orchards. What she did not know was that once she proved herself, showed herself to possess some bit of inner strength and decency and humor—to be a *chevraman* and not a *mefonekit*, or whiner—she would find herself surrounded by no truer friends, no finer family than these simple-living but never simple-minded Israelis.

Arik was in the stable, talking with a young man who was grooming a beautiful Arabian horse. He put out his arm, drawing her to him even as he spoke. Close to him once more she felt warm again, content, even though she could not understand what he and the other were saying. Somehow it did not matter.

He turned to her. "Can you ride?"

"Of course."

The young man smiled slightly, looking at Arik as if to ask, "Can she really? These are not plough horses."

That they were not. It was the first time Meri had seen any horses in Israel, and she was immediately taken with the beauty of these animals. She was sure they were pure Arabian. She went up to one and easily, with the manner of one who was familiar with horses, made friends. The young man nodded appreciatively. It would be all right.

Arik smiled. "Come on then."

*   *   *

128

It was good to ride again, especially in this green open country. The three of them galloped like Indians, Ami taking the lead, then Meri, with Arik in the rear. When at last they drew the horses up, Arik pointed ahead. "There's the border. Want to see Lebanon?"

"You're joking. Really? We're that close to it?"

"That's it."

"We still to patrol," Ami said in his faltering English. "Is quiet since the war. No more Fatahland. But good not to take chances, you understand?" He patted the black stallion, and Meri saw now that he had a rifle with him. "The general must to be run anyway." He smiled shyly at Meri. "You ride okay. Anytime you like to ride is okay."

"Where is your friend tonight?"

"Asleep. Amos?"

"At the committee meeting. I'll make some coffee."

"Good." He sat down on the narrow sofa which had served as his bed on former visits and flipped through a magazine. Ilana and Amos had one of the newer apartments, two rooms, the living room equipped with a small kitchen, the bedroom closed off by a folding curtain-screen. The boys slept in the children's quarters, but Daniella still had a cot in her parents' cottage. She was asleep now in the bedroom alcove.

"How does she find kibbutz life?"

"Meri? She's not complaining. I wouldn't say it's exactly her style, though," he added wryly.

"Or yours. You've always preferred Tel Aviv."

"That's true." He tossed the magazine back on the table. "What do you think of her?"

"Lovely. Like a movie star."

"Come on, Ilana."

"What do you want me to say? You've never brought a woman here before."

"You may be seeing a lot of her."

"Are you serious?"

129

"Can't you see that I am?"

She was silent, busy with the coffee, setting out cakes on a platter. "Arik," she said at last, "can this truly be what you want?"

"Meri? Yes."

"She is not one of us."

"She can learn to be."

"She would become a Jew?"

"That part of it is up to her. I would not ask it."

"Why not? How can you—"

"Since when are you such a *rebbitzan?*" he broke in angrily. "Come off it, Ilana. We were both brought up to respect others' beliefs."

"To respect, yes! But to—" She turned away that he might not see the tears that had come to her eyes, and began to busy herself dusting imaginary cobwebs from a corner of the immaculate room. When at last she spoke, her voice was low, as composed as she could make it. "I have always loved you," she said. "Not just because you are my brother, but because you have always seemed to me to be the finest, the best—" She could not go on.

"Ilana—"

"No, it's all right." She took a deep breath. "I see nothing but problems ahead for you." She sighed. "But it is not what I want that matters but what makes you happy. Only—" Her eyes suddenly filled with fear. "Arik, you won't become a *yured*, will you?"

"Leave Israel forever? *Motik*—" Smiling, he took her in his arms. "Little Chinese Eyes, had I wanted to do that I could have done so long ago."

"It's bad enough when one's parents—"

"Enough, Ilana," he said gently.

She sighed. "All right."

"What do you hear from them?" he asked in a light tone. "You must have had a letter."

130

"The usual nonsense. When are we coming to visit, and so forth. She sent the children beautiful sweaters for the winter. Much too fine for here."

"*Abba?*"

"You know he never writes. I suppose he's well. They live in a dream world, both of them. He with his numbers and formulae and she—oh, I don't know. You should see those sweaters." She laughed. "Assaf has already got his full of mud. Kids. . . ." The almond eyes met his, questioning.

"You're going too far, too fast, too soon," he said softly. "I don't know what will be. She may leave tomorrow. Go back to America and her fine life there. I couldn't blame her if she did."

"Women don't leave you, Arik," his sister said, with a slight smile.

"What are you talking about?"

"All the girls I went to school with, every one of them was mad for you. You could have had any one of them. I don't understand it. Why this one?"

He shrugged. "It happened."

"She is beautiful, yes, but surely—"

"Who can say why one person is right for another? It happens. Ilana, don't push me. I don't like it. You know how I am." He pushed a book of matches around the table, flicking it forward with his thumb, retrieving it, flicking it away again. "The truth is, I don't know myself what will be. It's something I never thought of, to become involved with someone like her. A good time, yes, but not like this, the way it is with us."

"You really love her?"

"She is good, Ilana. Lovely inside as she looks. There is no meanness in her." He used an old Hebrew expression. "She has an innocent heart."

"How does she feel about . . . what you do?"

He threw back his head and laughed. "She is totally untouched by it. It's fantastic. She is so innocent of our harsh

131

reality that when she says good-bye to me, it is like a woman saying, 'Have a good day at the office, sweetheart, and don't forget we're going to a party next week.'"

She had to laugh with him. "And that is what you want?"

He grinned. "I'm telling you, it's wonderful. To look into her eyes and not see the fear. . . . She asks no questions. . . . It's wonderful," he repeated.

"Wonderful, yes, but enough to—"

"I told you. I don't know. I'm telling you the truth—even though it is none of your business."

"Arik—"

"And because if it does happen, I'll expect you to be her friend—her true friend—as well as her sister. God knows, she'll need one."

"You expect me to call a *goy* 'sister'?"

The word shocked him. "Why must you say that? It's ugly."

"It's the truth."

He was uneasy again. "Let's drop it, all right?"

"You had better begin to face the reality of the situation."

"Ilana, in a few days I'll be back where I have all the reality I can possibly face. Right now I'm on holiday, and frankly, I don't need or want any more discussions like this one. From you or anyone else. As far as I'm concerned, for this little while, today is all that counts—today is forever."

He went out into the night. The *shomerim*—kibbutz guards—were making their rounds; they would drive the length and width of the settlement until the dawn. They were young, maybe nineteen or twenty years old, but fully skilled in the use of the Uzis they carried with them in the jeep. For a moment Arik thought of riding with them, but then he saw that they had their girl friends for company. He smiled, remembering how it used to be, patrolling all night, going afterwards to the kitchen to fry up chips and eggs while the girls made tea. There would be laughing and joking. Alone and awake in the

132

sleeping kibbutz, they would know a special camaraderie, born of being young and free and having successfully completed the important mission of seeing to the safety of their families and friends. They would sleep late tomorrow, and they would sleep well.

She was asleep on her stomach, her hair covering her face. He stood by the side of the bed for a moment, looking down at her; then he took off his clothes and got in bed beside her. She turned toward him as if sensing his presence. He took her in his arms and began to make love to her.

The worst part about the orchards, she decided, was the wet grass. Her shoes had not been dry for days. She wished she had a pair of the sturdy clodhoppers she'd seen on the others. Tennis shoes just didn't make it in the morning dew. Other than that, pear picking wasn't all that bad. There was a lot of singing—Israeli folk tunes from the *kibbutzniks*, some kind of Arab "Jingle Bells" from the Lebanese workers, and assorted rock songs from the young American volunteers. The sun was warm, the air smelled sweet and fruity; it really wasn't so bad, just boring. When the truck came to load the fruit, she awarded herself a break. She found Ilana alone in the laundry room, ironing again, as she had been the day they'd arrived at the kibbutz. "Hi."

"*Shalom.* How does it go with you?"

"Oh, fine, thanks."

"Where is Arik? This is the first I see you without him."

"I don't know. I can't find him."

"Well, never mind. He is probably off with Ami. He is crazy for horses."

"So it seems. He rides very well. We have a hunt club back home that I know he'll love."

Ilana looked up at her.

"I didn't realize you had such beautiful horses here. They're really superb. Can I help?"

"If you like. You can fold those towels there. Yes, the

133

horses are quite fine. They are an unusual addition to the kibbutz."

"They are pure Arabian, aren't they?"

"Yes, the offspring of a gift to the kibbutz—Galil-Aleph, that is—by a friendly sheikh. It was even before Israel was a state. It is rather a nice story."

"Tell me, please."

"The grandfather of Ami was a *chalutza*—a pioneer, you would say. I believe he came over with Trumpeldor. Anyway, he was a leader of one of the first settlements in the Galil. There was an Arab village near the kibbutz and relations between the inhabitants and the Jews were quite harmonious, believe it or not. It happened that one day the grandfather of Ami found a young Arab who had been badly beaten and left to die. He took him back to the kibbutz where he was eventually returned to health. As it turned out, he was of a tribe other than that of the village but had fallen in love with one of the girls there. Her brothers had set themselves upon him because he was a stranger to them, but as it turned out, he was the son of a very powerful Bedouin sheikh in the south. When he was well again, he returned to his father's tent. He later came back to the village with his own men, killed the girl's brothers and took her with him to be one of his wives. He knew the kibbutz was in need of work animals and in his gratitude for their care of him, he gave to them two beautiful horses, a stallion and a mare, from which the ones you see are descended. The grandfather of Ami knew the animals were too splendid to be used for ploughing and such, and he talked his *chevra* into allowing him to care for them and breed them and to use them not for the heavy work but for patrolling the area against bandits and to summon help when needed. The horses became a great source of pleasure and pride to the kibbutz as well as being useful and profitable. The stallion was quite active, you see."

"It's like a movie."

"Yes, it must seem so to you. But it is all quite true."

"What happened with the Arab village? Are they still friendly to you?"

"The village was razed by the Arab Legion in the war of '48 and the villagers driven from it. The elders were hanged in the market square. It was, you see, for being friends with the Jews."

Meri was silent a moment. "What of your people?" she asked. "Arik said you are seventh-generation *sabras*."

"On my mother's side. Our grandfather fled Russia at the time of the Bolsheviks." She looked directly into Meri's eyes. "Arik and I are a mixture of many bloods, both Sephardic and Ashkenazic. East and West. We are not what you call 'blue bloods.' We are perhaps like mongrels, yes?"

Meri made a face. "I never went in for that sort of thing. I suppose the Sloanes have a horse thief or indentured servant somewhere in the family closet. Maybe even a Catholic." She put down the towel she was folding. "I can't believe I just said that." She sighed. "Ilana, let's be open with one another. Until we are, I'm just going to go on making a fool of myself."

"As you like."

"Are you bothered by the fact that your brother and I—I mean, because I'm not Jewish."

"Yes."

"Well, that's open, all right."

"It would be difficult enough if it were simply that you are not Israeli. But to have no feeling for our past is to have no understanding for what we are now and why we behave as we must."

"That's unfair. And I resent it."

"Marriage is difficult enough—believe me—when you share a similar background. How would your children be brought up? What would they be?"

"Citizens of the world. Human beings."

"What nonsense you talk. Anne Frank was a human being. It did not save her from being taken to Belsen to die."

"You don't honestly believe that's going to happen again."

135

"How do I know what will happen? We are a people with a tragic history and we have been duped many times by governments promising sanctuary, security, freedom. Each time we have believed the promises, settled, prospered, only to be driven away finally or murdered by our 'protectors.' "

"But not in America. It will never happen in America."

"Can you say so? In a hundred years' time, when your children's children have been thoroughly assimilated, good little Americans who have forgotten that some long-ago grandfather was Israeli, can you say then there might never be the midnight knock on the door, recalling for those American descendants of yours their ancestor who was a Jew?"

"You're paranoid. You're all paranoid."

"Why don't you use the term your American press is so fond of? Say that we have a Masada complex."

"You do."

"With reason. An earned privilege of dubious honor. Never mind. Let us say that you remain in Israel. You know it is no easy life here. If you do not believe in the necessity of a Jewish state, a Jewish homeland—believe in it not just with the mind but with every part of your being—there is little reason to stay. For what? The climate? The beaches? Go to the Riviera, go to California. Certainly not for luxuries. There are many more pleasant places to be, easier places to live. Why should you stay here?"

"Because I love him. I love Arik. But I agree with you that there are easier places to live. You spoke of children. Why deprive them of the advantages they would enjoy in my country?"

"What will you give them in America? Television? Toys? Santa Claus? Here they will grow up with less. But with more. They will know who they are. They will have the sea and the desert and the hills of Jerusalem and the Galilee. They will have each other. They will know who they are," she repeated. "And they will be proud."

136

"They can be Jews in America, Ilana. If that is what Arik wants."

"Jews? Do you think I give a damn for your synagogues and temples? Jews? I am talking about being Israeli."

She was dumbfounded. What did the woman want? "Why must we speak of children?" she said at last, grabbing up another towel and folding it nervously. "That is a long way off. Maybe I don't want to be a mother. Certainly not now, this minute. Maybe never. I don't know."

It was the other woman's turn to be astounded. "What is life without the children?"

"Very pleasurable, I can assure you," Meri replied firmly, patting her stack of folded towels.

"Is that what you learn in America?" The Israeli woman did not bother to hide the pity in her eyes. She was silent a moment. "Then sleep with him," she said shortly, "and let it be only that."

Meri opened her mouth but no words came forth. Silently, she turned away and walked out of the laundry room.

"Where have you been?" she asked peevishly at lunch.

"Around. What's wrong?"

"Arik, how much longer are we going to stay here? I really should be back in Jerusalem finishing up my work." Besides, she thought, she'd really had about as much of Brook Farm as she could take.

He was about to answer her when the others joined them, and he started talking to them in Hebrew.

She put her elbows on the table and her chin in her hands and stared morosely at the salt and pepper shakers and the napkin holder. The napkins were the dumbest things she'd ever seen, tiny squares of hard, shiny paper that were terrific for writing home on but terrible on the face. All the napkins in Israel were lousy. The toilet paper was worse.

"Meri, do you want soup?"

"I'm sorry, what did you say?"

"Do you want soup?"

She looked up. A large woman waited impassively at the end of the table, a ladle in her hand.

"Oh," she said absently. "What kind is it?"

He reddened. "Do you want it or not?"

"How do I know? What kind is it?"

Tersely, in Hebrew, he relayed the question to the woman, who looked surprised. She shrugged. "Soup," she said. "Soup."

"I think it's barley," Ilana murmured.

"All right. Yes, I'll have some, please. Thank you," Meri said politely to the woman as the bowl was passed down to her.

"Bavakasha," the woman replied, nodding graciously as she moved off to the other tables.

"That was the dumbest thing I ever heard," he said later, in their room.

"I don't know what you're talking about."

"Asking what kind of soup it was."

"What's wrong with that?"

"You don't do that on kibbutz. You eat or you don't eat, but you don't ask what's on the menu. It's not the Four Seasons."

"I'm well aware of that. But I still don't see what's so terrible about asking what kind of soup she was serving."

"Because she's not your waitress. She's your comrade. How the hell does she know what they put in the damn soup?"

"I still don't see what I did that was so terrible."

"You wouldn't," he said, disgusted."

She took a deep breath. "Now look, I have had just about as much of this scout camp as I care to take. Picking pears and peeling cucumbers in the kitchen—in the kitchen, mind you— is not my idea of a good time. Nor do I enjoy sitting around every night in your sister's shack or that stupid clubhouse listening to all of you carry on in Hebrew—you don't even

138

bother to translate for me anymore. Or watching black and white t.v. shows that haven't been shown in the States for at least ten years. And every time I suggest going out somewhere, everyone looks at me as if I'm crazy, as if how could there possibly be anything more interesting in the world than life 'on kibbutz.' And I never see you anymore. I came up here to be with you, not to pick pears. And I never see you. You're always off somewhere. And I know that girl with the big breasts who's always in shorts—I don't know how it is she doesn't freeze—she's always hanging around you as well as all those little teenyboppers, and they're all stacked too. Or else you're playing chess at night. And your sister hates me, in case you didn't know. And I don't give a damn." She sat down on the bed. "I want to go home. What are you laughing about?"

"I was just realizing how all this must seem to you." He knelt beside her. "Ilana doesn't hate you. She's just concerned. In any case, you might as well know that I have no intention of living permanently on a kibbutz. In a lot of ways it's terrific—but it's not for me. I get too restless."

"Arik—" she threw her arms around him.

"Your shoes are wet."

"They're always wet."

He untied the laces, slipped them off her feet. "You're ice-cold. Why didn't you wear socks?"

"I don't have any."

"Stupid. You should have asked."

"What are you doing?" He was unzipping her jeans.

"Guess."

"But it's the afternoon."

"So what? You have a date with a pear tree? Or maybe one of our friends in the field?"

"Don't be silly."

"Then shut up."

Cold air struck her skin and then she was warm, warm. . . .

He looked up for a moment. "Besides," he said, in that way he had in which she could never tell if he was serious or

not, "I wouldn't want you to get the wrong idea. Kibbutz life can really be very interesting."

Dawn was breaking over the Galilee, the first golden rays touching the reeds and rushes that grew beside the Jordan River, the light settling like a star on the white cap of Mount Hermon on the Syrian border. A truckload of Lebanese workers, their papers checked by a border guard, passed through the wire fence into Israel and headed for the fields of Galil-Bet. The morning was clear, not a sign of rain. It promised to be a beautiful day.

At the kibbutz gate, the truck was waved through by the morning guard; it then proceeded to the parking lot a short distance from the center of the settlement. The driver pulled carefully into the lot, cautiously avoiding a small, new-model Fiat. The workers descended from the truck, some to go to the cotton field, others to work in the orchard.

Dov Ben Asher softly closed the door to his cottage, wiping the last drops of tea from his mouth. He was an old *kibbutznik*, had spent more than half of his fifty-three years in the hills of the Galilee since coming to Israel from Cyprus as an illegal immigrant smuggled into the country along with a half-dozen other "displaced persons" from Eastern Europe. This morning, something bothered him. It was too quiet. Usually, the 'Lebans' set up a chatter among themselves that never failed to annoy him. It was not so much the noise that bothered him but his inability to understand what was being said and to catch any insults that might be tossed in his direction. The absence of such chatter this morning drew his attention, causing him to take more than his usual disgusted notice of the foreign workers. Five of them were headed for the cotton field. Five? There ought to have been eight. He looked around. None was going to the orchard. Three, no, four were dawdling by the truck. One seemed to be headed in the direction of the children's quarters. Dov Ben Asher raised his hand and waved at the man. "Hey!" he called. "Where do you

140

think you're going?" The Arab turned, drew out a gun from his jacket and started shooting. After that, all hell broke loose.

Meri was getting dressed when the firing began. She was in good spirits; Arik had promised they would leave after breakfast. He had already gone out to the fields—to "pay for breakfast." Everything was still, peaceful, the early light reaching through the window promising a warm, sunny day. She was trying to decide whether she would prefer to return to Jerusalem or to talk him into going down to Eilat, when she heard the shouting and the gunfire. She ran out of the volunteers' dormitory, where they had been housed. People were running through the area, some of them only half-dressed. A siren had begun to wail. Not far off there was a flash and an explosion as a grenade hit one of the buildings. A teenage boy ran past her. "Get to the shelter!" he shouted. "They may have bazooka cover."

She ran after him. "What is it? What's happened?"

"Fatah attack. They came over with the Lebanese. Take cover!" He sprinted for the dining hall, first pushing her against a wall as another grenade went flying.

"Wait! Wait!" She followed blindly, not knowing where she was running. Someone heading toward her grabbed her arm, spun her around. He was a tall man, covered with mud, a snub-nosed Uzi under his arm. "Arik!"

"It's all right. Just do as I say. Get to the shelter by the children's house. The area is clear there, but they may start shelling from the border. They must have control of the town."

"Arik!"

"Just do it, Meri. Now!"

She could not move. A toddler wandered out of one of the cottages, crying. "Damn," he swore, sweeping the child up in his arms. He thrust the child at her. "Take the kid with you to the shelter. Come on, move!"

She stared at him, uncomprehending, frozen. Their eyes locked. It was only a second, a moment, before he realized she

must be helped, but it seemed an eternity. Suddenly a woman ran toward them and snatched the boy from him. He spoke to her in Hebrew; she nodded and pulled Meri along with her and the child.

She called after him but he was already off, not even looking back.

The woman guided her to the shelter. "Not to be afraid," she said in a soft voice. "Everything, it will be all right. *Sha, sha,*" she murmured to the child in Hebrew. "Everything is all right. It is only a lot of noise. Mommy is with you. Mommy is here." It was only when the woman reached for a chair that Meri saw how her hands trembled.

All *kibbutzim* were equipped with underground shelters such as this one—as were all apartment houses, hotels, office buildings, schools, factories, and country clubs in Israel. For the children of settlements near the borders, sleeping in these basement dormitories every night was not unusual. Before the Syrian artillery was cleared from the Golan Heights, daily shelling was common in that area.

Meri walked through the underground chamber, wandering as in a dream. In addition to the outside entrance through which she had stumbled, there was an entrance to the shelter from the children's quarters above. Some of the children were crying, not from fear as she might have supposed but from empty stomachs or dismay at having been snatched from their warm beds. Biscuits were found, juice prepared for them. Meri sat numbly on one of the cots, watching the women as they tended the children. She saw Ilana with Daniella in her arms, rocking the little girl, and trying at the same time to appease her sons, who wanted to join their father outside.

One of the women began to sing some sort of nursery song. Soon all the children were singing and clapping hands with her, the other mothers joining in too. It might have been a kindergarten scene anywhere in the world but for the fact that somewhere above the singing was the sound of rifle fire, the staccato of submachine guns, the explosion of grenades, the

wailing of the siren; and at the door, listening, a teenage boy and girl, rifles in hand, stood guard.

She was alone in the midst of this. She did not see Ilana beckoning to her, sending Assaf finally to bring her to them. The boy ran to her but turned shy as he came close. The pretty American lady was crying. Assaf put his hand on her shoulder. *"Hacol beseder,"* he told her. "Everything is all right. Don't be afraid. I shall look after you."

He was coming out of the dining room when he heard the shots. Dov Ben Asher was on the ground, moaning and cursing; one of the Arab workers was firing wildly in all directions. Instinctively, Arik hit the ground. A shot from the direction of the building behind him downed the gunman and at the same time the kibbutz siren went off, alerting the settlement. Cautiously, he got up, saw Amos and some of the men already armed. One of them got to Dov, saw that he was alive, called the others to help move him inside. Amos gestured with his thumb to Arik, who nodded and raced back to the weapons room. He was handed an M-16. "Uzi," he snapped.

"All gone."

He grabbed the rifle and raced back outside, heading straight for the sound of gunfire, found a teenager pressed against one of the trucks and snatched the submachine gun cradled in the lad's arms. He tossed the rifle to him. *"Sliha,"* he apologized. "Sorry. Thanks."

Four Arabs were firing from the truck. They had Kalechnikovs and grenades.

He found Amos. "What's happening?"

The *kibbutznik* lifted his chin. "You've got eyes."

"There must be more. You have at least a dozen coming over every day. Where are the others?"

"There seem to be only eight of them. The rest are Lebanese. They say they were forced to go along. Their families are being held hostage in the village."

"I thought the town was Christian-controlled."

"Evidently the 'peace-keepers' from Syria are letting our old friends return to their old haunts."

"Terrific." He let off a volley of shots. "Where the hell are the border police?"

"Soon, soon. Take it easy."

"You take it easy. Shit. This is supposed to be my holiday."

Amos was too busy firing at the truck to reply.

"Try not to kill them all. We'll want them for questioning."

One of the men murmured something to Amos, who nodded appreciatively. "He asks us to be careful. The car beside their truck—the Fiat—belongs to his cousin who is in *meloim*."

"Oh, great. Like Jerusalem in '67. Any other holy of holies?"

"Well, it would be good if you would watch out for the tractor there on the left. It is a new model. They are very hard to get."

"Which one?"

"There—" As he spoke, a grenade tossed from the truck destroyed the machine in question. Amos swallowed and raised the Uzi, "Now they go too far," he said.

Ami reached their side. "What about giving them some of their own?" He held out two grenades. "I lifted them from the body of the one that shot Dov."

Amos looked at Arik. The latter shook his head. "We can wait them out. Where can they go?"

"If they manage to get inside and start the engine. . . ."

"Any of your men on the other side?"

"I don't know. Hold your fire and we shall see."

"Never mind. Hold on to those," Arik told the boy. "If the truck starts moving, all right. Let's see first if we can get them to surrender."

"You think there's a chance?"

"Depends on how hard-line they are."

Suddenly one of the terrorists jumped down and sprinted

for the fields, firing in all directions. He was cut down a few yards from the truck. A genade rolled from his hand back toward the truck. In a moment, it was all over, the vehicle ripped apart by the blast as well as the explosion of the ammunition within. Stunned, the Israelis watched as flames engulfed the area. Then, as one, they ran for the fire extinguishers, calling to others to keep away as they tried to keep the fire from spreading. Amos stared morosely at the devastated parking lot. "Oh my God," he said slowly, forgetting even the loss of the new tractor. "Moshe's Fiat."

There were three more of them at large in the kibbutz. Somehow they had managed to get to the school building and were holding five people hostage there. The border patrol had arrived and the people in the shelters were notified that it was safe to emerge into the open as there was no danger of shelling from the border in a coordinated attack on the settlement. A crowd of *kibbutzniks* now stood near the school building, held back by the police and their own armed men. Some were angrily shouting and arguing with the police for not foreseeing this attack and protecting them from it; some were crying, others trying to comfort those whose relatives were among the hostages, particularly the hysterical mother of a young girl who had been dragged screaming into the building. The usual propaganda pamphlets fluttered down from the third-floor window, the usual demands for the release of Palestinian prisoners held by Israel were made, the usual rhetoric couched in Marxist-Maoist jargon was delivered to the crowd, all this accompanied by the usual threats to the lives and well-being of the hostages.

Captain Medar awaited word from Jerusalem. He knew there would be no orders to negotiate. That was policy. To rush the building, however, was certain death for the Israelis inside. He went over the plans of the school with the secretary of the kibbutz, looking for some way his men might enter the building unnoticed. The problem was not getting in, but get-

ting to the terrorists (now identified as members of Black July, Jayez Jaber Brigade) before they could turn on their prisoners. If only they could get the terrorists outside. A few strategically placed sharpshooters. . . . Of course, such men would have to be brought in. But it could be done. The captain had spoken with the one who had identified himself as an officer with Special Forces; no doubt he would be equal to such a plan. The two men agreed that much depended upon the character of the terrorists and whether one of them was an "officer" of their organization. Already there were five dead terrorists, one Israeli woman killed by grenade fragments, and three others wounded, two seriously. What now? Would these three hold stubbornly to the dream of some kind of deal with Jerusalem? Could they be persuaded to surrender? Or were they fanatics who would choose a "heroic" death, taking with them five more Jews?

The American girl, Meredith Sloane, was in the watching crowd, her hand held firmly by eight-year-old Assaf Bar-Ner. Various leaders within the kibbutz hierarchy urged everyone to return to the dining room or the clubhouse or their cottages (obviously no work would be done today), but naturally no one listened, and they went instead to the school site.

She looked about for Arik, half-fearing to go to him even as she sought him. There had been something in his eyes; he had seemed so cold. No, that was not true. He had cared, he had come looking for her, wanting to see that she was safe, wanting her to be safe. Still, there was something—that moment when he'd thrust that child at her. She had not understood what he wanted of her. It had been so confusing. The noise, the running. . . . She had not understood. . . .

She could see him now. He had his head together with Amos and a man in uniform; the Uzi was still in his hand. Amos was also armed. She looked back at Ilana. The woman's face was impassive. What kind of people were these? Didn't they feel anything? Was this grotesque scene so common to them

that it made no dent on their emotions? What had once been the parking lot. . . . That was blood on the ground, bits of flesh intermingled with burnt metal and pieces of glass. God, there were dead people in this place and now these lunatics were shoving people's faces out a third-floor window so everyone would know there were not just three Arabs in the building in case they cared to blow the place up. They had pushed a young girl almost all the way out the window, letting her dangle above the ground before pulling her back. The girl's mother had fainted. Meri tried to avert Assaf's eyes but the boy pulled free. "Let him see," Ilana said fiercely. "Let him know."

The child worked his way through the crowd until he came to his father. Amos turned to the child, giving Arik his gun, and carried him back through the crowd to Ilana. She lifted her chin inquisitively but said nothing. The others around them bombarded Amos with questions. He answered calmly, briefly, then returned to his former position.

"What is it?" Meri implored. "What's happening over there? What are they going to do?"

"They must wait for a representative from the government," Ilana answered, her eyes still on her husband's departing figure. "Also, the Fatah have asked for the French ambassador to come."

"Will he come?"

She shrugged. "I suppose so. It will make him feel important."

"What of the people inside? Will they let them go?"

"Certainly," an old man said. "All we have to do is give them Tel Aviv."

The others laughed.

Meri reddened. "I don't think it's funny. That girl—"

"What do you want us to do?" Ilana said angrily. "What? What can we do? They have given a deadline of two hours," she added.

Meri turned away, looking back at Amos and the police

captain. They were talking, their faces serious. Arik had disappeared.

He came out of the kibbutz office and nodded to Amos. "*Beseder*. I have the authority. Medar is on the phone with them now. I've asked for another man, someone in my unit. They'll helicopter him in with the ambassador. Give me a cigarette, will you. I seem to have lost mine."

"Why you, Arik?"

"Why? Because I'm here, stupid," he said good-naturedly.

Amos shook his head sadly. "What is it called—'The Busman's Holiday'?"

Arik laughed. "Never mind. There's always *Shabbat*. Listen, they want everything as quick and quiet as possible. A minor incident, you understand?"

"A minor incident. . . ."

"They don't want anything to spoil the new peace initiatives. The Christians have been alerted and are taking care of things on their side. They don't like this any more than we do. Now, if we can handle this quickly and quietly by ourselves— the kibbutz aided by the border police—it will be a good thing. Show the importance of strong border settlements and the ability of Israelis to look after themselves."

Amos nodded alowly. To him, all that was important was getting his *chevramen* out of danger. With governments, it seemed to be a different story. "There will be no negotiation then," he stated.

"You know better than that. Every Israeli citizen is considered a front-line soldier. We will appear to negotiate, however—we'll get the ambassador and so forth—to buy ourselves a little time. But no, we're not handing out any tickets to Libya."

"*Beseder.*"

"They weren't too happy about the truck. MOSAD wants at least one of them alive."

"That will be difficult now."

"Agreed. Did you see the one with the beard? Hear his accent? He's not an Arab. I've heard that inflection before. Brazil. That's where it was. Brazil." He sighed. "I bet he's just aching to die for Che's memory."

"Who?"

"Doesn't matter. Just a feeling I have. Yeah. He sees himself as some kind of grand revolutionary star, all right."

"You mean he's crazy," Amos said matter-of-factly.

"Yep. He's crazy. He's also the one I want."

"What do you want me to do?"

"Try to keep everyone calm, if possible. Don't let any hotheads try storming the building."

"Arik, our people are in there. I appreciate your orders—but to hell with MOSAD. Get our people out. Alive."

"It won't be another Maalot, I promise you. We've worked out a few contingency plans since then. We'll get the kids. But I must bring that fucker out alive."

Captain Medar came out of the office. "*Gan-Aluf* Vashinsky, my orders are to inform the terrorists that the French ambassador has been contacted and is on his way with a representative of the government of Israel. I am to tell you that a Sergeant Ron Segal has been located and will be flown in as well. It is Operation Shiloah, as you suggested." He checked his watch. "We have about three-quarters of an hour."

"Good."

"I must go now to inform the Fatah." He paused, reached out to shake the commando's hand, then left.

Amos looked at his brother-in-law, who was now staring rather absently in the direction of the school building. "What are you thinking?" he asked.

"What? Oh. I better change my shirt. This one's full of mud." He turned to go, stopped suddenly and turned back to Amos. "Have you seen Meri? She all right?"

"She's with Ilana."

"Good. Poor kid. She must be scared stiff."

"Who isn't?"

"Well . . . keep an eye on her, will you?"

"A hundred percent. Don't worry."

He stamped out the Israeli cigarette. "How can you smoke these? They're the worst. Really bad."

She watched Ilana put Daniella to bed for a morning nap. The two boys were jubilant: there was no school today. Ilana turned to her. "Would you like a cup of tea?"

"Yes, thank you, I would."

"There is coffee as well, if you prefer," she went on politely. "Nescafé. Is that all right?"

"Anything. It doesn't matter." It was absurd. Three crazy men with guns and grenades were holding five people prisoner in a school building, the parking lot was the scene of a bombed-out truck and burnt cars and the pieces of what had once been human beings, there were wounded men in the infirmary, bullet holes in the buildings, fires that had to be put out—and this woman wanted to know whether she preferred coffee or tea. One lump or two?

"Sugar?" Ilana asked.

A short hysterical laugh erupted from her throat.

"Are you all right?"

Meri swallowed. She took a deep breath and managed to nod in the affirmative.

Ilana gave the boys some biscuits. They were anxious to play outside. When a neighbor stuck her head in the doorway, Ilana sent them off with her. She sat down and stared at Meri as though wondering how this stranger came to be in her house, as though surprised to see her still there. The American was staring into her teacup with the preoccupation of a fortune-teller reading leaves.

"Before the war in Lebanon," Ilana said calmly, "there was a great deal of shelling by the *fedayeen* from across the border. Bazookas, you know? But it has not been so bad since then. In the *kibbutzim* under the Golan Heights—before the

150

'67 war—there was hardly a day when someone was not killed or wounded by the Syrian artillery and the snipers. They were under fire constantly. That was bad."

Meri sighed. "But why do you stay then . . . so near to danger?"

"The soil is good. Why should we leave?" She laughed suddenly. "You think we are like you? When the black people move into your streets, you sell your houses and run away."

"At least we are not the ones to push them out of their houses," Meri retorted.

Ilana was amused. "But you let them push you out of yours. America is such a big place, not like Israel. I should think there would be room for everyone. But I suppose there is only enough room to run. From sea to shining sea, yes?"

Meri put down the cup and stood up. "I have no stomach for this kind of debate. It may be nothing to you, but I've never seen people shot at before or killed. For that matter, I've never before seen anyone dangled out of a window. While we sit here, five people are being held hostage by a bunch of fanatics. I guess it just doesn't put me in the mood for tea and cookies and this kind of conversation. Excuse me. I'm going to find Arik."

"Meri." Ilana also stood up. "Wait. Forgive me." She made a vague gesture. "I don't know what I've been saying to you. It doesn't matter. It's just talk, do you understand? It isn't you. Niza, the one they held out the window, I've known her since . . . my God, I remember the day she got her first *vessit*, her menstruation. You don't know, you cannot know. . . . I'm sorry, really I am. It isn't you. . . ." She sat down abruptly, covering her eyes with her hands.

Meri stood by the door a moment, but she had no words for the stricken woman and she left abruptly, returning to the volunteer dormitory, where she found him in the room they shared. He was changing his shirt as though nothing had happened. She rushed to him, so happy to see him that she did

151

not notice his startled expression or the absent manner in which he accepted her embrace.

"Thank God you're all right! Is it all over? Have they been released?"

"No, they're still in there."

She closed her eyes. "Please, please can we go away from here? Please, Arik, I don't want to see any more, I don't want to know—we can read about it in the papers or watch it on the news." She laughed nervously. "I've never been the kind who could stand around at street accidents, watching the ambulances, counting the victims. Oh please! Let's go! Arik, please, take me home, take me away from this. I don't want to see it! I don't want to know!"

He stared at her as though she had spoken in a language unintelligible to him, as though she were someone he did not know.

"Thank God you're all right," she said again. "I just thank God we're both all right, and now please can't we go? Won't they let anyone leave, is that it? Of course, I'm so stupid. Security. Nobody comes in, nobody goes out. All right, I'll stay here. In this room. That's all right, isn't it? I'll just stay here. We can stay here until it's over."

"Meri." He caught her to him, held her trembling body tight against his. Then he let her go and forced her to sit down. "Stay in the room if you like. I'd rather you were with the others, but I have no time to argue. I can't stay with you. If you like, I'll arrange for you to be taken out of the kibbutz, but I can't go with you. I can't leave."

"But why? Why?"

"The people in the school. I have to get them out."

Now she saw the Uzi propped against the wall, watched stunned as he picked up the weapon and started for the door. "You," she whispered. "Why does it have to be you? I don't understand. I mean, the border police are here. The army. . . ." she stopped.

He nodded. "It's my job, Meri. I tried to tell you. This is

152

what I do." For a long moment they looked at each other. Then he moved toward the door again.

"But the French ambassador is coming," she blurted. "A government representative is coming. You can talk to them. You can negotiate."

You don't negotiate with terror, his eyes told her. You don't make deals with those who have come to kill you. "It is written in the Talmud that if you let a murderer go free, you are as guilty as he; for who can say how many more will be slain by the one you have excused. No," he said, matter-of-factly. "I don't think we are prepared to give them what they want."

"But they've got five of your people in there!"

"Five today. Five hundred tomorrow. That's what it's all about." He paused. "*L'hitrahot*," he said gently. "See you later."

She closed her eyes. When she opened them, he was gone.

The terrorists were getting jittery; they threatened to push the deadline forward if they were not given some kind of assurance about their demands. Captain Medar quoted logistics of time and distance to them, repeated again and again that the ambassador was on his way. There was a period of quiet, then the one with the beard appeared at the window to announce a change in demands. Now they wanted safe conduct across the border into Lebanon. They would take the hostages with them and release them to the Syrian army. Captain Medar said he would transmit this message to his superiors. There was yet another demand. They wanted American and European media representatives notified. They wanted t.v. cameras present.

Meanwhile an army helicopter had landed a few kilometers away, its two passengers driven by jeep along a back road to the kibbutz.

Arik entered the office of the kibbutz to find Zadok waiting for him "*Shalom*," the MOSAD agent said. "Is there any

tea? I've had no breakfast and that skyride has played bad tricks with my gastrointestinal tract." He grimaced. "If God had meant man to fly. . . ."

In the kibbutz kitchen, a young man with black curly hair and the classic profile of a Minoan bull-jumper was charming a flustered middle-aged female into making him a cup of coffee and maybe buttering a roll or two as well. In jeans and sweater, twenty-two-year-old Ron Segal might have been another *kibbutznik*, the kind whose flashing smile and flirting banter conquered many a young miss. At the moment, however, he was throwing all his considerable charm in the direction of fifty-five-year-old Ruchela, who had the distinction of running the kitchen. One more smile and "sexy devil, you," and the grandmother would be insisting he allow her to fry up an egg or two as well. The enterprising soldier jumped to his feet when he saw Arik, but was motioned down again. He relaxed slightly. "Where did they pull you from?" he asked respectfully. "I thought you were on holiday."

"This is it. My sister's kibbutz."

The young sergeant let out a whistle.

"I hate to disturb your meal, knowing how you're still a growing boy and all, but do you think you could spare me a minute or two in the office? No, take the coffee. Why waste it?"

"Yes, sir. Sir. . . ."

"Yes?"

"Thanks for asking for me."

"Had no choice. You're the only one in the unit who smokes my brand."

Sergeant Segal grinned and brought out the pack of American cigarettes.

"I'm glad you have a rich father, Segal," Arik noted as he took one.

"Stewardesses," Segal corrected his commanding officer

154

as he followed him into the small office. "My father doesn't approve of smoking."

Another helicopter had landed, this time on the grounds of the kibbutz. Several persons emerged, including a gentleman in uniform and, ostensibly, the French ambassador. It was during this arrival, which took place in full view of the school building, that the two commandos slipped into the school by means of a connecting bomb shelter, and began silently working their way up to the third floor. After what seemed like hours of restless pacing in her room, Meri had finally left the empty quarters and joined the anxious crowd that was milling around the school and the blood-stained area that had once been used as a parking lot. The bodies of the dead had been removed; a group of men was hosing down the area. She pushed her way through the onlookers, seeking him yet terrified by the thought of what she might see. Then she saw the army officer and the men coming out of the helicopter, and for a moment she thought it was going to be all right. They would negotiate. They would talk it out like civilized people and come to terms with one another. They would make some sort of compromise and the terrorists would go back where they came from and the hostages would go free and he would not have to go in there maybe never to come out. Give them what they want, she prayed, only let everyone come out of that school alive. But even as these thoughts went through her mind, she knew it was not going to be like that. She could see the tension in Amos as he stood beside the police captain. She could see something in his eyes. . . . Oh my God, she thought, he's in there now. Her throat went dry; at the same time her muscles went flaccid and her bladder released itself, which went unnoticed by everyone, including herself. Yet she did not fall to the ground but stood there, limp, hurting and numb all at the same time. He was in there. She was sure of it.

The man with the beard appeared at the window. There was some kind of exchange with the people on the ground.

155

They were asking to see the hostages, to see if they were alive. They wanted to send someone up to see if this were so. The man with the beard shook his head vehemently. The "French ambassador" started to approach the building, hands in the air, calling out that he was unarmed. The man with the beard shouted something angrily, then turned away, called away it seemed by his comrades. There was a long moment of silence, then the sound of gunfire and screaming and crying from the crowd outside or the people within, she could not tell which. At the same time, it seemed, the border police rushed the school. It all was done quickly, but to her it seemed that time had stopped, suspended within her own agony. Suddenly the face of Captain Medar appeared at the window. He gave a jubilant wave, and the entire kibbutz seemed to race to the building. The freed hostages were embraced by one and all as they shared tears and laughter together. The police had to push the angry crowd away from the one surviving, wounded terrorist as they rushed him to the helicopter; the mob would have torn him to pieces had they been able to get their hands on him.

Slowly the sap began to flow through her limbs again, and she ran toward the building. An arm reached out, stopped her. It was Amos. "He is all right," he said quietly. "Come with me. Arik is all right." She was crying. He put his arm around her, thinking she had not understood. "It is all right," he repeated, leading her away. "He will come to you soon. He is not hurt. *Hacol beseder. Hacol beseder.*"

They spoke little during the ride back to Jerusalem. The terrorist attack was news now, on the radio even as they drove away from the kibbutz. There would be film tapes, interviews with members of Galil-Bet on television that very evening. The reports, government-censored, would make no mention of the two commandos nor of the fact that one of them had a relative living in the attacked settlement. Chaim Zadok, against Arik's wishes and to his anger, had managed to have a

quick, quiet talk with Meri. He had been toying with the idea of getting her to work for him, but her obvious bewilderment and fear at the day's events caused him to abandon these plans for the moment. He had managed to impress upon her, however, the absolute necessity of anonymity for her "friend in Paratroops."

"When you return to America," he had suggested, "it would be best not even to keep a photograph."

When she returned to America. . . . How had he managed to read her mind?

She turned to look at the man beside her. Once before —it seemed so long ago—they had driven away together from an ugly scene. She would never forget that mob in Jericho.

"Well," she said, thinking it would make him smile, "at least I didn't faint."

But he didn't remember. "What?" he asked, startled out of his reverie.

"Nothing. Never mind." She turned away, looking out the window once more.

This is my job, he'd said. . . . This is what I do. . . . I'm part of a commando unit. . . . We strike against terrorist operations. . . .

Where have you been? she'd asked.

Beirut.

You're joking. Have you ever killed anyone?

I've seen men die.

Arik is a very important officer, Elie Ben Levi had said. He is with Special Forces, his daughter, Tal, had told her that first night. I can't say any more, you must ask him yourself. . . .

Once before, long ago it seemed, they had sat beside each other like this. She had only just met him, yet he had not been so much a stranger to her then as he was now.

He did not want to go into the apartment with her. He could not stay, he explained. He had to report back. She

nodded, but sat unmoving in the car. He got out at last, taking her suitcase up to the door. Slowly she followed, fumbling with the keys until he took them from her and opened the door for her. "You're so efficient," she said bitterly. "Nothing rattles you, does it?"

He followed her inside, shutting the door behind them. "I told you life is hard here. What happened today doesn't happen every day. But it happens."

She bit her lip.

He took her in his arms, tilting her face up to his. His eyes, the color of Eilat stones, looked deeply into hers. He bent his head to kiss her, but she avoided him, stepping away from his embrace. "You know, she said, looking away from him, "my work here is really just about done. I really ought to be presenting my findings in New York, to the museum board. I imagine they're all wondering what has become of me."

He waited.

She took a deep breath. "And maybe it would be better . . . I mean, if I went home, saw my family. . . ." She looked up at him.

He nodded thoughtfully. "Yes," he said quietly. "It's probably a good idea. Maybe it's best."

"You're not angry, are you." It was a statement, not a question.

"No, I'm not angry. Maybe we both need time to think things over. It's probably a good idea," he repeated.

It was her turn to nod.

"Well," he said. "I'd better go."

"I won't be leaving right away. I mean, I have to make arrangements and so forth."

"That shouldn't take long. You get VIP treatment, don't you?"

Her face flushed.

"I'll call you in a day or two." He brushed her lips with his. *"L'hitrahot."*

After he'd gone, she went into the bedroom and lay down,

exhausted by the day's events. She pulled the eiderdown coverlet like a cocoon around her. The flat was cold. She was cold. Her insides felt as though they were made of broken glass.

She was awakened by an urgent knocking. The flat was dark; she had no idea what time it was. Sleepily she stumbled to the door. There stood Eleazar Ben Levi, an anxious expression on his face. "Meri! Are you all right? We heard the news and called the kibbutz, but they said you had already left. Where is Arik? He is with you?"

"He had to go back."

"He is unhurt? You are both all right?"

"*Hacol beseder,*" she said automatically. "Come in. What has been happening at the Tel? Wait, let me turn on the lights."

"Never mind that. Leah has sent me to fetch you. You are to come and spend the night with us."

"Oh no, there's no need for that. I'm quite all right. Really." She was embarrassed by his concern.

"Nonsense. This is no time for you to be alone. You must be with friends now and tell us everything that happened. You know what *yentas* we all are," he joked. "Come, get your things."

"No, really, it isn't necessary," she stammered, backing away.

"Miss Sloane. This is no time for Yankee reticence. An experience such as you have had today must be exorcised from the soul with tea and talk and companionship until it becomes just that: an experience—and not a nightmare that will return to haunt you." He put his arm around her. "Tea and talk. Jewish first aid. Come, get your things, my girl. I am sure you have not yet had your dinner, and Leah is waiting."

To her surprise, there were a number of people waiting for her at the Levi residence. Linda Meyers was there, along

with several members of the expedition with whom she had become friendly. Later in the evening, university personnel she had come to know also called or dropped by. She was a bit overwhelmed by this attention, embarrassed to be holding court as it were, and amazed that all these people had come not simply out of curiosity, but with real concern for her. Again and again she had to relate the events as she knew them, omitting, as Zadok had coached her, any mention of Arik's part in the business concerning the hostages. (The official communiqué would state that members of the army and border police had aided the *kibbutzniks* in the capture of the terrorists.) As the night went on, the room growing warm with people and brandy (one neighbor brought a box of chocolates to be passed around; Uri, the student at the Tel, arrived with a bouquet of flowers for her), reminiscences flowed forth of army days and kibbutz attacks and hijacked planes until the horror of the day subsided in her heart, became, as Elie had promised, an experience now shared with the experiences of others. The interesting thing, Meri would later recall, was that the most remembered parts of these true tales of war and Arab attacks and hijackings were the funny moments, the hilarious inconsistencies of behavior under stress. One woman recalled how she had managed to crochet an entire sweater while her hijacked plane sat on Libyan soil, thinking crazily that for once she had the time to do it. "Didn't you ever think that you might not ever get to wear it?" Linda Meyers asked. "No," the woman confessed. "All I could think of was the money I'd spent on the wool—even in London it was dear—and I was damned if I would let it go for nothing. I lost everything else I had with me when they blew up the plane after releasing us." She laughed. "But can you believe it? I managed to take that sweater with me."

"What must you think when you wear it?" Leah wondered.

"Oh, I gave it away. The fit was all wrong."

Tom Jordan had rushed over as soon as he heard Meri was there. He wanted an interview, but she begged off. "Don't want to talk about it?" he asked.

She had to laugh. "It seems to me I've been doing nothing but that for the last two hours. The whole thing is starting to sound unreal to me, like a crazy dream or—well, not something that really happened." She started to laugh again, but suddenly she had a vision of that parking lot and a dismembered arm she'd seen lying on the ground there, an arm that had once belonged to a living person. The expression on her face changed.

"Must have been terrifying for you," he said sympathetically.

"Well. . . ." She swallowed. "It wasn't the sort of thing I've ever been exposed to before—except maybe in the movies."

"Were you scared?" he asked bluntly.

She looked at him and nodded. "I wet my pants," she said solemnly.

He smiled. "Good girl," he said, patting her on the back. "Now you're one of us."

She looked at him. "Are you Jewish, Tom?"

"Church of England, luv. Ever since Henry the Eighth was around."

"But you said 'us'."

"Right. And I meant it."

The strange thing was she understood. For the first time in all her weeks here, she felt that indeed she was "one of them"; and when all the visitors had left at last, she went to sleep in Tal's bed, and she slept peacefully and without dreams. But in the morning she was depressed. Alone in the sand and rubble of Tel Shalazar with Elie, under that bright, blue white sky which stripped one naked of makeup and mask, she let it all out. "I was no good," she confessed morosely. "I didn't help. All I did was whine and get in everyone's way. I know he's ashamed of me—but no more than I am of myself."

161

"You are too hard on yourself," Eleazar Ben Levi said calmly. "In the first place, I do not see that there is anything you might have done to save the situation. Surely the other women did not grab up guns and swords with which to fight your attackers. It is only in films that such things happen. What could you have done?"

"I was truly frightened," she whispered. "I was terrified."

"And you think the others were not?"

"But they all seemed so . . . so . . . I don't know," she said helplessly. "All I know is I was no good at all. I behaved selfishly and cowardly. And Arik . . . Arik . . . oh Elie, I saw him just before—" She bit her lip and turned away. "I ought not to say anything more."

"It's all right. I know about Arik. He is a commando officer. I am sure I can imagine the part he played in the rescue of the hostages yesterday. I was wondering how much you knew."

"He might have been killed and I didn't even tell him. . . . He went without a word, without an embrace. . . . What must he have thought of me?"

"His thoughts were all on the task at hand, that is all. And he was happy to know that you were in no danger."

"That isn't all." She sighed. "I wanted to run away. While those poor people were being held in that building, I just wanted to go away and I wanted him to go with me. I asked him to leave. Can you imagine it? I actually asked him to run away from what was happening." She laughed bitterly. "Oh wow. I am really the right girl for him, aren't I? I'm sorry," she said suddenly. "I ought not to be bothering you with all this."

"On the contrary. I am pleased our friendship is such that you feel you can speak so to me. It is difficult, being so far from one's home. And no matter how adult one thinks one is, there is always the child inside needing to talk to *abba*, eh?"

"*Abba*? My father? I don't think I've ever had a talk with him in my life. He's always been too busy running the world to say much more than, 'Need anything, Princess?' Besides,

Sloanes don't talk about their feelings. I'm not sure we're supposed to have any."

"Meri. . . ."

"Do you know what I used to do when I was in school? I used to run away. I was about fourteen or fifteen. I used to take the train into Center City, Philadelphia, and just wander around, deliberately trying to get myself lost in those narrow little side streets. Once I walked all the way down to South Philadelphia. That's where all the toughs were supposed to live. I saw people sitting out on their front steps talking to each other. There was a street market with stalls of fruit and vegetables right on the sidewalk. I've never forgotten it. The place smelled of everything you can imagine. I thought it was heaven. Blacks and Italians and Jews and even Chinese . . . and I was walking along with them, accepted by them. I thought I was the bravest thing in the world. I went back to school thinking I had it all over the other girls, that I was really something special. Because I hadn't been afraid to eat an unwashed apple or talk to a boy who was obviously poor and Italian."

"But it was courageous, considering the obviously sheltered existence in which you had been conditioned."

"Courageous? You can say that? I know you're trying to make me feel better, Elie, but don't insult my intelligence. No, I'm not brave. I'm used to a very rich and easy life. When I'm too tired to walk, I take a cab. When I want a new dress, I go out and buy one. I don't mind getting dirty so long as I know there's a hot shower waiting, and I rather like squalor so long as it's picturesque and not happening to me. I like adventure. But not when the bullets are real, not when you can smell real blood. No," she repeated. "I'm not brave like you. Like Leah and Ilana and Arik and everyone else here."

"You are too hard on yourself. Courage is within us all, waiting, like love, for the chance to emerge."

She sighed. "No, it's no good. The whole affair has become so complicated . . . I don't think either of us is sure of his

feelings now. Anyway"—she took a deep breath—"there really isn't any good reason to prolong my stay here much longer. My findings are fairly complete. I ought to be getting back to New York."

"What? You're not going to help me find your Holy Grail? You're giving up the quest?"

"On Elie, you know it's just a dream. You'll never find it."

"Perhaps. But look at the artifacts we have unearthed. The scarab ring. The silver comb. The letters. And most importantly, definite proof of a small Christian community living here at approximately the same time as the destruction of Jerusalem by Titus in 70 C.E.."

"You know, I've always wondered how you came to be involved in this project, why you've concerned yourself with something that, well, really has nothing to do with your people."

"Anything that concerns Israel is of interest to me. And you are quite wrong about this having nothing to do with 'my people.' You will allow me to remind you that your Christ was a Jewish rabbi concerned primarily with bettering the lot and increasing the spiritual awareness of his brethren—the Jews of the Roman province of Judea. He did not seek to create a new Church—if our historical analysis is correct—but to enlarge upon the tradition and knowledge in which he was raised. To tell you the truth, I have always been fascinated by Jesus the Nazarene. Did he live among the Essenes, learning their skills of prophecy and healing? Was he a revolutionary, as so many in the Galilee were, chafing beneath the Roman yoke? One whose philosophy came at last to transcend the concerns of earthly power struggles? Was he simply an angry young man rebelling against his elders, and was all the rest the work of his followers seeking to justify him to themselves? Who can say? But of this I am certain: the man was a Jew. And he loved Israel." He cleared his throat. "Well now! Can't I even tempt

164

you to remain with us until the contents of a particular reed basket discovered at site nine are fully investigated?"

Her eyes opened wide. "I told you there had to be something there! I knew it! When? What did you find?"

"It happened while you were away. Yigael discovered it. He has the longest arms of anyone. The basket was full of wonderful things—a wooden box, sandals, keys, a mirror. But—here is the best part—in the crevice behind the basket— it was wonderfully woven—lay a complete and rolled scroll of parchment with a string tied around it. We could not of course open it there and then, but I managed to peep into its inner parts through its end. I must tell you, I could see no traces of writing. It may very well be a blank scroll, just material prepared for writing. In any event, Professor Biebermann has it now and we should know very soon—"

The expression on his face changed suddenly. She had been about to congratulate him, her own spirits lifted by this news. She turned now, trying to see what it was that had made him so grave, and saw a small figure stumble over the ridge of the excavated mound and fall, tumbling down the sandy, stony hill to a spot some few yards away. They both ran to the boy. It was Raffi, all bloody and badly beaten. A noise caused them to look up, and they saw a group of children poised at the top of the hill, their upraised hands filled with stones which they were about to hurl. Ben Levi advanced menacingly toward them. "Get out of here!" he shouted in Arabic. "Go away!" They hesitated, intimidated by the ferocity of his manner. But he was only one man, at the bottom of the hill; they would have unleashed the stones had not Uri and several of the students suddenly appeared. The urchins ran away, shouting insults as they went.

"Dear Lord," Meri whispered, taking the boy into her arms.

"Is he dead?" one of the students asked fearfully.

Raffi opened an eye. "Of course I'm not dead," he man-

165

aged to say. "But if I had not pretended to be they would have killed me for certain."

Ben Levi let out his breath. "Exaggerating as usual," he muttered angrily. "That's what you get for stealing. What did you take from them?"

The boy struggled to sit up. "Nothing. I took nothing," he said, his fists closing in anger.

Uri took out a handkerchief and wiped the blood from the boy's cheek where he had been cut by a stone. He spoke softly in Hebrew to him. Raffi shrugged and looked down. Uri looked up at Ben Levi: "They have been giving him a hard time for coming here. They don't want him to be friendly with us. I heard one of the big fellows warning him a few days ago. They call him the Jew-lover."

"They wanted me to take things from the camp for them and not to be your friend," Raffi admitted sullenly, wincing as Uri cleaned his face. "They wanted me to set fires. They are only children," he explained. "They do not understand. They do not know this work you do is important."

"Important for the Jews?" Ben Levi asked him.

"For history," the boy exclaimed. "For all the world."

"Is that why you come here?" Meri asked.

Raffi shrugged. "I like it here. I learn things. You are my friends."

"But they told you we cannot be friends," Ben Levi said.

"No one can tell me that," Raffi said angrily. "No one shall tell me who may be my friends and who not. I am a man. I shall tell myself what to do."

"Raffi—" Meri tried to take him in her arms. Her eyes had filled with tears.

The child struggled free of her embrace. "I am a man," he repeated firmly. "No one shall tell me how I must be." He brushed himself off and stood as tall as his years would allow. "I must go," he said, and started up the hill. At the top of it, he turned and grinned that sweet, impish smile that was his alone. "Don't worry," he assured them cheerfully. "I will be back."

166

Eleazar Ben Levi watched the child disappear toward the village. It seemed to Meri that whatever pain Raffi might be feeling in that thin, bruised little body was reflected now in the man's eyes. Ben Levi turned to her. "We speak of bravery, you and I," he said. "There must be many kinds. Perhaps the greatest of all is the courage to love."

7

It was snowing in New York; but the hookers on Eighth Avenue were showing at least five inches of thigh between boot top and skirt bottom as they hopped from one foot to the other, clutching their short fur jackets close to their bodies with more honest passion than they would ever show their customers. A few city blocks and several worlds away, on Fifth Avenue, Madison, and Park, ladies in longer skirts and furs went through the revolving doors of department stores, got in and out of cabs, nodded to each other across small, crowded restaurants as they lunched on quiche and potage du jour. It was almost Christmas. The city was tinseled and garlanded, occupied by troops of Santas ringing their bells on every corner, newspapers and television counting the shopping days until the birthday of the Prince of Peace.

She threw herself into holiday partying with a ferocity previously alien to her. No invitation was refused; nights stretched to dawn; she even, on occasion, came to the office still in evening dress. On this particular morning she was suitably attired in an oatmeal-colored cashmere sweater and

skirt, her fading tan and tawny hair still golden enough to draw attention in Manhattan crowds and the cool marble halls of the museum. But there were dark circles under the blue gray eyes, and she could not suppress a yawn as she entered the private offices of the Metropolitan.

" 'A dillar, a dollar, a ten o'clock scholar,' " Diane Whitney recited tartly. " 'What makes you come so soon?' "

She laughed sheepishly. "Any coffee?"

"You know I detest paper cups lying around. Try the restaurant."

"Too tired to move." She plopped into a chair.

"Um. I don't doubt. You made the columns again. That's the third time this week. 'It's a "Meri" Christmas for Prince Dimitri. The Gorgeous Greek has found his Venus in the Golden Goddess from the Main Line—Meredith Sloane, daughter of Philadelphia banker Jonathan Harris Sloane and presently brightening the halls of our town's Metropolitan. Meri has just returned from a rather extended stay in the Holy Land. Looks like she's acquired a taste for things Mediterranean.' "

"Just *shish kebab.*"

Diane Whitney raised an eyebrow. "And what does Prince Dimitri's taste run to?"

Licking toes, Meri thought. The creep had really made some weird propositions. It had been easy enough to push him out the door, though, he'd been so high. "He likes to dance," she said.

I just bet he does, the other woman thought. She regarded the slender blonde with a certain envy. Meri had always been attractive, but since her trip to Israel, she was quite astonishingly beautiful. Something in her seemed to have warmed, ripened. Thank God that tan was finally fading. It really wasn't fair.

Meri leafed through the papers on her desk. There was another school tour this afternoon.

"Max wants to see you. I almost forgot."

170

"Thanks. Can I go in, or has he got someone with him?"

"He said soon as you arrived."

Maxwell Radnor's office was a small museum unto itself. Relics of the ancient past dotted his desk like so many ashtrays and pen holders. Among the many photographs on the wall, Meri now recognized one of Eleazar Ben Levi, his arm around the white-haired curator, both men smiling and squinting in the Negev sun. Radnor smiled at the girl now as she came in. A near-fatal heart attack had not dimmed the diminutive man's energy and zest for life. Even as he sat behind the desk he was like a small tornado momentarily in repose.

"Ah, here she is! Meri! Come in, come in! I want you to meet Donald Lawrence, a member of our team over at the UN."

An attractive man in his thirties came forward now, his hand extended. His eyes expressed some small shock which quickly changed to unveiled admiration. He cleared his throat. "Well. Miss Sloane. I've been looking forward to meeting you."

"Then why do you look so surprised?" she asked, smiling.

He laughed. "Frankly, I was expecting someone—ah—well, not as—" He shook his head ruefully. "Some diplomat. You've got me tongue-tied."

"Ha!" Radnor chortled. "Since she got back from Israel she comes at you like a *sabra*. Right to the point. No shilly-shallying."

"What I mean to say," Donald Lawrence went on, "is that we're all very impressed with your report on the Tel Shalazar project. In fact, we're incorporating it into our platform regarding the—in our view—unwarranted UNESCO decision."

"You mean you're not going to support the condemnation?"

"That's right, Miss Sloane. Furthermore, you may be interested to know that a rather influential group of people—writers, artists, actors, politicians—are instigating a boycott of

171

UNESCO activities because of the committee's obvious bias. Your report has made waves."

"That's wonderful." She beamed. "Oh Max, isn't it wonderful?"

"Yes, it is. That's why I wanted you to hear it for yourself."

"Does Elie know?"

"I've cabled."

"Thank you, Mr. Lawrence. You have really brightened my day."

"Not so much as you have mine, Miss Sloane. How about lunch? Dinner?"

"Not today, I'm afraid. Call me."

"I will. I certainly will do that." After she'd gone, he turned to Radnor enthusiastically. "She's sensational! How the hell do you manage to keep her here in this dusty, musty tomb?"

"Careful, Lawrence, or you'll lose points with me. This tomb, as you call it, is filled with more life than you'll ever see in that monument to absurdity in which you so fruitlessly endeavor."

"Well," the diplomat said, quickly changing the subject, "I imagine your Israeli colleague will be overjoyed to hear the news."

"Eleazar Ben Levi?" Maxwell Radnor grinned. "He couldn't care less."

"We all wish to thank you for your endeavor in our behalf," the archaeologist wrote to her. "Even Terza. It is perhaps a small victory—because, as I once told you, I am convinced that those who wish to see no good in us will continue to do so regardless of the facts. But small victories have a way of growing, and it gives us heart to know that we have friends in quarters where we had not thought to look. Demosthenes has also been served well.

"The scroll hidden behind the reed basket was, as I had feared, blank. We subjected it to infrared and ultraviolet pro-

172

cesses to see if there were some invisible traces of script, but all our efforts were for nothing. It must have been writing material, as I feared. We have, however, come upon a rich cache of scrolls—about twenty of them!—tightly rolled like cigars. Need I tell you who made this discovery? Raffi! We were most fortunate to come upon them when we did, for the rains are quite heavy now and all work at the Tel is suspended for the winter. The scrolls in question are in the hands of Professor Biebermann, who is proceeding most cautiously. As soon as I have more on this I will write. Perhaps you will see them for yourself in the spring? Eretz is very beautiful when the wild almond blooms. . . ."

Roger finally called. She had been dreading seeing him; and he was, in fact, quite cool when he rang her at last. She didn't blame him. She'd never answered his letters (there were only two) and had not even bothered to contact him when she returned to New York. They had lunch at the Plaza, where, conveniently, they both had committee meetings to attend. He seemed truly hurt. It was the first time anyone had ever dumped him, even temporarily.

"Sorry about not writing," she apologized. "The days just flew by. Time has a way of disappearing out there."

"Swept up in the desert wind, I suppose. Carried away by a flowing caftan and a white stallion."

She was amused. "What happened to *Fiddler*? That sounds more like *Lawrence of Arabia*."

"Well, I didn't think you'd get involved with some little Jew. It's not our style, is it, darling?"

"As a matter of fact," she replied coldly, "I was seeing an Israeli."

"An Isreali. Oh yes. Planting oranges in the desert and wiping out hordes of screaming Arabs. *Exodus*."

"You know, Roger, it's kind of scary to think America is being served by congressmen whose only frame of reference is the cinema."

"I choose my examples to fit the intelligence of my constituents."

"Then I suggest you reevaluate your constituency, because if people ever find out what you really think, you won't be able to get an endorsement for dogcatcher."

"You might have returned my call," he said sullenly. "Do you know what a mess I could be in if some reporter got record of that call? I go out on a limb, I put my whole future on the line because I'm concerned about you—did you know about the bomb in Jerusalem? Do you know what went through my mind? And you don't even have the decency to return my call or even write. I had to go to the most godawful boring party with Kay just so I could find out from that Whitney bitch that you were still alive. You think that wasn't sticky? I mean, I have taken risks, Meri. Risks."

"How is Kay?" she asked calmly.

"Well, she's not sick anymore, thank God. Just fat. Blooming like a goddamned lily. Now don't look at me like that. I swear all I have to do is breathe on her and she's pregnant. I married a goddamned rabbit. Not a bunny, mind you. A rabbit. Christ! We're not even Catholic. . . ."

"Poor Roger." She patted his hand.

"Look, I've got a meeting. Why don't we talk things over tonight at your place? Around ten? I'm willing to forgive and forget."

"That's very generous of you."

"Stop putting me on. I know I have no right to expect anything from you." He stared at her a moment. "Is it a game? To make me—if it's marriage you want, you know how I feel about you. It would take time but—"

"No . . . no. . . ."

He seemed to take a deep breath. "All right then. You had a holiday fling. Okay. We're two grown-ups in a grown-up world. Let's forget it."

What does he want with me, she wondered. I'm nothing with him, nothing like what I can be, what I have been with

174

. . . someone else. Why is he so willing to settle for so little? Or doesn't he know there's more?

"Why don't we just forget everything else," he was saying, ".and just go back to making each other happy?"

She stared at him.

His jaw tightened. "Or don't I measure up to your exotic Middle East playmates? I know a few tricks myself, you know. It's only out of decency I haven't—"

She stood up. "You don't know what decency is," she said. "You married Kay for her money, and the only reason you would consider divorcing her is because I'm even richer and my father more powerful than hers. She can get you into the House but I can get you the Senate. Isn't that it? I always found your ruthlessness attractive—I don't know why—but now I see it's just a big cover for what a baby you are. A spoiled baby. No, don't bother going into a recital of my character. I know what I am. But that doesn't mean I have to like you. Or sleep with you."

"Oh come on, Meri. Sit down. Please. Christ, what's come over you? You're all out of control. Stop being so damned—"

"Emotional?"

He stood up now, gesturing to the waiter, refusing to answer.

Outside, she caught her breath in the cold wind. Across the street, at the park entrance, a man was haggling with the driver of a hansom cab, his wife watching disgustedly. Meri remembered the bargaining that went on in the *shuk*, debates sweetened by cups of minted tea and thick, dark, cardamom-flavored coffee. Roger was putting his gloves on. She put her hand on his arm. "I just don't want to cheat you," she said. He frowned, said nothing, guiding her to the car. "Thanks, I feel like walking." Her eyes were the color of the December sky. She kissed him lightly. "Happy holiday, Roger. Give my best to Kay." Waving, she moved off into the crowd.

*   *   *

175

So Roger was out of her life. But there were others. The parties did not stop. Intimate dinners for twelve, dancing in private clubs, midnight forays into the city's glittering nooks and crannies. She had never been gayer, more charming, more witty, more beautiful. The Greek prince flew to Sardinia without her; he was replaced by an internationally renowned film producer who promised her anything, including an Oscar. When he left for the West Coast, a cosmetics magnate stepped in. The carousel whirled around and around, all the other riders astonished because she alone of them simply laughed at the brass ring. Had Dimitri and the producer and the magnate and several others had a drink or two together they might all have agreed that the Golden Goddess was gilded marble. The one item that didn't make the columns was the fact that Meredith Sloane slept alone.

It was just no good. She wanted to have an affair, to be swept beyond thought, but the first kiss served only to chill her, to turn her stony and skittish. She needed desperately to have a man's arms around her, yet everything in her rebelled against having these men touch her. And so she flirted and danced and bought extravagant Christmas presents for everyone she knew and had her apartment repainted and decorated. And in the few hours she grudgingly allowed for sleep, she dreamed about the desert, and saw herself wandering down unknown yet familiar streets.

She had seen Arik once more before she left Israel. He had come to the flat in Jerusalem to pick up his things and to say good-bye, of course. He had been very polite, very formal. And suddenly he had taken his hand and slapped it hard against the wall. "You are angry with me," she'd said, frightened and yet relieved.

"With you. With me. With the whole damn situation." And he had grabbed her, twisting his hand in her hair. "Forget me," he said. "Forget us. Do it!" he said fiercely. "If you can!"

And he had branded her with that kiss, marked her as

surely as if he had cut his name into her flesh, so that she tossed and turned alone in her bed high above the city streets and yet could not find solace with another.

The doorman sounded anxious. "There's a man here to see you, Miss Sloane. Big guy. With a beard. Talks kind of funny. What was that name again, buddy?"

She could hear the expletives in Arabic over the intercom. "It's all right, Eddie. Let him up. He's an artist," she added, as though that explained everything.

Yossi looked very much as he had the first time she'd seen him. There was the stocking cap perched atop the thick black hair streaked with gray, the quilted, army-issue winter jacket, the same black beard and mustache masking most of his face, split now by a huge grin. The combat boots, however, had been replaced by fine Italian leather. He had with him a large canvas wrapped in brown paper and tied with a jumble of knotted string. "For you," he said. It was the painting that had hung over the bed in the Jerusalem flat. She stared at the oil, overwhelmed by the gift. "But Sara—" she started to say.

"Sara will have me the rest of her life, poor thing. I will make a hundred others for her. Well, maybe not. Never mind. You shall have this one. It is a small thing to repay you for all you have done. The exhibit. The visa. . . ."

"Are you all set up?"

"I am to stay with Paul." That was Paul Simmons of the prestigious Simmons-Butler Gallery. "What a place! He has more *tsatskas* lying around than my Tanta Sasha kept in her china cupboard. And she was a collector, believe me. Sheets on the bed every color of the rainbow. Animals and flowers all over the pillowslips—what magnificent dreams I shall have!"

She laughed. It was good to see him again.

"I think he is a homosexual, yes? Never mind. He will get used to me."

"I'm sure you can defend yourself." She looked up at him.

177

"But I doubt the necessity." The elegant gallery owner had his pick of companions.

"Well, I have a cousin in the Bronx I can always move in with. But I want to find a place of my own. With good light. That is most important. The light is everything."

She remembered the brilliant sun of Jerusalem. Every hour of the day the sky was a different color. And then there was that moment before night when the city turned to gold. . . . "Will Sara be coming to the opening? I've been looking forward to meeting her."

"She is working like crazy in California. She wants me to come out there. We shall see. I like this dirty city of yours. It has much heart. It is—what is that word I like?—funky."

"Yossi, you are truly amazing."

"Give me time. I shall show you how amazing I can be. Or is it that I am still outranked?"

"Outranked?"

"The *Gan-Aluf*. Arik Blue-Eyes. Surely he is coming to America. Or do you go back to him?"

"Neither."

"Good. Then I have a chance."

"No, you don't," she said, laughing. "You are my friend and I love you dearly but—well, no. No."

"Why? You don't like the beard?"

She knew he was teasing her. "What about Sara?"

"You always worry about Sara. What do you care about her? You don't even know her."

"Never mind," she said, lifting her chin like an Israeli. "I've slept in her bed and lived in her flat." The woman was there in every hanging plant and handsewn curtain. "I think I like her as much as I do you."

He smiled. "She is a good girl, my Sara. A good woman. If only she were an American."

"Why?"

"I could marry her and get my citizenship papers in three years instead of five."

*   *   *

"I will always be Israeli," Yossi told her, his large bulk stretched out on the cream-colored sofa. "Nothing changes that. But I am an artist. I am hungry for the world and all its delights. I cannot deny my nature. 'If I am not for myself then who shall be?' " he recited. "Of course if I am needed, if—God forbid—there must be another war, then I shall go back. It would be unthinkable to do anything else. But meanwhile—" he looked around the apartment approvingly—"this is very pleasant."

"I wish someone else shared your view."

"The *Gan-Aluf*? He is a different breed. We are both Israeli, but he is a different sort of fellow. For him there is only Israel." He gave her a sharp glance. "Perhaps you would not like him in America."

"Why do you say that?"

He shrugged. "He would not be what he is. He would be something else. You as well."

"Do I seem different to you now from what I was in Israel?"

He thought about it. "I don't know. You are more elegant, of course. All smooth and sleek like a cat. In Jerusalem, you were not so refined. The cat was more like a young lioness. I liked that."

She laughed. She liked that too.

"Ah, there is the look I remember. You are not very happy here, are you? No, I think you were more happy in *Eretz*."

"How can you say that? I was positively miserable that weekend in Jerusalem. Don't you remember?"

"Miserable, yes. But happy."

"Happy living in a walk-up apartment with no heat, no telephone, and limited quantities of hot water? Happy worrying about bombs going off on the bus or in the SuperSol? Or maybe getting killed by one of your own crazy drivers? Not knowing half the time what any of you were talking about?"

179

"You were happy," he insisted mildly. "For the first time in your life you were free."

"It was a very interesting and exciting experience," she said carefully. "A nice place to visit, as the saying goes, but that's all. I couldn't live there. I . . . I just don't belong there."

He spread his hands as if to say who could tell where home was for anyone.

She got up, restless now, and went over to the painting he had given her. "I can't imagine Sara letting you give this up."

"I shall tell you a secret. It was not done with Sara in mind. I painted it before I ever knew her." He studied it critically. "It is not my best work. The composition leans too much to one side. Still it has a certain feeling. . . . I was in love with a dancer with the Batsheva company. What a beauty! She married a dentist she met while on tour in the States." He turned his attention back to her. "You are not happy," he repeated. "Your eyes have a certain look. . . . All the women in this city have such eyes. Why is that? It is very interesting. . . . Linda Meyers—you remember Linda? She also had that look when I first met her."

"Linda. How is she?" Meri asked eagerly. "I've been meaning to write. Is she seeing anyone?"

"You see how like a woman you are?" he teased. "First off you must know if she is in love—or more important, if there is someone who is in love with her."

"Well. . . ." She laughed sheepishly. "I like Linda. I'd like to know if she is happy."

"You see? Of course she is happy. She has her work, she has her self." He grinned. "Be at ease, my liberated American female friend. Linda has been swept up in the arms of an American neurosurgeon at Hadassah Hospital. He is a bit older than she—a widower, my cousin who is an intern there, informs me—but quite vigorous and not without charm." He laughed happily. "I can imagine what joy there will be in Ohio when Linda's mother learns her daughter is seeing a Jewish doctor. Of such things are happy endings made, yes?"

180

She smiled wryly. "I wouldn't know."

He stared at her a moment. "Go back to him," he said suddenly, softly. "Go back to Israel."

The voice on the telephone sounded vaguely familiar. "I've been trying to get you for days. You're one busy lady. There's a party tonight for the Ambassador of Somalia. I know it's short notice, but you didn't return any of my calls."

The message on her desk this afternoon. Donald Lawrence. The man from the United Nations. Of course. She had forgotten his name. "I just walked through the door. Can you give me an hour?"

"I think we can manage that. Eight o'clock?"

"Fine."

"Good. See you then."

He was easy to be with, a comfortable sort of man with the graceful assurance that came of good schools, old family, and a friendly acquaintance with the powerful. The law degree at Harvard had been a matter of course; he had no desire to join the family firm, preferring the world arena of diplomacy.

"Guess I got hooked during my Peace Corps days," he told her.

"Where did you serve?"

He laughed. "I'm embarrassed to tell you. Barbados. Paradise on earth."

"I know what you mean. My grandmother has a house there. We always used to fly down after Christmas and stay until the New Year. I think my parents are planning on going again this season."

"How about joining them? I can get a few days off. Let me show you the real island."

"Harry's Bar?"

"What a naughty girl you were, Miss Sloane. Or may I amend that to present tense?"

"Well, I never actually went there myself—"

"How about the Pepsi Bel Aire?"

"You've got me there."

"Ah ha! To all appearances, a simple native bar. But at two in the morning when the moon is full and the ships come in. . . ." He grinned. "Curious?"

"A little. But I think I can guess."

"Anyway, it's a beautiful island. Nice place to spend a couple of years. Or a Christmas holiday. In fact, the idea sounds better and better to me."

The party was the usual mix of diplomatic personnel and Manhattan upper crust. Donald Lawrence watched approvingly as Meri gracefully accepted the attention of his colleagues. He was particularly amused by Quincy Peterson's obvious admiration. Peterson had not been pleased with their stand on the UNESCO condemnation; he was concerned about Third World reaction, and had griped about "this dumb-ass report by some dumb-ass broad who just wants to go on digging up broken pieces of pottery." Donald Lawrence wondered what Peterson would say if he knew the beautiful young woman to whom he was telling his stale old jokes was in fact the "dumb-ass broad" who had dug up, in addition to pottery shards, a rather nice kettle of fish. He smiled. "I don't know if I mentioned it, Quincy, old boy, but Miss Sloane is the author of that report from the Metropolitan. You know—the one concerning the Israeli archaeological expedition in occupied Jordan."

It took a moment for this to sink in. Peterson's eyes widened. "Well," he said finally. "Well."

Meri turned to her escort. " 'Occupied Jordan?' " She raised an eyebrow.

He spread his hands apologetically. "Section twelve, paragraph four, of Resolution—"

"Never mind. I understand. I was so happy, Mr. Peterson, to hear that the United States delegation had decided the condemnation had no merit. Because it really wasn't true, you know. I mean, about disturbing an Islamic holy area. For one

182

thing, most of the people of Rannon are Christian Arabs."

He cleared his throat. "Really? I wasn't aware of that."

"Oh yes. When I first began to interview the villagers they were amazed that I wanted to know how they felt about the whole thing. But when I pressed them, and they finally understood that I was not a representative of the Israeli government, they sort of shrugged it off. It didn't seem to have much bearing on their lives one way or the other. Except, perhaps, they were rather proud to think Rannon had some importance."

"You mean none of the villagers minded the presence of the Israeli expedition?"

"There were one or two who were angry because they thought we were digging for treasure. Gold, diamonds, that kind of treasure. And they felt that if we found anything like that, it ought to belong to them. But as far as I could determine, no one in Rannon had made a complaint to warrant any investigation."

"But a complaint was filed with the organization."

"Yes, I know. I was taken to see a young man in the home of the village mayor. There were a number of elders in the room, but only this one young man spoke to me. He explained the feelings of the people of Rannon regarding the 'forced intrusion by the occupiers' in language very similar to that of the resolution drafted by the gentlemen from Rumania or Tanzania or wherever. He gave me quite a long lecture on 'Zionist colonialism,' 'American imperialism,' and a great many other isms with which I suppose you gentlemen are familiar. His jargon was impeccable. Anyway, after that little interview, nobody in Rannon had much time to talk to me. Everybody became very, very busy."

"Are you implying it was a set-up?"

"Well, Mr. Peterson, I should imagine you are more knowledgeable about such things than I."

"Yes, well, you must understand, my dear, world politics is not based on the simplistic formulas of right and wrong."

"More like supply and demand," Donald Lawrence murmured.

"We must consider the possibility that the emerging nations have a tendency perhaps to overreact. On the other hand, we have a situation in the Middle East of very real grievances. We cannot expect the Palestinian people to suffer gladly an interminable existence in those camps."

"Yes," she said thoughtfully. "I think most intelligent people will agree that it doesn't matter anymore how those people came to be displaced—that, as you know, it was the Arab governments that put them in those wretched camps, that it became more expedient to keep them there rather than integrate them into the mainstream of Jordanian or Egyptian life because the UN would foot the bill for their food, clothing, education—everything—so long as they had the status of refugees."

Quincy Peterson cleared his throat again. "We all know the United Nations has its share of detractors these days. On the other hand—"

"Oh, no." She flashed him a dazzling smile. "I didn't mean to attack the UN We all know how important, how vital it is to the world community." She put her hand on his arm.

Quincy Peterson smiled. He patted her hand.

"What I really started to say was that I think all intelligent people will agree that until the Palestinian Arabs have a real home—a territory, a place where they will feel content and secure—something to which I think all people of the world are entitled, even the Jews, why, they will continue to commit acts of desperation and terror."

Quincy Peterson slipped his arm around her waist.

"So you see," she went on sweetly, "I do understand your concern for the Palestinian Arabs. What I don't understand," she continued, accepting a glass of champagne from the tray proffered, "bearing in mind Maalot, Munich, the attack on Yom Kippur, is why the rest of the world expects Israel to be more forgiving, more tolerant, more generous than any other

184

nation or country has ever shown itself to be in all recorded history. I mean," she said, "how do you feel about giving the IRA observer status? Or perhaps returning Oklahoma to the Cherokee?"

"I don't believe Quincy Peterson knows what hit him," Donald Lawrence said later. "Last I saw, he was asking if anyone got the license number. I told him it didn't matter—it was a case of diplomatic immunity."

She laughed.

"I hope that means I can come up for coffee?"

"How can I refuse? You have diplomatic immunity."

"You're really into this Israel thing, aren't you?" he asked as she brought a tray into the living room.

"I? What do you mean?"

"You're one of them now."

She sat down. "If you only knew how funny that is."

"But you are. I can tell. Israelis have a peculiar way about them. They don't foam at the mouth the way their supporters sometimes do. Oh, they're passionate all right. But I always get the feeling they find it all bitterly humorous. It's as if they know the game is fixed—they'll give it a shot, but they intend to go on their way regardless of the outcome. Anyway, the way you handled Quincy—"

"But I understand his feelings. It's just that I can't help wondering why Arab blood—anyone's blood, for that matter— suddenly becomes so precious to us whenever the Jews are involved. No one gives a damn when thousands of Lebanese are killing each other. Nobody cares when whole populations in Laos get wiped out in civil upheaval. Or when Asians born in Africa are expelled en masse. Or when one African tribe exterminates another. Who even thinks about Biafra now?"

"Well, there are certain ramifications—"

"You mean, if they strike oil in Dimona, the hell with Arafat?"

"Hey wait, I'm on your side, remember?"

"My side?" She stared at him a moment. Was it "her side"? "I was at a kibbutz in the Galilee," she said slowly. "There was a terrorist attack and a woman was killed. She had come from Poland after the war in Europe. She came to Israel because the United Nations said this would be her country if she wished. The world body agreed that the Jews should have a homeland. The world body endorsed Zionism. And now, after all this time, they're saying, 'Sorry, we made a mistake. Everybody pack up and go back to Poland and Germany or wherever. Only be sure and leave the cities you have built, the fields you have planted. Real estate being what it is today, we wouldn't want the new owners to take a loss.' "

"Meri, Meri," he laughed. "You really are far gone on this."

"Oh dear," she said ruefully. "Talk about foaming at the mouth. How did I get started? I certainly didn't mean to. I just can't help thinking. . . ." She stood up. "Coffee's cold. Let me make a fresh pot. Would you like some brandy?"

"Fine. What were you doing in a kibbutz in the Galilee?"

"Oh, just visiting the sister of . . . of a friend."

"Do you write to him?"

"I beg your pardon?"

"Or is it over?"

She sat down again. "I do like you, Donald," she said quietly. "But if you tell me that you have had me investigated, I'm going to throw you out of here."

"Investigated? What on earth for? Hey, look, I was just trying to feel out my competition. I'm sorry, I didn't mean to scare you. I'm not involved in any security clearance business, if that's what you're thinking. Not that you couldn't pass. . . ." he looked at her strangely. "Did they do a number on you overseas?"

"I look like a courier for the Popular Front."

He let out a whistle. "Wow."

"Oh, it wasn't too bad. It was cleared up right away. It just

gives one a funny feeling to think of strangers knowing so much about you."

"Would it give you a funny feeling if this stranger knew more about you? He wouldn't be so much of a stranger then."

"You really are persistent. State Department training?"

"Well, I wouldn't want you to think American men are any less aggressive than Israeli men. . . ."

His eyes were blue gray, almost the same color as her own. "There was someone in Israel," she admitted.

"I thought there probably was." He raised the brandy glass to her. "I didn't think those fellows would let you just walk in and out of their domain without some kind of hot pursuit."

"You mean, The Blonde American?"

"Hell, you're more than that." He looked down into the glass and then back at her. "I pride myself on being an outspoken man. Maybe that's not such a good thing for the diplomatic corps. The thing is this—you've had me floored from the first minute I saw you. You are everything I want."

"You certainly are good for a girl's ego, Mr. Lawrence."

"I mean it."

"Let me ask you something. Have you ever thought what it would be like to fall in love with someone who was not everything you want?"

"Couldn't happen."

"You'd be surprised."

"You mean, 'opposites attract,' and so forth. I've had flings like that. But that's not what I'm talking about."

She was silent.

"You said you liked me. Then do something for me. Call him or write to him or do anything you want and then let me know where I stand. Unfinished business always bothers me."

She smiled. "He once told me that not knowing what you want is as bad as not wanting anything at all."

"I don't know about that. I just want to know if I have a chance."

"You see, Donald," she teased him, "if you were Israeli, you wouldn't ask that. As you said yourself, even if the game were fixed, you'd give it a shot."

"Maybe. I'd rather give you time."

"Thank you," she said quietly.

"Dinner tomorrow?"

"I can't. I promised—"

"Okay. I'll call you in a day or so."

"Fine."

At the door he took her in his arms. "My judgment is impeccable. I'm telling you we're right for one another."

She thought about it when he'd gone. The feel of him had not been unpleasant, had seemed almost familiar. Comfortable. The faint aroma of the subtle men's cologne, the smooth touch of fine wool. He would never smell of the sweat of the desert, of machinery oil and cigarettes, the fabric on his shoulder a rough patch of khaki. His gaze was clear, direct . . . but it was not the gaze of one who has looked across a vast, silent terrain or charted midnight marches by the pattern of the stars. His eyes were a calm blue, a steady gray . . . they were not the color of the sea, the hue of jewels found in King Solomon's mines.

Yossi made her feel like a tourist. He had the city in his pockets, taking out bits and pieces of it like small change to suit his pleasure. The owner of the delicatessen might have been one of his numerous cousins, so solicitous was he: "You got enough pickles, Yossi? Maybe you want a sour tomato? I got some beauties in the barrel." People came in and out of the restaurant; rarely was there one who did not know him, who did not say hello or (self-consciously but with great pleasure) *shalom*. The stocking cap could have been a crown.

"They are crazy here for Israelis," Yossi confided to her. "They think because I fight in '67 and Yom Kippur War I am a hero. *Meshugenas*. Crazy. But it is very nice all the same." He

was very happy. The exhibit had been a great success, he had
found a loft with good light and a seventeen-year-old music
student to keep him company while Sara brought Jerusalem to
the United Jewish Appeal in Chicago. Erin, the music student,
was not in the loft at the moment, but her presence was evident
in the cello and music stand allotted one small corner of the
place. The rest was given over to canvases, paints, easels—
Yossi had spent his newly-earned riches on art supplies with
the abandon of a long-deprived child given free rein in a toy or
candy store. But years of habit were hard to break; he was still
easiest with pen and ink, materials he could always count on
finding. In the bunkers of the Sinai he had spent the long
waiting hours drawing on typewriter paper with a ballpoint pen
"borrowed" from the captain.

There were a few of Sara's paintings in the loft. Meri
found herself drawn to them as she never had been before.
Now, so far from Israel, she understood their appeal. There it
was, Jerusalem, caught like a goldfish in a crystal bowl. It all
came back to her—the terraced hills of stone, the olive trees,
the white skyscrapers surrounding the mountain city like a
modern citadel, the old, old streets where donkeys led by men
in desert robes ambled in the dust of blue-jeaned riders on
their motorbikes. She could see the moonlike craters of the
Negev, the sun breaking open the sky as though no day had
ever dawned before this one. She thought of the nights, sweet
in that sudden, heavy darkness, the wind spiced with cypress
and sandalwood and lemon. . . .

And suddenly she seemed to understand it all, the pull
this tiny piece of land exerted on so many different peoples.
She was neither Jew nor Arab. She had grown up on sandy
stretches of Middle Atlantic beaches, in the greenery of Penn's
Woods, with the stone and brick and steel of America's great
cities. There was nothing in all her frame of reference to lead
her to this sudden shock of melancholy, this wishing to be in a
country that was not hers. Yet there it was.

So, in the end, it was neither politics nor religion but an

189

inexplicable pull, a longing for a place where each day was lived to the fullest degree, where love, grasped within the frailty of time, was treasured for the moment and was talisman to the future.

She looked at Sara's paintings, and she saw Eleazar Ben Levi on the balcony of the King David Hotel, watching the city of his birth work its magic. She saw Arik, standing on the hilltop of Megiddo, looking out over the Valley of Jezreel where the battle of Armageddon would take place. She saw herself, standing on the balcony of an impossible palace built by a mad king for the princess he loved and later killed, looking out upon the steely surface of the Dead Sea and the lavender mountains of Moab, feeling as if her very soul had flown up and out into that clear bright sky.

Yossi saw her hunger. "Now you know the meaning of *Gola*," he said softly. "Now you understand what the exile was for us."

"I am not in exile," she replied coldly. "This is my home. I am an American."

"Bavakasha," he said amiably. "As you wish."

"People ought to stay where they . . . fit in. With their own set. It's just . . . easier . . . that's all."

"A man and a woman in love make their own place in the world."

"You don't understand, Yossi. I don't belong there. I'm . . . extraneous. I don't fit in."

"Nonsense. Go to him. He needs you as much as you need him."

"He doesn't need anyone. He has *Eretz*. He has Israel. You said it yourself. For him there is only Israel."

He did not reply to this. Instead he took up a sketch pad and a charcoal pencil. "Did you know that the *Gan-Aluf* had a brother?"

"Dani? He was killed in the Yom Kippur War."

"Yes, he was killed." He began outlining her figure. "Is that all you know of it?"

190

"He was the youngest in the family. Arik. Ilana. And Dani."

"He was twenty when the war came upon us. Very promising. He was to go for officer training. I know all this because I have a cousin on the same kibbutz as Arik's sister," he explained.

"Yes, I know." She smiled. "Israel is a small country."

"Exactly. Well, Dani was in the army down in the Sinai. He was a tank commander.

"The Egyptians came across one morning. There was no warning. They hit us with hundreds of tanks and thousands of men. They had missiles, cannon. . . . It was Yom Kippur, the Day of Atonement—the holiest day of the year. We had only a few reserves.

"Dani Vashinsky was in the very worst of it. One minute they heard him on the radio, trying to protect a pass with his tank. Then his radio went dead. He was reported missing.

"Later, after the fighting, when the mountain pass the young men had bought with so much blood was sold by the old men for a few pieces of paper, Ariel Vashinsky walked through the battlefields in the Sinai looking for his brother. The army had been unable to find Dani's tank.

"One month searching alone in the desert. Ilana—his sister—told my cousin of it. One month looking for Dani."

"Did he find him?" Her voice was hardly more than a whisper.

Yossi nodded. "Yes, he found him. Dead, of course. I do not know if the pieces are buried on the kibbutz or in the military cemetery. It was a direct hit, you see. There was very little left."

The fireplace in the study at Woodside was garlanded with holly and pine. The great house was ablaze with light, its windows shining in the night like the yellow eyes of a cat. Dozens of parked cars lined the long driveway and cul-de-sac. Christmas was always the occasion for open house, the stream

191

of friends and guests beginning after church service and continuing throughout the day and evening. Tomorrow the estate would be silent, the Sloanes flying off to winter in a warmer climate.

Meredith Sloane stood before the fire in the paneled room with the great mahogany desk and walls of moroccan-bound books. She looked at the leather sofa, the sea paintings, the Oriental rug. She had never really looked at the rug before; now she wondered at the beauty underfoot and unnoticed for so much of her life. She looked up at the volumes of Dickens and Thackeray and Scott. She could not recall ever opening any of the books that lined these shelves. When she needed one for school, she bought a paperback edition in the college bookstore; it did not occur to her then to touch these, here in her own home. Now she wondered why.

She loved the great willow that brushed against the window in this room. The grounds of Woodside were dominated by beautiful trees. In the spring, when it rained, the trunks turned black as coal, and the leaves and grass were a rich wet green, a blinding green, a green that could be found nowhere else in the world. April and autumn were dazzling in this part of Pennsylvania. There were no wild almond or olive trees, but there was dogwood, white and pink, and weeping cherry, and willows and white birch. . . .

She would miss the seasons.

Jonathan Sloane came into the room, saw his daughter standing there, staring into the fire, and hesitated. "Princess? Everything all right?"

"What? Oh. Fine. Everything's . . . fine."

There was something in her voice. He came closer. He was not given to outbursts of emotion, lavish with praise, or demonstratively affectionate. He had never had what he would call a "cuddly" relationship with his daughter. Yet he was proud of her and loved her perhaps more than any other living creature. Early on, he had recognized the restlessness in her, the seeking nature that had led Sloanes across oceans and

continents in clipper ships and wagon trains, that had, for him, found expression within the empires of business and finance. If she had been male, he would have trained her to be his heir in a very practical way. Maybe, he thought suddenly, those women's libbers had something after all. Meri was as bright as any of those young puppies in the office. He wondered if this museum business was enough for her. There had been something about her since that Mideast junket. All sorts of items in the society pages. Tish had been delighted. He had been less pleased. But he knew there were no real shenanigans. Not with Meri. She was his daughter. And she was a thoroughbred.

"You always loved a fire," he said. "Remember Nana's wire corn popper? You had us eating tons of that stuff one year. You would stare into the flames for hours. Loved bonfires on the beach too."

All my life looking to get warm, she thought. Aloud she said, "That was because of the toasted marshmallows. You forgot that."

"Guess I did at that. Still like them?"

"Sure." She smiled. "Whatever happened to that old corn popper anyway?"

"Around somewhere, I imagine. If your mother didn't give it away. Everything goes to the hospital thrift shop. I don't dare lay anything down anymore. Turn around and it's gone. Hospital thrift shop."

"Is that this month's charity?"

"I must say I prefer the ones that just want money. Taking a man's golf jacket just because it's a few years old. Why, it was just beginning to feel right."

"Dad." She turned to face him. "I'm going back to Israel."

"Oh? More work for the museum?"

"No. I'm going on my own."

"I thought you might consider coming with us for the holidays. The Paines asked about you. They—"

"I'm not going on a holiday. I'm going for good. It's what

they call 'making *aliya.*' I'm taking out a temporary resident visa."

He stared at her a moment, then turned and shut the door to the room. Their privacy ensured, he went to the desk, put down the crystal cup of Fish House punch, and poured some Scotch into a glass. "That's a big move, Princess."

"Yes, I know."

"What is it? A man?"

"Yes."

"Someone in the embassy?"

"He's Israeli. A soldier."

"Oh, my God. Meri."

"You don't have to say it. I've said it all myself. A hundred times. And none of it matters."

"An Israeli soldier. Meri." He shook his head. "You've always been so level-headed. You're like me. You're my daughter."

"Maybe that's why. You don't let anything stand in the way when you want something."

"Yes, but—" He studied her. If she had made a big dramatic scene of it he could have understood it better, dealt with it. But her voice was quiet. It was his own voice when he'd made up his mind. He stared thoughtfully at his daughter. There was a new maturity about her. When she had first come back she was all restless gaiety and deliberate charm. She had been more like her mother than he had ever imagined she could be. But this time home she was different. She was his Princess again and yet changed, altered in some subtle and not unattractive way. He recognized now what that change was. She had become her own woman. Still. . . .

"All right," he said. "You met someone. You like him. Fine. Bring him over, let's take a look at him."

She laughed. "You think it's one of Chessie Greene's busboys, don't you? You think once he's here, I'll see it in what you feel is the proper light."

"Afraid to find out?"

194

"No." She was still smiling. "When you meet him, you'll know how wrong you are in what you're thinking."

"Swell guy, huh?"

"Swell guy."

"I still say, bring him over," he continued smoothly. "I'm sure we can find something for him. Maybe not in banking but—"

"You don't understand. He doesn't want to live here."

"Oh come on, they all want to live here. Everybody wants to live here. Why shouldn't they?"

"He's Israeli."

"He's a Jew." He almost choked on the word. "And I've yet to meet one who didn't prefer champagne to beer."

"Who doesn't? Besides, he doesn't drink."

"Very funny, daughter. All right, let's get down to the bottom line. You go overseas on a business trip, meet someone, and now you think you're in love with him. Happens all the time when you girls are far from home."

"I was fifteen when I made my first tour of Europe." she reminded him.

"Well, you had more sense then, that's all I have to say." But he had indeed a great deal more to say. "Now look, I know these types—Jews, Italians, Greeks. They have a certain appeal, I suppose, for some women. But I never thought my own daughter—"

"I told you, I'm not Chessie Greene. You've never cared about my private life before," she said suddenly. "What I did, who I was with. Why the sudden concern? Because he's Jewish?"

"It's because I don't know him, dammit! Who he is, what he wants—"

"He doesn't want anything."

"Nobody doesn't want anything."

"You don't understand," she said calmly. "He doesn't need any of this."

"What has he got to offer? A girl like you—"

195

"Nothing. A hard life. A hundred problems for us to face. And if it makes you feel any better, I don't even know if he'll have me."

That stopped him.

"It was sort of over when I left," she went on, explaining. "Not in so many words, but. . . ." She took a deep breath. "I've written him a letter. I mailed it before I came down here. If he still wants me, that's it. I'm going to him."

"And if he doesn't want you?"

"I think I'll go anyway," she said in that new quiet voice. "If I have to track him across that whole damned desert."

He had to smile. She was his daughter, all right. "He must be some guy."

"He's everything I want."

He was not sure what that meant. "Have you told your mother?"

"I haven't spoken of it to anyone. I'd sort of like to wait. Until I hear from him."

"I thought you were going anyway."

"I am. I'd just like to hear from him first."

His daughter, all right. "Meri . . . I'm not going to insult you by asking if you've given this a great deal of thought because I'm sure you have. But I must remind you of the difficulties you will face. Living in a foreign country is not the same thing as going there on a visit. Especially a Levantine country. God," he muttered, "the water alone would be enough to kill you."

"I think my fine WASP sensibilities can withstand the trauma."

"Your fine WASP sensibilities, as you put it, are more than a match for anything this world has to offer. Your great-great-aunt took six kids out to California by wagon train to join your uncle who'd gone on ahead to mine for gold. There's been a Sloane fighting in every war this country—hell, you know your background." It's what makes you stand up now, he

196

thought. "All I'm trying to say," he went on more gently, "is that you may find yourself out of place . . . alone. . . ."

"I know. But I feel that way now. Ever since I got back. The parties, the people—it all seems so meaningless, so false to me. Oh, I'm not saying there aren't good people and worthwhile things around. It's just that I can't seem to relate to anything but . . . what I found over there. I'm going to feel out of place and alone anywhere I am unless I know that he's somewhere near, knowing that I love him, knowing that we're there for each other."

"That's all very nice, I'm sure. Very romantic. But don't you think your sentiments are a little out of place? Don't you think the setting is a little wrong for hearts and flowers? I mean, we're talking about my daughter going off to live in a country that has existed in a virtual state of war for nearly thirty years. You talk of love. I think of terrorist attacks, bombs going off, hijackings. What the hell kind of a place is that for love?"

"You're wrong. You're very wrong. This morning, when we were sitting in church, I suddenly wondered why I have never found God in any of His houses. I always accepted being a Christian because, well, that's what I was. But I never had any real concept of Christ, any real feeling for Jesus, until I went to Israel, until I saw the towns and villages where He had walked and taught, the sky above Jerusalem, the desert night. And sitting in church this morning, I suddenly realized that the only thing that made any sense to me was His message. Love. Even in the midst of violence. Especially in the midst of violence."

Jonathan Harris Sloane looked at his daughter. He had been right. She was a thoroughbred. "You are very brave, Meredith," he said softly.

"No, I'm not brave. But I'm not afraid anymore. Arik once told me that people in battle very seldom have the ideology or motivation to make them courageous. What is important, he

197

said, the thing that makes the difference, is their loyalty to their friends, their love for their comrades. I understand now what he was trying to tell me. Love is the only true measure of courage."

The day after Christmas, the Sloanes flew off for a West Indies vacation. Their daughter, Meredith, according to Joseph Dexter's column in the Philadelphia *Evening Bulletin*, had returned to her Manhattan apartment to brighten the Gotham scene as well as the halls of the Metropolitan. There was no announcement of the Main Line beauty's forthcoming emigration to the Middle East. Meri had promised her father she would not make any move until she heard from Arik. At least, Jonathan Sloane thought as he looked out the jet's window at the blue green waters below, at least he had bought some time. Even as he handed his luggage over to the native customs official, his own men were checking into the identity of one Ariel Vashinsky, Lieutenant Colonel in the Israeli Defense Forces.

"Your mother," he had said with a sigh to his daughter, "is going to have a fit."

"Who cares?" the girl had replied mildly and without malice. "It's my life."

So she sat in the bedroom of her East Side apartment now, brushing her hair, preparing to go out for the evening. It was New Year's Eve, more than a week since she had sent the letter. It took approximately five days for a letter to reach Israel, presuming everything went as it should. She had addressed it to the kibbutz as he had told her to do should she want to contact him. Approximately five days there, five days back. . . . Still, she had hoped for some bit of providential kindness, some small miracle or omen with which to start the new year. Even a letter from Elie or Linda. . . .

She opened her jewel box, looking for something to wear with her gown. It was a simple white crepe, cut along the classic lines she favored. Perhaps a gold pin. . . .

Her fingers touched a silver chain caught in the jumble of beads and brooches. Untangled, the chain held a pendant of what appeared to be silver filigree set with a large blue green stone. She had wanted an omen. . . .

Okay, she thought, half-laughing at herself, half-filled with the same anxiety that had led her long ago to clap for Tinkerbell. Okay. Work a little magic for me. Come on, she thought. I eat my carrots. I say please and thank you and help little old ladies up the museum steps. Just a little magic. Straight from King Solomon's mines. . . .

The phone rang.

Startled, she jumped, the necklace slipping from her hand. Laughing at herself, she went to answer it. It was probably Max Radnor. He was taking her to the Bennetts' dinner party tonight. Donald Lawrence was in Washington. Maybe it was Donald. She rather hoped not. After all, there was no point. . . .

"Yes? Hello?"

"Shalom."

Everything went still in her, breath suspended, heart bursting.

"Hello? Meri? Are you there? Hello? Is this 371-84——"

"Yes, yes," she breathed. "It's me. I'm here. I . . . I'm here."

His voice relaxed. "I thought maybe I had the wrong number. Or you'd moved."

"No," she repeated. "I'm here."

"Good."

Silence.

"How are you?" he asked politely.

"I'm fine." She laughed. "I'm fine."

He laughed too.

It all came in a rush. "Did you get my letter? I wrote to you—I sent it to the kibbutz. I would have called but I didn't know where. Did you get the letter?"

"No. I've been on maneuvers. You wrote?"

"I'm coming back. I'm coming back if you want me. It's all in the letter—"

"Never mind. It doesn't matter. I love you. Yes, I want you. I want you to come back."

"Oh, Arik." She started to cry. "I love you."

"Sshh. Sshh. Don't cry. Meri, don't cry."

"I can't help it, I'm so happy."

He was happy too. She could hear it in his voice. "Miss me?" he asked.

"Yes."

"Want to see me?"

"Yes. Yes."

"Tonight?"

She caught her breath. "You rotten, no-good—"

"Hey! I thought you loved me."

"Where are you?"

"Princeton. New Jersey. The army gave me leave to come over and see my folks. My mother's been ill."

"Oh. I didn't know. I'm sorry."

"She's okay. Listen, I have the train schedule here. There's an 11:10 train I can catch. That will get me in to Penn Station at 12:14. I'll grab a cab—"

"You'll never get one. It's New Year's Eve."

"You're kidding. Damn, I forgot. The Gregorian year. Sure. That's what all the noise is about."

"Wait at the station. I'll pick you up there. At the ticket counter."

"Good. Did you get the time?"

"12:14. I'll be there."

"Good. *L'hitrahot.*"

"*L'hitrahot.*" How easy the words came back to her. "I love you."

"*Anni ohev otah gam ken.*" His voice was like fingers on her skin. "I love you too."

She had no sooner put the receiver back on the hook when the intercom buzzed. Eddie, the doorman, was letting her

200

know that Maxwell Radnor was on his way up to the apartment.

"You look radiant. Positively radiant," the curator beamed. "Gad, I shall have the most beautiful woman in New York on my arm tonight!"

"Max." She kissed him. "Please don't be upset. I can't go with you."

"What is it? What's happened?"

"Someone I met in Israel. He—he's here in the States. It's very important to me or I wouldn't—please understand."

"Someone from Israel?" His eyes lit up. "The young officer! He's come to claim you!"

"How did you know—"

"Elie mentioned it in one of his letters. He thought you might need a friendly shoulder."

She laughed. "Jewish first aid."

"When do you expect him? This is all very exciting. He can come along with us to dinner. I want to meet him."

"He's coming by train from Princeton. About midnight. I'm to meet him at the station."

"That's hours away. I think we'll just go on to the Bennetts as planned and when it's time for you to meet your young man, we'll put you in a car and send you off to him. How does that sound?"

She kissed him again. "You are a dear, sweet, understanding man."

"When you reach my age, that's about all you can be, my darling. Now . . . I want to hear all about it."

Edward Bennett's limousine moved slowly through the heavy lines of traffic. "Don't worry, miss," the chauffeur kept saying. "We'll make it. We'll get you there."

Sure, she thought miserably. Tomorrow. The lobster bisque she'd eaten earlier, the Black Forest cake, were beginning to peak into a tidal wave in her stomach. She had been too excited to do more than nibble at the elegant supper, but whatever had gone down was now threatening to come up. She

had been careful to leave the party with a good allowance of time to get to the station. The crowds and traffic had been as great as she had expected, yet she had not thought it would take so long to make a simple trip from Sutton Place to Thirty-second and Seventh Avenue. The streets were mobbed.

"Some kind of accident ahead," the chauffeur was saying. "Don't worry though. We'll get you there. Only a few more blocks."

I'm going to have a heart attack, she thought. I'm not going to make it. Oh God, why did I eat that cake? I'm going to throw up. She clutched the silver pendant suspended from the chain around her neck. ("What a lovely necklace," Cynthia Bennett had cooed. "Such an interesting design.") "What time is it?" she asked the driver.

"Eleven forty-three. Plenty of time, Miss. Those trains are always late."

She leaned her head back against the seat, taking deep breaths, hoping the earthquake inside her would subside to just a quiet rumble. Suddenly the car stopped. She shot forward, hand on the door. "That accident." He stuck his head out the window. "Jeez, looks like a bad one. I can't get through."

"Oh no, no. . . ."

"Lemme see. Maybe they'll let me turn around. . . ."

"Never mind! Uh. . . ." Her mind was in a whirl. "Look, I'm getting out."

"But—"

"Just meet me at the station." She was out of the car.

"Hey, Miss, wait!"

But she was off, running, pushing through the crowd, a slender figure all in white, her hair tumbling about her face and shoulders like a moonlit cloud.

How she got there she would never know. Later, days later, she would remember only a mass of bodies that she pushed, elbowed, slid through somehow . . . hands reaching for her, a drunken boy trying to kiss her . . . some woman's voice saying sympathetically, "Aw, she must have lost her date. See, I told you, Harry, hang onto me because a person

could get lost." Other voices . . . "Hey sister, where ya goin'
in such a hurry?" "You okay, lady?" "Happy New Year, baby!"

Suddenly, like a dream, the people vanished. She was on
Seventh Avenue, running down the dark, deserted street,
running alone in this concrete canyon of the garment district,
the sound of her slippers tapping on the pavement, echoing
eerily through the night.

She ran and she ran and suddenly she was there. People
were coming out of the station, looking about for cabs. Someone held open the heavy glass door for her. She hesitated at the
top of the stairs. The place was almost deserted. Only a solitary
ticket counter was open. She stepped onto the escalator. And
then she saw him, standing in the center of the silent room, a
tall figure in blue jeans and a suede jacket. He was lighting a
cigarette. There was a small leather satchel on the floor at his
feet, the kind they sold in the Arab marketplace, the leather
from Turkey. She wanted to laugh with love. He looked like a
cowboy. An Israeli cowboy.

He looked up and saw her, gliding down toward him like
some angel or *deus ex machina*. He smiled.

I'm going to love you all my life, she thought.

The escalator deposited her at the bottom of the stairs.
They were close to each other once more.

"Shalom," she whispered.

"Hi," he said.

And then they were in each other's arms, and there were
no more words for a time.

A man and a woman walked out of Pennsylvania Station in
the first hour of the new year. He was a tall man, casually
dressed in dungarees and a turtleneck sweater, and despite the
cold, an unbuttoned brown suede jacket. His hair was very
thick, tawny-colored and curly; and his face was bronzed as if
by some distant, fierce sun. The woman was in a white evening
dress and fur jacket. She was fair, with eyes that in this light
seemed the color of violets and hair that was somewhat lighter
than the man's. Around her throat she wore a silver chain from

203

which hung a silver pendant set with a large stone that, if one looked closely at it, was the very color of the man's eyes.

They had their arms around each other as they walked out into the night. Had there been a passerby he would have seen how much in love they were.

As they walked down the street, a limousine drove up to them and stopped. Without a word they got into the car and drove off into the morning.

8

His hands awakened her from the soft deep sleep into which she had fallen. His knees pushed her legs apart. With a will of its own her body arched to meet his, seemed to tremble and sigh. And then they were both swimming in the sky, lost in the giving and the taking. And she was whole again.

"There's nothing wrong with me at all," she wondered, as they lay content beside each other.

"What are you talking about?"

"I thought there was something wrong with me. I couldn't—while we were apart—I mean there's been no one. No one has. . . ."

His kiss silenced her. "I told you," he said at last. "We belong with each other. That's the way it is." He sat up, looking for a cigarette on the night table. There was none there, so he got out of bed and began rummaging through the clothes scattered on the floor.

She watched him lovingly. He was a beautifully made man. She enjoyed looking at him as much as touching him. In this light, the angle of his body so, he looked like a piece of

Greek sculpture. No wonder it had been difficult sometimes walking through the halls of the museum; there was so much there to remind her of him. She watched him pulling pockets inside out. "You smoke too much," she said mildly.

He looked up and grinned. "Good old Micah. He's never wrong."

"Who's Micah?"

"The 'Old Fox.' Fifteen years ago he was one of my instructors. Now he serves under me." He laughed. "And I still go to him with all my troubles." He found the pack of cigarettes finally and returned to bed with them. "He's not as fast as he used to be, but he has great instincts. A real sense for survival."

She was confused. "Are you talking about the army?"

He laughed again. " 'Go and see her,' Micah said. 'Get it out of your system. Now you think she's different from the others, but soon she'll be telling you you smoke too much or you drive too fast or you never listen when she talks to you.' "

She leaned her head against his shoulder. "I like the way you drive. But you do smoke too much." She lifted her head. "Do you think we'll really become like that? You know, me talking all the time and you never hearing a word I say?"

"How's that?"

She snatched the cigarette from his mouth. "What else did Micah say?"

"You'd put on weight, get headaches, and be angry with me for going off and leaving you with the kids."

"I gather Micah is married?"

"How'd you guess?"

"Woman's intuition." She snuffed out the cigarette. "Terrific guy, that Micah."

"He is. God knows how many times he's saved my skin. He's the best. You know, the British sentenced him to hang. He—"

"Arik." She took a deep breath. "Back there . . . I wasn't very brave. . . . I don't just mean what happened at the kibbutz. I mean all of it."

206

"Meri—"

"It's just that when it hit me, really hit me, all that we'd have to face together, what we each had to face alone, I just, I couldn't deal with it."

"I know. Don't blame yourself. I was just as bad."

"You?"

"I didn't show that I had much faith in us. Why should you?"

"Don't be charitable, Arik. I can't bear that."

"It's not charity. I knew the terrain. You didn't. No, listen to me. There are only two words an Israeli officer has to know: 'Follow me.' I can't expect my men to go willingly into a dangerous situation unless they see me go first. And I can't ask you to be strong if I'm not." He paused. "I'll try to make it as easy as I can for you." He was very serious. "Get an American-style flat with central heating and all that other junk you probably need."

She started to laugh. It had never occurred to her to be concerned about such things.

He laughed too. "And you'd better learn to speak Hebrew, lady. You can get into a hell of a lot of trouble if you don't."

"Umm. And Arabic too. But Hebrew first. I'd like to know what you're saying when you talk in your sleep."

He had bent his head to kiss her, but now he straightened up, surprised. "I talk in my sleep?"

"Sometimes."

"What do I say?"

She bit his ear. "That is what I'd like to know. In the meantime, I am going to take a shower. I'm all sticky."

"Mind if I join you?"

"Do I have a choice?"

He caught her to him. He was smiling, but his voice was serious. "You always have a choice. Always."

She kissed the hand on her shoulder. " 'Whither thou goest. . . .' "

207

"How about that shower?"

"Thy soap shall be my soap, and thy towel—"

"—Shall be smacked across thy bottom." He drew her tight against him. "We'll make it," he whispered into her hair. "It'll be rough. But we'll make it."

They had less than three weeks this time. Eighteen days. And it was as good as it had been before—the living together, the loving, the exploration of every pleasure. Only now they had New York too. Instead of the Carmel Market, there was Orchard Street; and Chinatown, and a funny little bar he remembered on Pell Street; and cappuccino at Ferrara's; and a chocolate egg cream at a candy store-newsstand on Second Avenue (how did he know about chocolate egg creams?). She had never known anyone so hungry for life, so full of appreciation for different modes of living. Uptown, downtown, Eighth Avenue, Seventh, Fifth; Fourteenth Street, Fifty-seventh, Eighty-sixth. . . . It was he who pointed out to her the various subcultures, the microworlds existing within the small space of a city. It was he who wanted to hear Gregorian chants at the Cloisters, wondering if they were still played in the courtyard each day at three. It was he who took her for the first time ever to the Apollo Theatre in Harlem, who bought her a piña colada drink at a Forty-second Street stand. It was he who spotted the Fifth Avenue lingerie shop with its display of red garters and porno negligees and the distinguished-looking gentleman and woman in a full-length sable who hesitated before the window. It was he who made her wait to see if the couple would enter the shop, and when they did, it was he who grinned and gave thumbs up to the man who turned nervously to look at them.

She had never laughed so much in her life, eaten so much, made love so much, or walked so much as she did now in this time with him. He walked everywhere. Once when she protested against a 2 A.M. foray, saying that it really wasn't safe to

go out, he gave her a scornful look. "Don't think like a victim," he said.

He bought her a pair of suede jeans, and the first thing he did when she put them on back at the apartment was to take them off.

They dressed casually most of the time they were together, but when, for an evening sponsored by the museum, they borrowed evening clothes for him, he took to black tie as easily as he had worn his uniform. She watched him across the crowded hall of glittering guests. There was a small group around him; he seemed to be involved in a serious discussion. She suddenly wished her father were present to see this man she loved. Chessie Greene's busboys indeed. As if sensing her attention, Arik looked up and caught her eye. He winked.

That was the night they ended up in the West Side apartment of a middle-aged but still attractive movie star with a well-known affinity for handsome young men. Meri's breakfast omelet was cooked to perfection by another film star, a well-known heartbreaker who had spearheaded the UNESCO boycott. It was almost six in the morning when she and Arik finally left the party. They walked home through the park, both silent as the hour, cool to each other as the crystal wind that carried the noisy sparrows. He stopped and picked up stones to skip across the lake. She leaned back against a tree, hugging her coat to her body, waiting. Finally he turned. Their eyes met, and together they started to laugh. They had both been jealous. They walked the rest of the way back to her apartment with their arms around each other and spent the remainder of the day in bed.

She went with him to Princeton. His mother was small-boned and beautiful but obviously a creature of finely strung nerves. Her features were similar to Ilana's, except for the eyes, which were the same color as Arik's. They shone with disconcerting intensity. It was Chaim Vashinsky who pos-

209

sessed that oblique slant, that Russian eyelid which gave his daughter's face its Oriental expression. Meri wondered what the brother, Dani, had looked like. There were no photographs in the living room except for one of Ilana's children. Rina Vashinsky has already accumulated a heap of parcels for her daughter and grandchildren which Arik was to take back to Israel with him.

"She hasn't been out of the stores since you arrived," Chaim Vashinsky said good-naturedly to his son. "I told her to mail them, but she says they will pay a fortune in tax."

"It's all right," Arik said. "I don't mind."

"It isn't the tax," his mother said. "They will all be broken if you send them by post. You know nothing ever arrives in one piece." She paused. "Broken," she repeated in a strange voice. "Everything gets broken."

Arik and his father exchanged glances.

"The house is lovely," Meri said. "I almost feel as if I'm back in Israel." The Scandinavian furniture in dark rosewood, the artfully arranged shelves of books and art objects, the paintings by various Israeli artists seemed to mark all the apartments she'd visited in Israel. She recognized one painting. "That's a Reuven Rubin, isn't it? I suppose since his death his work has become quite valuable."

Arik's mother looked up at the painting. "We bought that one years ago. You remember Chaim? The little dealer on Ben Yehuda Street?"

Chaim Vashinsky nodded. "Yes, yes, of course." He hadn't the faintest recollection of it. The mathematical minutia he stored in that brain was truly astounding. On the other hand, he couldn't be trusted to go out to the store for eggs, as he would more than likely return with cheese.

Meri touched the bowl of flowers on the coffee table. "What a lovely arrangement."

"Flower arranging is one of *Imma*'s specialties," Arik said. "The neighbors were always coming to her."

"Perhaps you can teach me," Meri said smiling.

210

"With pleasure. My daughter has no time for it. She can do it very well—I taught her myself—but she has no time for such things. She is too busy ploughing fields in kibbutz." There was no mistaking the flare of nostril and curl of lip that accompanied the word kibbutz. Rina Gurion Vashinsky was a citizen of Tel Aviv. She bought only a few new store outfits each year (Israel had an abundance of good seamstresses), but these were from Paris or, at the least, Rome. She took coffee on Dizengoff each afternoon with her friends, sitting at one of the many outdoor cafes, watching her acquaintances pass by and gossiping about the ones who didn't. Her nights were filled with weddings, bar mitzvahs, parties, and *Shabbat* dinners for at least six guests each Friday. Jerusalem held little appeal for her; there was no theatre, and besides, it was too cold in winter. She suffered greatly from the winters in America, although the Princeton house was a good deal warmer than the tile-floored flat on Rehov Zircon Yacov had ever been. Never mind. Who stayed indoors in Israel? There was too much going on outside. Besides, one could always wear a sweater. But in America, such winds. So much snow. And then the houses were too warm, it was really unhealthy. And one needed a car for everything. . . .

"Meri has met Ilana," Arik was saying.

"Yes? You were on kibbutz? You liked it?"

"Well. . . ." She took a deep breath. "It's an interesting experience." From the corner of her eye she saw Arik grinning. "Frankly," she admitted sheepishly, "I hated it."

"Of course you hated it!" his mother exclaimed. "Anyone of any sense hates it. Kibbutz is only good if you are a cow or an orange." She leaned forward. "My daughter is a fool."

"Ilana is a very capable girl," her husband said in his mild-mannered way. "And Amos is a good husband and father. He is first class."

Arik nodded. "A hundred percent."

Rina Vashinsky sniffed. "A first-class farmer. What is that?"

211

Dr. Vashinsky shook his head. "You are too hard, Rina. Too hard."

"Is it so wrong to want a little pleasure from my children? To sleep at night knowing they are warm and safe in their beds? No, one sticks herself and her babies a few kilometers from the border, living in a shack half the size of a Yemenite's flat. And the other one—this one here—half the time who knows where he is, what he is doing?" Her eyes darted to her son and then quickly away from him. She sniffed again.

"Why don't you make us some tea, *Imma*?" Arik suggested quietly.

"Yes, all right." She pulled at Meri's sleeve. "Come into the kitchen with me. We must talk without the men. And you must tell me where you bought your shoes. They have great style. I like things to have style. I love beauty. It is my great weakness." She steered the girl before her into the other room, went to the stove, put on the water to boil. Her movements were quick, nervous ones. "I want to talk to you," she said. "I know how it is with you and Arik, and I want to tell you that I am glad. I am glad of it. It is what I have prayed for."

Meri had not been prepared for this. "I'm glad you feel that way. I thought . . . Ilana—"

"Never mind Ilana. I can imagine what she said to you. Golda Meir, that one. My daughter and I," she added, "do not get along."

Meri nodded, biting her lip. She was not sure if it was a good time to smile or not.

"I know you are a Christian," the woman went on, "and I want you to know I don't care. The important thing is you are not Israeli. It is what I have prayed for." The blue green eyes were blinding. "You will keep him here, yes? You need not live near us," she went on quickly. "You need not even come and visit. I don't care about that. But you will keep him here in America, yes? You must. You must."

"No," Meri answered, confused. "No. We're going back. Didn't you know? I'm going to Israel with Arik."

"No, no! You must make him stay here! You must! You must!"

"But you know that's impossible. Arik will never live outside Israel. Not permanently."

"Then you must pretend it is for a little while. And when that is finished you must ask for more time, just a little more. And then again and again and on and on. Lie to him, do whatever you must do to keep him here. But don't let him go back! Why do you think I stay here?" she asked suddenly. "I thought . . . I kept hoping . . . if we are here then he will come—" The teapot whistled on the stove. She went to shut off the light under it. "If you go back," she said in a low tone, "they will kill him. Each time it is harder and more dangerous. They think I don't know. I know everything. What do they want with him?" she demanded.

Meri took the cup from the woman's trembling hand, placed it on the tray with the sugar and the dish of sliced lemon. Rina Vashinsky stared vacantly at the teapot. "It is always the best who go first," she said. "Never the ones who deserve to die. Why does God take the best ones from us, do you suppose? Can He be jealous of our love?"

"You mustn't talk like that," Meri murmured.

"I had another son, did you know? My Danitchka. He had a smile . . . he used to play the guitar and sing for us. He made everyone happy. Everyone loved him. Twenty years old. What did he know of life? Nothing. It was all there before him, waiting for him. My baby. My child. Arik brought him home to us . . . only there was nothing there. They wouldn't tell me but I knew. I knew. There was nothing left of my smiling boy."

Meri put the spoons on the tray. She could not bear to look into the woman's eyes.

"And now Arik. My first-born. He does not even have to serve in *Zahal*, did you know that? He is the sole surviving son. It is the law. He can be excused from military duty."

"I didn't know—"

"You must keep him here. You—"

213

"What are you saying, *Imma*?" He stood in the doorway of the kitchen. His voice was quiet, but his jaw was set in that way he had when he was angry.

Rina Vashinsky smiled a dazzling smile. "I was saying how happy I am that you have found yourself such a girl. A beauty. A real beauty. Much nicer than Yordana. I never liked that one." She put her arm around Meri and kissed her and petted her and pressed her cheek against the girl's, all the while beaming at her son. "It will be wonderful," she said breathlessly. "Perhaps you will not live far from us and we can see each other now and again. We could have dinner together on *Shabbat*—"

"*Imma*, stop it. You know we will be living in Israel."

Her face seemed to grow small, her features to age. "I thought . . . perhaps. . . ."

"We'll come back to visit," Meri said kindly. "After all, my parents are also here."

"That isn't what she wants," Arik said stonily.

"What do I want? What? For you to lead a good life? For you to outlive me?"

"Stop it, *Imma*. Don't go on with it. Please. You know how I feel. I know you love me, but—"

"But nothing! Go! Go back to Israel! Both of you, go! And when your children become food for machine guns, then come back and tell me how you feel!"

His face paled. He took a step forward. "I'll take the tray in," he said at last. His voice was gentle. "*Abba* is waiting for his tea."

His mother looked up blankly. "What? Yes. Yes, the tea. It is all prepared for you."

He went to her, bent his head and brushed her cheek with his lips. A sob escaped her; but as he turned to go, she raised her chin and called to him in a strong, steady voice. "Arik, I am not crazy."

He turned back to her.

"I am not crazy," she repeated. "It is you who are mad, not I. Both of you."

It was only when they were outside, alone, walking about the campus grounds of the Ivy League university, that he allowed his anger to surface. "She shouldn't say things like that. How can she do it? She knows there's no choice. How can she talk like that?"

"She is a mother. Don't be angry with her. I can understand how she must feel. One son killed, the other . . . no, she wouldn't think about that. She mustn't think about it."

"You think I don't know? You think I'm some kind of damn fool? Don't you think I want to live to be a hundred and have a good fat life like everyone else? You think I like—"

He stopped and said nothing for a moment. He was holding her hand as they walked. His grip was so tight she could not move her fingers. "There are over three hundred terrorist organizations in the world—those are your government's figures, not mine, Meri. Each one is crazier than the next." He let go of her hand and turned to face her. "I do what I do because someone has to," he said bluntly. He let go of her hand and turned to face her. "It's necessary, Meri. You've got to believe that. There isn't any doubt in my mind that it is necessary to fight these groups. Not just for my country, but for all of us. Everyone who believes in a world of sanity. Of simple decency."

She leaned her head against his chest and held tightly to him.

"You've got to promise me you won't become . . . the way she is. No matter what happens to me. Don't dirty what I believe in. Don't make it for nothing. Promise me, Meri. Promise."

But even as she gave her word, she saw him with the Uzi in his hand going toward a terrorist-held schoolhouse; sitting in a command car as he had that first day; walking alone through

215

the mine fields of the Sinai. If only she could keep him safe, keep him where there were no wild-eyed men with grenades, no tanks and missiles, no teacherous traps laid out in the sand, hidden behind the rocks and stones, waiting in the distant hills.

She clung to him, as though by holding him so she could protect him always, wanting to draw him inside her where he would be forever hers.

He kissed her with all the passion of his love for her, and still she clung to him. "Give me a child," she whispered. "I want to have your baby. I want you inside me. Oh Arik, give me your child!"

He was not really happy again until they were back in New York.

I must never show that I am afraid for him, Meri thought. It was the one cowardice he would not accept.

The phone was ringing as they entered her apartment. She rushed to answer it, leaving him to turn on the lights. She did not speak long, and her face was grave as she replaced the receiver on the hook. "That was Diane Whitney. Max has had another heart attack."

He was pale and tired, but alert and in good spirits. "Meri . . . Arik. . . . Good of you both to come, but really, it wasn't necessary. I'm fine. Fine. Just a little tired, that's all." His face brightened. "Did you see the nurse that just left? Her face . . . positively Byzantine . . . amazing. . . . I shall call her Theodora. . . ."

"You must rest, Max. Try not to talk."

"That's hardly entertaining, is it?"

"We didn't come here to be amused, sir. We came to see how you are feeling. And if there's anything we can do."

"Ah. The young officer. What is the name? Ariel. . . ."

"Just Arik, sir. You had it right before."

"Arik is short for Ariel, isn't it? Yes, I thought so. Let me

216

see how much of my Hebrew I remember. I used to speak it quite well. Back in forty-six . . . with Elie and Leah . . . and Rachel. . . ."

"Rachel?" Meri looked wonderingly at Arik.

"Long ago . . . by the waterfall in Ein Gedi. . . ." He closed his eyes for a moment. "Ariel," he repeated, his eyes opening once more. " 'The Lion of God.' Correct?"

"A hundred percent."

Max Radnor smiled and closed his eyes again. They thought he had fallen asleep and were about to leave when his voice stopped them. "We'll be getting the Tel Shalazar items in a few weeks, Meri. I received a cable from Elie . . . before all this happened. It isn't complete—he's hoping to continue in the spring. But we can have a nice showing in conjunction with the benefit dinner in March." He raised his hand, then let it fall back again. "Seems I'll be out of commission for a few months." He made a face. "Complete rest and all that rot." He smiled. "But I know you can take care of it. That's the only reason I'm giving in to these doctors. I know you can handle it."

She looked at Arik. He squeezed her hand.

"I knew from the first you had it in you. Like Rachel. I knew you had it. . . ." He closed his eyes again and now he was in fact asleep. They took their leave quietly.

"I don't know what to do," she said when they were outside. "I thought I'd be going back with you. But now . . . I hate to let him down."

"Don't. I think you ought to stay and do your job."

"But we—"

"We've got a lifetime, Meri." He gave her a penetrating look. "You believe that, don't you?"

"Yes," she stammered. "Yes. It's just—"

"Listen to me. You've got to start thinking like one of us. Like an Israeli. That means believing in the future. Live, work, love as if every day were your last. But never, ever doubt that there will be a tomorrow." He smiled. "Don't worry. Once you get the idea, anything less is boring."

She smiled ruefully. "I know." It was Max Radnor who had spoken once of a passion for life. Some people were born with it, he's said, while others had to learn it. She wondered if Rachel had been his teacher.

"We haven't talked much about it," Arik was saying, "but I'm proud of the work you've done. Not just the UNESCO business. All of it. At first I thought you were just doing some society broad play-job number. But you're okay, lady. First class. A hundred percent."

She hugged him.

"Elie thinks you're terrific. He told me how you pitched in at the dig. Did I tell you I saw him before I left?"

"You saw Elie? Leah too? How are they?"

"Great. From what I gather, Elie's kind of adopted some Arab kid. Talks about getting him into the university when he's old enough. . . ."

The sun was shining in Jerusalem. The winter rains came and then stopped and then began again each day. Eleazar Ben Levi stood at the window of his office on the Hebrew University campus. To all appearances a beautiful day, he thought. But out in the hills, where he would have liked to be, the ground was a pool of mud; and the wadis presented the hazard of flash floods with each sudden torrential outburst. He sighed. Another day of classrooms, lectures. . . .

Terza entered the room. "The mail has come," she announced. "Weeks late, of course. Since the letter-bomb to the prime minister's office, they are running everything through the scanners again. What a bother."

"Better old news, my girl, than the loss of a hand. Or worse."

She shuddered. "Imbeciles. The world is full of imbeciles."

"Many of whom I shall be addressing after lunch today," he murmured, leafing through the envelopes and periodicals she had given him. "I tell you, Raffi has more of a grasp

of—what is this? From New York. I am afraid to look. The shipment we sent to the museum is lost, I'm sure of it. Stolen. Broken beyond recognition. Nothing goes right in winter. I should have brought it over myself." As he read through the letter he began to smile.

"It is not bad news after all?"

"It is lovely news. Lovely. You remember the American girl? Meri Sloane? She is coming back to us."

"What now?" the secretary said in dismay. "Everything has been catalogued and sent. I promise you, I forgot nothing—"

"No, no. She is coming to stay. To live."

Terza was astounded. "She is making *aliya*? She is Jewish?"

"Terza, make some tea for us, would you be so kind?" he asked impatiently.

"I didn't know she was Jewish."

He was still busy with the letter. "She's not."

"So why does she come to Israel then?"

He looked up briefly. It had started to rain again. "For the climate, of course," he said.

9

It was a hard winter, colder than most in recent years. But even as the last days of February were blown away by the winds of March and New Yorkers were still pulling their collars up and their hats down, coats were coming off in Jerusalem and coffee was served outside the Tel Aviv cafés once more. In the hills of the Galilee, the poppy and anemone began to color the landscape, while throughout the land the wild almond began to bud. Toward the end of March, in the beginning of the Hebrew month of *Nisan*, the rains began to subside and the evenings to become mild, so that lovers stayed long outside watching the stars that always seemed so near. On this particular night, the moon shone full upon the border area of Northern Israel, illuminating the figures of a small group of men as they crossed into Lebanon.

"I don't like it," Micah said. "Why can't the Americans get their own people out?"

Arik shrugged. "I know as much as you."

"They're important?"

"Two agents that have managed to infiltrate the Palestine Liberation Army."

Micah spat on the ground.

"Our orders are to get them out of Lebanon fast. Tonight!"

Sergeant Ron Segal, the young marksman that had been at Galil-Bet, moved alongside. "Maybe their cover has been broken," he suggested.

"All I know is they want them out fast."

"So let them fly TWA," Micah growled.

Arik grinned. "Don't you like Uncle Sam coming to us for help?"

"I don't like it, period. Something stinks—and it isn't herring."

"Listen, we owe the Americans a lot of money," Segal said. "Maybe this is a good way to pay them off. Figure a thousand dollars a man per hour."

"A thousand dollars an hour, huh?" The grizzled veteran looked at the F-N rifle with telescopic lens. The rest of them had Uzis. "You figure that's what you're worth, Segal?"

The young man grinned. "Depends on what services I'm asked to perform. Sir."

"He's a wild one, that Segal," Micah muttered to Arik as they pulled ahead of the unit. "Did you see the two pieces who drove in with him from Tel Aviv? Where does he get the strength?"

"Ron's okay."

"You know what he calls that rifle of his? Bubbala."

"Bubbala's okay too." He thought of the schoolroom in Galil-Bet. Segal was a wild kid, but he was also a dead shot.

"Just check his ammo belt. Last time he had sandwiches in it instead of bullets."

He had to smile. "That sounds familiar."

"You used to do the same thing, don't think I've forgotten. Well . . . we'll see what kind of officer this one makes."

"Ron's okay," Arik said again. He looked back at the men. He knew each of them as well as any man could. There was not one among them who was not, in his opinion, first class.

222

"I still don't like this operation," Micah grumbled. "Zadok involves us more and more in his intrigue."

"Our orders come from Hatar, Micah. I answer only to the general. You know that."

The older man looked away. "All right." He sighed. "I hope Beni knows what he is doing."

"Don't tell me you'd rather be spending the night in a soft bed than out here under the stars. You're getting old, Micah."

"Older, yes, my commander. Also smarter." He looked up at the sky. "It is too bright. Good for romance. Bad for war. Light can kill."

"Romance as well."

For the first time, the soldier smiled. "When does she come?"

"Next week."

"So you found a flat?"

"I only hope she likes it."

"Don't worry, she won't. Women always want to pick out everything themselves. They—"

Arik's raised hand stopped him. A figure was approaching. The commando squad immediately took up positions. However, the signaling flashlight revealed the stranger to be a friend. Or someone who knows the signal, Micah thought. His scalp had been tingling ever since they set out on this mission, always a bad sign.

It was Samir, an officer in the Christian militia. He came right to the point. "It's a trap."

Micah spat on the ground and turned away, disgusted.

Arik brought out his cigarettes, offered one to the Lebanese, took one himself. "All right," he said calmly. "What's the story?"

"It's a set-up. They're waiting for you outside Marjayun."

"Who's in on it?"

"Everyone. Except, my friend, your government."

The Israeli gave a half-smile. "Well, that's something."

"The Americans too?" Segal asked.

"It has been a cold winter," Samir replied. "A legitimate denouncement of an unprovoked military incursion into Lebanon by Israeli forces—a UN resolution, of course, backed by the Americans for once—might please the oil cartel."

"As well as signaling a more receptive attitude toward the PLO," Arik added.

The Christian Phalangist nodded. "Which neither of us cares to see."

"Well," Micah said. "That's it, then. Let's go home."

"Wait a minute—"

"He's right, Arik. It is senseless to stay." Samir laughed wryly. "I too wish I could see a way out of this. I can tell you something the Americans do not know. One of their men is a double agent."

Arik whistled softly. "Wow. You sure about that?"

"As you say, one hundred percent."

"Corroboration?"

"A man named Anton Vlastok. He is presently in Algiers using the name LeFracque. Your agents know of him."

Arik blew a smoke ring out into the night. "So," he said thoughtfully. "We go into Syrian-occupied Lebanon to bring out two American agents. Who's waiting for us? Syrian regulars?"

"Fatah. They're supposed to turn you over to the peacekeeping league. But I wouldn't count on it."

"I thought they'd turned in their weapons. They were supposed to hand everything over before they could return south."

Samir's jaw tightened. "They are well armed. Believe it."

"And your men?"

"Also."

The Israeli and the Lebanese looked at each other. "What happens if we don't show?"

Samir shrugged. "Your agents will drop a story to cover me."

Arik blew out another smoke ring. "Any idea how many men there?"

"Twenty—maybe twenty-five."

"Syrians?" Micah asked.

"No. I am sure of that."

Arik put out the cigarette. "Will they follow?"

"The Syrians are out of it. They are looking for the diplomatic victory."

"No, I mean, do you think the *fedayeen* would leave Marjayun, say, to give chase?"

A slow smile spread over Samir's face. "No doubt. It would be unfortunate," the Lebanese added, "should they penetrate our territory, armed as they are. My men would feel disturbed by their presence."

"I kind of thought they wouldn't look too kindly on it."

"We would be defending ourselves against unprovoked attack," Samir asserted solemnly. "What else could it be?"

"There's just one thing," Micah put in dryly. "They're waiting for us. Have you forgotten? We're expected."

"Well," said Arik, "here's what I've been thinking. . . ."

The commander of the Palestine Liberation Army unit in the Lebanese town of Marjayun looked with unconcealed hostility at the man brought in to him. The Lebanese, for his part, harbored no liking for these intruders; he did not waste words: "They have called it off. We received this an hour ago." He handed him a piece of paper. "It is to be tomorrow. Same plan of action."

The Palestinian read the message carefully. "Too bright for them, eh? Can you believe it?" he said to an aide. "The Israelis are planning their moves by the moon."

"Maybe they are superstitious."

"No. They are quite right. One can see everything on a night like this." He crumpled up the paper and threw it against the wall in a sudden fit of exasperation. "All right," he said, calming himself. "Tell the men."

"Have you any message for me to take back?" the Lebanese asked.

"No. Wait. Has there been any confirmation from Beirut?"

"We cannot get a line through. Perhaps you will have better luck."

As he spoke, another Palestinian came into the room. "The Israelis have changed the date of their operation. They notified the Americans about an hour ago. Damascus just got through. It is to be tomorrow."

The commander of the *fedayeen* nodded. "All right then. Everyone relax." He smiled and went over to the television set in the middle of the room. Broadcasting had ceased since the civil war, but programs from Israel and Syria could still be picked up. "At least we won't miss 'Kojak,'" he said.

"The evening is a great success," Donald Lawrence said. "I believe Max is as proud as if he'd done it all himself."

"There were times when I wished he had," Meri replied, looking at the coterie of guests in the museum. "We had a bomb threat at one point. Can you imagine? Over a museum exhibit? Anyway, I'm happy that it turned out well, and I'm glad I had this opportunity to do something for Max—even though it has delayed my departure."

"You're really going through with it?"

"Of course. Didn't you think I would?"

"I was hoping—"

"Ah, Donald, you really are good for my ego."

"I wish I could say the same for you. When are you leaving?"

"Next week. Three days and two hours from now, to be exact."

"You're really counting time, aren't you?"

"Yes, I guess I am."

"Well . . . keep in touch, will you? There's no reason we can't be friends."

She put her hand on his. "We are friends, Donald. Nothing will change that."

"If they don't treat you right over there, you just let me know. We can always order up a UN investigation."

"Thanks," she said, laughing. "But I think I can do without that."

"Couldn't we all," he admitted, smiling too. "Couldn't we all."

The sleeping man was awakened by the beam of a flashlight in his eyes. He put up his hand to block the light. A pleasant voice addressed him. "Taylor?"

"Wha—who—"

"Ed Taylor?"

"What's going on?" he answered in Arabic.

"Cool it, Taylor," the voice said in perfect, American-accented English. "Get your clothes on. Your partner is waiting for you. We've come to take you home."

The others were waiting outside, shadows pressed against the walls, silent figures in doorways. Arik signaled Micah. The sign was passed along and one by one, swiftly, silently, the commandos moved out with the two American agents. At one point Taylor seemed about to fall, and he would have sent a steel drum clattering on the cobblestones had not the tall soldier caught him by the arm. "Careful," the Israeli murmured. Taylor looked at him; he could have sworn the man was smiling.

At the outskirts of town, two cars were waiting. One was a jeep, the other a green Mercedes. The Israelis scattered, hiding in the hills. Arik raised a walkie-talkie to his mouth and gave a short order. The cars started up, moving out on the road that would lead some thirty kilometers straight ahead to the Israeli border. Reaction was instantaneous. The lights went on in Marjayun. From their hiding places, the commandos could hear the shouting of orders, the firing of weapons as the *fedayeen* moved off in noisy pursuit. The machine gun

227

mounted on the escaping jeep opened fire and certain plastique explosions that had been set at various points went off, adding to the confusion.

Taylor looked at the man beside him. The walkie-talkie was in use again. Taylor understood Hebrew; he strained his ears but could not pick up anything. "What now?" he asked, watching the last car disappear past them.

The Israeli answered without looking up. "We wait."

"And then?"

"We walk."

The American ambassador to the State of Israel was sleeping. His valet did not wish to disturb him, but the caller was insistent. Reluctantly, he touched Harding Graham's shoulder. "Sir?"

"Eh? What is it, John?"

"Samuel North is on the line."

Graham was up. "Thank you, John." He reached for the bedside phone. "Sam? Is that you? What's happened, man?"

The voice was careful. Both men had no doubts about the line being tapped. "Just got word from Damascus, Harding. Taylor and Norton are being escorted home by friendly parties."

"What?" Mechanically, he reached for his glasses, looked at the clock on the night table. "They called me just a few hours ago. Said it was off for tonight."

"Yes, that was the word given out." The CIA man paused. "Clever, wouldn't you say?"

"I suppose so," Graham said slowly. "Are they in Israel now?"

"Not yet. Should be before daybreak unless they're stopped before the border."

"Any chance of that?"

"Your guess is as good as mine. No one seems to know where the hell they are except somewhere in southern Lebanon."

228

"What about the Phalangists?"

"They're more likely to occupy themselves with the leftists if they cross into their territory. You know what hatred exists between those groups."

"Yes," the ambassador said carefully. "I imagine any future collaboration—in the quest of peace—among the Lebanese factions must be looked upon as being quite fragile." He paused. "I cannot imagine why the Israeli command misinformed me."

"No doubt you will discover that in the morning. We all will, I suspect."

"Indeed. Thanks for calling. Sam. . . ."

"Yes, Harding?"

"I hope they make it back. I really do."

The call ended, he leaned back thoughtfully. He hadn't liked this piece of business from the beginning. It was a dirty affair and, to his mind, quite unnecessary. Governments, Harding Graham believed, ought to be above that kind of manipulation. It wasn't honorable.

And now, the plot had failed. The trouble was, Graham thought, they'd all forgotten how good the Israelis were at this sort of thing. He wondered if the Israelis had known it was a trap. They're just too good, he thought, chuckling softly. "Just too damn good," he said aloud, and reached for a cigar.

The moon slipped in through the windows, illuminating the statues of young gods and classic heroes with the simple divinity of light. She had slipped away from the others, a chiffon butterfly fluttering among the silent marble figures of the museum. She could hear the laughter of the partygoers down the hall like some distant echo. She smiled to herself, running her finger down the profile of "A Young Greek Athlete," and looked up at the ageless beauty of the gods. "Soon," she whispered to the Periclean Apollo. "Soon, my love." The moonlight caught her, turning her pale as the statues to whom she raised her glass.

"My God," Maxwell Radnor breathed, finding her so. "I thought for a moment we had a new acquisition. What an exquisite study. But what are you doing here alone? Everyone's asking for you. . . ."

She laughed. "Saying good-bye." She saluted the statue with her glass of champagne.

"Ah, but I hate good-byes."

"So do I," she admitted.

"*Shalom* is more fitting in any case, wouldn't you say?"

"*Shalom*. Peace. A lovely word. *Shalom*." She rolled it in her mouth. "Goes nicely with champagne. But then everything goes nicely with champagne, doesn't it?" She laughed and whirled about. "I'm a little high, you know. Feels lovely. Come and dance, Max. You can just hear the music."

"But they've stopped playing," he said, smiling.

"That is very odd because I tell you, I hear music. Lovely, lovely music. Oh, Max, I'm so happy. So very, very happy."

"I'm truly glad, Meri. I must confess I have had the guilts, keeping you from your young man these past months." He spread his hands apologetically. "I love you madly, but—"

"But not so much as you love the museum," she finished, laughing.

"You don't hate me for it?"

"Of course not. Arik and I both agreed that I should stay. And now that the time is almost here for me to leave, I can't imagine where the days have gone. I could use another month just to pack."

"I'm glad you feel that way."

"Dear Max. I admit there were moments. . . . It was hardest just after he left. But that's all done with now. We'll have a lifetime together. All our lives."

He kissed her. "Just love each other. And the rest will work itself out."

She started to say something, then stopped herself. "I—

I—no, I can't. I wanted to tell you—but no, not yet. It's a secret."

"A secret? Now you cannot do that to me. You know how I am—"

"Not now." She took his arm and walked back with him to the party. "But speaking of secrets, there is something that I am curious to know." She paused dramatically. "Who is Rachel?"

"Rachel?" She had taken him by surprise.

"You mentioned the name when you were in the hospital. Who is—or was—she?"

"Rachel." He smiled and patted her hand. "That, my darling, is another story."

The moon shone down on the small band of men as they made their way to a point some fifteen kilometers from the border. A convoy would be waiting there to take them home. Micah cast an uneasy eye up at the sky. The brightness of this night continued to bother him. Arik had stopped a few meters ahead and was looking back at them. It was so bright that Micah had no trouble making out the smile on the *Gan-Aluf*'s face. "Well," he grunted. "You are pleased with yourself. It is too early for that."

"I was just looking at you and Segal. You're a real pair. You keep looking up at the sky as though you expect a bomb to drop any minute—and he won't take his eyes off the ground."

"Mines," Segal muttered as he came up to him. "I don't want to go that way. Anything else, I don't care. But I don't want to go that way."

"Relax. Our information says this area is clear."

"Can't help it, sir. It's a thing with me."

"Well, stay behind me then. If I don't go up, you won't. And if I do, well, step over the pieces, boy."

"It doesn't bother you?"

The officer laughed softly. "It's not how you die that matters, Segal. It's how you live."

231

"You are in a good mood tonight," Micah said out of the corner of his mouth as they continued forward.

"It went well."

"It is not over."

"I know." He smiled. "Maybe it's the moon—"

"Too bright."

"I just feel good."

"Don't say that. Bite your tongue and spit. You want to bring bad luck?" He gestured with his chin at the Americans. "Think they'll try anything?"

"Not now. They don't know where the hell they are—or which end is up."

They went on another kilometer before they began to hear the sound of artillery. At that point, Samir appeared. Arik signaled his men; they waited as the Christian officer approached.

"What's happening?"

"A little noise. They will wait for daybreak to make a real move. Your people have changed their position. I will take you as close as I can to them."

"How does it go with you? Any losses?"

Samir grinned. "It is a good night for us. We had been feeling very frustrated lately. You had no trouble in Marjayun?"

"Like going to the movies."

The Lebanese sighed. "We could have taken that town. Before the Syrians occupied our country. Well, come. Soon it will be dawn."

What a mess, she thought, entering her apartment. The place was beginning to show the effects of her sporadic packing and sorting. She really must straighten things up. Her father was coming in tomorrow. They were to have lunch together. There just wasn't enough time for everything. . . .

She yawned, kicking off her shoes on the way to the bedroom. She would clean everything up in the morning. It

was hardly midnight and yet she felt so tired. Lately, all she wanted to do was to sleep.

It had been a nice evening. There had been only two things to mar it—the first, of course, that he was not there. The second . . . she frowned. Somehow, somewhere during the night the blue green stone in the necklace Arik had given her had worked loose and been lost. She would call in the morning and ask the security guards if they had come across it, but she doubted they'd find it. She could replace it soon enough—next week, in fact—but the loss was annoying. It bothered her.

She went to the medicine cabinet in the bathroom. After all that wine and champagne it might be best to take some aspirin before she went to sleep. She was about to fill the toothbrush cup with water when she stopped. No pills allowed. Of any kind. Just vitamins. Enormous yellow vitamins. She smiled at her reflection and touched her breasts. She wondered if he'd like her being so voluptuous. Personally, she thought she looked pretty good right now. If only he were here. . . .

April might be the cruelest month but a full-moon night in late March could be lonely as hell.

Samir had returned to his men. "Be careful," he had warned before leaving them. "The *fedayeen* are concentrated near the village but they may have fanned out to snipe at your border patrols or to look for an opening to cross over. This is the first excuse they have to come so close to Israel again, and they are anxious to prove they are not intimidated by either your warnings or ours." He pointed to Arik's uniform, identical to his own. "They may think you are one of us." A wry smile crossed his face. "And they don't like us any better than they like you."

"I hope this work tonight brings no sorrow to you," Arik said.

"This would have come sooner or later. Better now, before we are forced to disarm by the Arab League. Your people are waiting for you. It is less than a kilometer."

Arik gave a brief salute. "Israel thanks you, Major."

The Lebanese grinned. "Israel, eh? Why not? In this matter I would trade with the devil if I had to."

It was the Israeli's turn to smile. "In that case, the devil thanks you." He put out his hand. *"Shalom."*

Samir clasped his hand with his own. "Go with God, my friend." He paused. "We have come to know each other well these months, you and I. Tell your sons I say they are fortunate to call you father."

Arik's eyes widened. "My sons?"

"Why not? It happens to the best of us. Only the best."

"As they moved off again toward home, Taylor moved beside him. "You seem to have a good thing going with the rightists."

Arik shrugged.

"You work with that man often?"

The Israeli looked at him. What the hell, he thought. "We're friends," he said, "if that's what you want to know. That's what it's all about, Taylor. One-to-one. Like a stone in water. Throw one in and watch the circles build. The rings keep getting bigger and bigger."

"I don't follow."

"No? Yeah, well, maybe my English isn't so great," the blue-eyed man replied good-naturedly. "See, I think in Hebrew."

The night was almost over. They were almost home. He heard the sound almost the same instant as Micah did. It was just a small sound, but enough for them to freeze. As he gave the signal to take cover, shots rang out. They went into action, their Uzis splattering the night, blasting away the last pieces of darkness into the coming day. As suddenly as it had begun it was over. In the stillness that followed they heard Micah gasp. Arik crawled to his side.

"Watch it," Micah said, wincing. "I know I got one of them. But there are more. Two. Maybe three. No more than

that. Samir was right about snipers. The asses. They think we're Christian Phalangists."

Arik nodded. He was busy making a tourniquet for the wounded man's leg.

"The shoulder as well. Just grazed, but coming from the other side like that—can you believe it? They think we're Lebanese!"

"Shut up, will you?" He picked up the Uzi, his eyes scanning the hills. Suddenly the Uzi spoke; the sniper let out one short final cry and then it was still again. He waited. Finally, cautiously, Arik signaled his men. Segal returned the wave. "Okay," Arik murmured, bending down to Micah once more. The man was unconscious. "Damn," Arik said.

The sun was rising over the hill now. A ray of light shot out from the east, blinding him as he raised Micah in his arms. He turned away from it toward the waiting group of men, a dark figure silhouetted against the sky. They raised their hands to their faces, shielding their eyes from the sun. One shot echoed in the hills of the valley of Lebanon and Arik fell forward, sending Micah rolling on the ground. He tried to get up, fell forward again. In an instant Ron was at his side, covering the officer's body with his own. The others were on the ground, dragging Micah to cover. Ron heard a sound; he shifted his weight, bent his head to Arik's mouth. "Wait," Arik whispered. "Wait." The soldier nodded. He did not take his eyes from the horizon, waiting silently as the sun rose higher over the hill. Then, like a finger, the light pointed to something metal, and Ron knew where to look. He raised the F-N to his shoulder, waiting. A head began to peer out from behind a rock. Ron shot him square between the eyes.

He looked down at Arik, nodded. The officer managed a smile. "Good," he said faintly. Suddenly he looked startled; his eyes became like glass. They were the color of the sea, Ron thought. It was like looking down into the waters of the Galilee.

"The sun is in my eyes," Arik whispered. "The light . . . I

235

can't see. . . ." A great sigh went out of him. His eyes closed.

The young soldier stared disbelieving at the figure in his arms. He bent down, listening for some sign of life. Finally, he raised his head. *"Shma Yisroel,"* he whispered. *"Adonoi elohenu, adonoi ehad."* He stood up now, like a crazy man, turning in a circle, the rifle pointing at the rocks and hills as though daring himself to be shot. But the valley was still.

Sergeant Ron Segal turned to the waiting men. He wondered why they looked at him so strangely. He did not realize there were tears running down his face. He motioned them up, two to carry Micah, one to guard the rear. He slung Arik's body over his shoulder and moved to the head of the unit. Morning had dawned. The air was cool and clean, the light fair in the cloudless sky. He looked back briefly. "All right," he said. "Follow me."

10

"She's only eighteen," the woman was saying. "Naturally we were very proud, her wanting to spend a year on the kibbutz before starting college. My husband and I are both very active in Jewish affairs. Marty is an officer in our B'nai Brith chapter and I'm very active in our Temple sisterhood. I don't mind telling you I've given three years of my life as program chairman for those women and they can thank me for getting Cantor Rosenbluth to do 'Fiddler on the Roof' for their membership luncheon last September. Marty and I are very active. So when my Cheryl joined Young Judea, it was a very natural thing for her to do. She's a beautiful girl, my daughter. A face like a doll. You should see her. So here is this girl. With everything. Beauty, Brains. A nice home—you should see the room we fixed up for her. Everything coordinated—bedspread, curtains. Out of a magazine. All right, my husband says, a year in Israel before starting college. Why not? I mean, we are both very proud. The women in my organization gave me a standing ovation when they heard. All right. Lovely. Wonderful." She sighed. "So now she wants to stay. What can I

do? I ask you, did we raise her, give her everything, for her to go live on a kibbutz? I mean, as an experience, it's wonderful. Marty and I are very proud of her. But as a way of life. . . ." She shook her head. "I can't see it. I just can't see it."

Meri motioned the stewardess to remove the luncheon tray. She turned back to the passenger beside her. "Have you ever been to Israel?" she asked the woman.

"Are you serious? This is our fourth trip. After the Yom Kippur War, we went on a fact-finding mission with our area's UJA chapter. Marty shooks hands with Moshe Dayan. I love Israel. I would come every year if I could. We have a wonderful time. We even have relatives in Natanya. Distant cousins. Wonderful people, wonderful. They lost a son in the war, a terrible tragedy. Oh God," she groaned. "And now Scott wants to go join his sister. My son. Fifteen years old and now he wants to spend his summer vacation on a kibbutz. I told Marty, no. Not this one too. It's bad enough having to go drag Cheryl home, but my Scottie? No. No way will I let him go. My God, he'll want to join the army!" She sighed again. "I just don't understand it. We've given them everything. And don't misunderstand—I love Israel. I give my life for it in sisterhood. But my children, what can they find there? My Cheryl has a scholarship to college waiting for her. She has her own car. I don't know. I just don't know."

"Well. . . ." Meri smiled sympathetically. "Israel is a very seductive country. . . ."

"Seductive?" The woman stared at her. "Oh, my God," she said. "She's met someone. I should have known. Marty! Marty!" Her husband was in the front of the plane with a group of passengers, trying to photograph the Alps through the clouds. "Excuse me," the woman said hastily, and went to join him.

Meri leaned back and closed her eyes. It all sounded vaguely familiar. The words were different but the idea was the same one expressed in the hysterical monologues that had come her way the last two months. Her father had been more

238

subtle than her mother, silent for the most part, evidently saving it all up for that last scene before she left. He was coming to town for a business meeting, he'd said, and offered to take her to lunch. He had arrived at her apartment early, quickly taking in the suitcases, piles of clothes, and cartons of belongings. "You've really made up your mind," he said.

"I don't mean to be disrespectful, Daddy, but what does it look like to you?"

He threw his hat atop one of the cartons. "I thought perhaps. . . . You hadn't said anything lately. . . ."

"There's nothing to say. I know how you and Mother feel, and you both know how I feel. You knew I'd arranged a flight, sublet the apartment. What did you think it was all about?"

"You might have given us the courtesy of—"

"—a weekend in Valhalla? Tish playing *Philadelphia Story* for all it's worth? No thanks. I'm not about to have my private life served up like a goddamned macadamia nut to your Saturday night regulars."

"Now, look here, young lady—"

"Oh, let's not have a scene." She sighed. "Look, I'm sorry. Really I am. The truth is I'm a bit hung over this morning. I feel really rotten. In fact, I've just made a pot of coffee. Would you like a cup?"

"I've reserved a table at the Athletic Club. We ought to be moving on."

"I really don't feel much like eating anything. Could we let it go?"

"All right. Perhaps a private talk would be better— especially as I may not be seeing you for quite a while." He took off his coat. "You pour that cup of coffee. I'll call the club."

When she returned from the kitchen, he was looking at a strip of photos, the four-for-a-quarter kind taken in curtained booths in penny arcades.

"Good Lord," he said. "Where did you get these? I haven't seen these since—remember when we used to go down to Atlantic City? The boardwalk?"

She looked over his shoulder and laughed. "We took them on the subway platform at Forty-second Street."

"The subway?"

"Arik wanted to ride the A train. You know, from the song?" She laughed again, remembering the night in Harlem.

"Hmm. Nice-looking fellow. I imagined him darker, somehow."

"Oh, you can't tell anything from that. They're terrible photos and we were making all sorts of faces. But you're right, he is fair. That is, he would be if he weren't so tanned."

"Yes, I suppose it's quite hot over there. Thank you." He took the mug of coffee from her. "You do look pale. Are you sure you're all right?"

"Just a little queasy." She laughed sheepishly. "It's nothing to worry about. I'll be fine." She sat down. "Okay, J.H. Out with it. Say what you want to say."

He took a deep breath. "I want you to know I respect your decision, Meredith. You're a grown woman, capable of running your own life. I wouldn't have it any other way."

"But?"

"But I'm still a father. So I guess I have to act like one." He leaned forward. "It isn't that I don't want to see you happy. It's just that I don't want to see you hurt."

"What makes you think I will be?"

"Oh, it's not your soldier. I'm satisfied as to his character, his background, education. He has a master's degree in philosophy, I'm told. From Harvard."

She blinked. "I didn't know that. He never told me."

"No? Well, perhaps there are other things he's never told you."

"Daddy—"

"No, I don't mean some dark dreadful secret, another wife, whatever. I'm sorry, I didn't mean it to sound that way. No, from all I've learned, he is quite a fine young man. Quite . . . fine."

"How did you find out about Harvard?" She was still intrigued by that bit of information.

"Meri—now don't be angry—I had my people look into this."

"An investigation? You had him investigated?"

"Yes."

She grinned. "Well, good for you, J.H."

"You're not angry?"

"I think it's super. Sort of evens the score. The Israeli military had a dossier on me," she explained.

His eyes widened. "Well I'll be—" He started to laugh. "Well, now they've got a file on your father too."

"You?"

"Shortly after I, ah, started to ask questions, I received a call at the office from a gentleman who identified himself as being associated with the United States government. Seems somebody wanted to know why I wanted to know about your Arik. I explained it was a personal matter. Well, the upshot was I was told—not asked, mind you, but told—to stop snooping around. That amuses you, does it? Well I can't say I found it so funny. Needless to say I made a few more calls—I am not without friends, as you know—and got pretty much the same answer. But I managed to find out a few things that I think you ought to know."

"Okay."

"Do you know what your 'Israeli soldier' really is?"

"Do you?"

"He is an officer in an elite corps the Israelis call Special Forces. From what I understand, these are men that are pulled from various outfits within the military—"

"I believe the term is commando."

"Then you do know."

"Yes."

"There's more—and I doubt if you know what I am about to tell you. There is talk—quiet talk—of a new organization

241

being set up, basically an American-Israeli venture, although a few other countries are involved—a highly trained, highly motivated emergency unit directed solely against international terrorism." He paused. "And your Arik would be an important part of that team."

She remained silent for some time. At last she said, "Do you honestly believe what you've just told me is going to make any difference?"

"I don't know. But I think you ought to realize what you're getting yourself into besides the more obvious problems. No matter how you look at it, you're going to have to be very strong, Meri."

"I know."

"At least consider living here in the States. If this new group is realized, I can make a few calls. It should be easy enough to get Arik stationed here."

She shook her head. "I promised his children would be *sabras*, as he is—that they would be raised in Israel."

"Well, God, Meri, there's plenty of time for that—"

"No, there isn't. I'm pregnant. I'm going to have his child."

Eleazar Ben Levi was waiting at Lod Airport. He embraced her warmly. "No, Arik is not here," he said before she could ask. "I saw him last week. He thought he might be called away and asked me to come and meet you. Here, he gave me this note to give to you."

She read it hastily, then laughed. "He always forgets the vowels. Look at this—'I lve you.' Reading one of his letters is like trying to break a code."

"It is because of the Hebrew. We do the words differently," he said lamely.

She looked up at him curiously. He sounded strange.

"Come," he said. "Here is the car. You have everything?"

"Yes. I shipped some things by sea. I don't suppose they'll arrive for weeks."

"We shall have to go to Haifa for them."

"So I was told. Well, where are we headed? Arik wrote that he had found a flat—"

"Leah and I thought you would stay with us . . . until—"

"—until Arik comes for me. Wonderful. I'd like nothing better." She took a deep breath. "You can just smell the sunshine. Oh Elie, it's good to be back."

"It is good to see you, dear girl. I just wish. . . ." There was that funny tone again. She looked at him.

He cleared his throat. "Meri. . . ."

She knew before he told her.

The road was as crowded and noisy as ever, crammed with buses, bikes, jeeps, cars, and an occasional tank. At various points along the way, young soldier boys and girls waited, looking for lifts from the passing cars. There were flowers on the trees alongside the road. The wild almond, she thought, and wondered if the haze that clouded her view was from the heat or the dust.

He took her to the cemetery where Arik had been buried. It was a military cemetery, the same one in which the remains of his brother had been laid to rest. "There is no stone," Elie explained. "It is our way to mark the grave when a year has passed and not before then."

She looked at the patch of earth and nodded. "We will be here," she said. "The child and I will be here."

"Meri—"

"We had better be on our way. Traffic is so bad. And Leah must be waiting."

"If you want to stay a bit longer—"

"No." She smiled gently. "Thank you, but it isn't necessary. Arik isn't here, Elie. Not for me. He's with me. In me. Nothing can change that." At last the tears came, but still her voice was calm and steady. "We belong with each other," she said softly. "That's the way it is."

*   *   *

243

There was much to do. She took the necklace to the Yemenite to replace the stone that had been lost. Then she rented a car—another little Fiat—and drove down the Jericho Highway to the Dead Sea. The old man that operated the cable car at Masada smiled at her, and she wondered if he remembered. There was a group of schoolchildren at the top of the mountain fortress, listening attentively as the history of the place was explained to them. She watched them for a while; they seemed so impressed. She found her way to the Northern Palace where they had once stood together, and stood alone on the terrace there, looking out upon the breathtaking view, seeing him there in the sky and the sea and the tawny canyons of the Judean wilderness. When she left, the sky was red as a child's ball and the cliffs were the color of gold.

In the days that followed, she drove from one end of the country to the other, always heading northward, to the Galilee. There was no hurry; she stopped at Safed, at Tiberius, and at Capernaum. She went again to Megiddo, site of Armageddon, to Nazareth, and still northward, passing Arab villages and Jewish cities, *kibbutzim* and *moshavim*, factories and farms, giving lifts to the soldiers on the road, watching spring unfold in the miracle of life renewed in the Holy Land. And then finally, one day she was there, at Galil-Bet, in the Upper Galilee.

She parked the car and walked toward the cluster of dwellings that housed the families of the kibbutz. A new building was going up alongside the barn. A group of children ran past her, laughing as they chased one another. A young boy and girl brushed by, their arms around each other's waists, involved in what seemed to be a very serious discussion.

It was not hard to find the cottage. The door was open. Ilana was putting some clothes away, her back to the entrance. As if sensing Meri's presence, she turned and saw the American girl standing in the doorway. She stared at Meri for a moment. Then, slowly, she put out her arms to her.

244